M

CW00381874

NOBBY

GROG

For Mum

Table of Contents

All For Me Grog

Traditional Shanty

Oh it's all for me grog me nobby, nobby grog

It's all for me rum and tobacco

I've a spent all me tin with the lassies drinking gin

Oh across the stormy ocean I must wan – der

Verses:

Here is me coat me nobby knobby coat

Me coat's seen a lot of rough weather

For the sides are wore out and the back is flying about

Oh the lining's looking out for better wea – ther…

CHORUS

Here are me britches me knobby knobby, britches

Britches a seen a lot of rough weather

Oh the pouch is near wore out and the seat's all flying about

And the knees are looking out for better wea-ther

Here is me shirt me nobby nobby shirt

Me shirt's a seen a lot of rough weather

Oh the collar's all worn out and the sleeves are flying about

And the tails looking out for better wea-ther......

CHORUS

And look at me boots me nobby nobby boots

Me boots seen a lot of rough weather

Oh the soles are wore out and the heels are flying
about

And me toes are looking out for better wea-ther....

CHORUS

Look at me hat me nobby nobby hat

Me hat's seen a lot of rough weather

Oh the brim is wore out and the crown is flying about

And the lining's looking out for better wea-ther ...

CHORUS

I'm sick Oh me head well I haven't been to bed

Since first I came ashore from me slumber

I've spent all me dough on the lassies don't you know

Far across the western ocean I must wan-der......

CHORUS

Name of writer ot shanty anon/lost

CHAPTER 1

Sunday 12th September 2018 – Robin Hood's Bay, North Yorkshire

'I'm dead, aren't I?' said the young woman standing immediately behind DI Elsie Storm.

Elsie turned slowly round to look at the young woman – who was the spectral image of the corpse lying on the beach at her feet.

The morning sky had settled into a vague unde-fined mist and the sea breeze had gone. There was a sense of timelessness which pervaded the air, as if Elsie and the young woman were suspended in some hazy undefined space in which they were the sole inhabitants.

The young woman was dressed in a long, dark, vel-vet skirt and a fitted blouse, the colour of merlot.

Her pale face was beautiful - her eyes large, grey and glassy.

On her Sunday morning walk along the beach of Robin Hood's Bay, Elsie had spied what she thought was a mound of seaweed. Closer inspection had revealed the mound to be a tangle of seaweed wrapped around a corpse.

Over the last few years, Elsie had often seen the spectres of murder victims she was investigating. She was a detective inspector for the North Yorkshire Police Force, with its headquarters, a few miles further down the coast, in Scarborough.

Elsie had no idea why these spectres presented themselves to her and had long given up questioning their presence. They rarely interacted with her but did sometimes speak. On fear of losing her job she never told anyone about them. Although they were unnerving, they were harmless and she felt far more sympathy for them than fear.

A number of gleaming silver bangles dangled from the young woman's arms. She was wearing high heeled lace up boots and her hair was a mass of tumbled tendrils caught up in a haphazard way: a shiny black colour which contrasted starkly with her pale skin.

'Who did this?' Elsie asked – her voice came out as a croak and she coughed and asked again, more loudly this time. 'Who did it?'

'Will you tell my family that I love them?' the girl asked quietly.

'Who are your family?' asked Elsie, knowing that the girl would never answer her questions. They rarely did.

'I shouldn't be here.' The girl said gazing sadly down at the corpse; 'I shouldn't be here, should I?'

Swollen with melancholy, Elsie looked at her and replied, 'No, you shouldn't.'

Elsie's mobile phone buzzed to notify a text and she glanced down at her jacket pocket instinctively. She looked back up quickly but the girl had gone. Elsie angrily took out her phone, the text was another inconsequential one; life insurance wouldn't you know. Disregarding it, she furiously rang the body in.

Suniya, the district pathologist, arrived before long; shortly followed by the others. Suniya had a fluid and efficient manner. Her dark eyes missed nothing with their laser-like precision. Her brows were generally drawn together in an expression of focused intensity.

Everyone had to move quickly as the tide would only be out for a few hours and locals and tourists were already beginning to gather some distance away. A hastily erected white plastic hut was soon flapping disconsolately around the body and a SOCO team was busily searching the nearby vicinity for any clues washed up on the shore. A crime scene photographer was meticulously taking myriad photos.

'Elsie,' Suniya said, by way of greeting as she and Elsie entered the tent erected around the body. Suniya was a woman of few words but Elsie knew that Suniya was particularly saddened when the victims were young. A barely visible tell-tale twitch intermittently pinched the side of one of Suniya's eyes as she looked down at the body of the young woman.

Suniya sighed after a cursory inspection. She stood up and again looked morosely down at the body.

'Any thoughts, Suniya?'

'The body has hardly had chance to decompose and she hasn't been in the water long. I'd say death occurred in the last ten hours or so – I'd need to run tests to confirm that.'

'Of course, do you think she drowned?'

'Perhaps, but I'm unsure at this stage. There's a head wound that shows massive impact; looks as if it were caused by a blunt instrument - possibly sometime yesterday, but I would need to verify all this back in the lab.'

Elsie spoke her thoughts aloud: 'If it was suicide, how did the girl sustain that kind of head injury? If it was an accident, how had the body found its way into the sea to be washed up on the beach?'

'She might have drowned with the injury being caused on rocks, post-death,' said Suniya. 'Although that is speculation, of course, at this stage'.

Elsie nodded and then said, 'She could have perhaps been in a boat which sank in the storm, last night. But she hardly looks dressed for seafaring – especially with a storm on its way. Perhaps she fell off one of the cliffs – that would explain the head injury, I guess, and then the tide carried her body out.'

Anything is possible until it isn't, Elsie thought to herself. That was one of Ian Lansdowne's mantras – the Superintendent of Scarborough Police Station who had nurtured and mentored Elsie since she was a constable. 'Anything is possible,' she began.

'Until it isn't,' completed Suniya who too, had known Ian Lansdowne for a long time.

Both she and Suniya looked down at the girl with an expression of grim solemnity.

'And of course, murder is possible too,' said Elsie.

CHAPTER 2

Sunday 12th September 2018 - Mick Harper's Residence - Robin Hood's Bay.

The village of Robin Hood's Bay (or Baytown as it is known to locals), a few miles down coast of the thriving fishing port and tourist town of Whitby, was once one of the most prosperous villages in all of England: officially, due to its fishing; unofficially, due to its smuggling enterprises. Nowadays, it is the tourists that provide the largesse. The village has hardly changed in the last few centuries and its cobbled ginnels and lanes weave labyrinth-like up the bank of the sloping cliff, onto the vast, heathery, Yorkshire moors.

Mick Harper lived just outside the village, in a large prosperous house set down a lane overlooking the bay. Mick Harper was becoming uneasy. Demeris, his twenty year old daughter, had not been answering her home number or her mobile. He had made a couple of phone calls to her best friend, Gemma, and to Demeris' boyfriend, Jimmy, but there had been no reply. Demmy (as she was known to her friends) had moved out a few months ago into a little cottage in Robin Hood's Bay – left to her by her great aunt, Jessie. He hadn't been happy about this but knew she wanted her independence. He had insisted though, that she rang home regularly and visited often. She had said she would be here at twelve for lunch, with him and her brother Sam. Demmy was a little absent minded and she had already lost two phones but he tried her number again to remind her of the arrangement. There was no answer. He rang Gemma again,

'Hi, Mr Harper, sorry I didn't ring back but I've only just checked my phone.'

'Was Demmy with you last night, Gemma?'

'No, Mr Harper, she wasn't. We were all in The Angel, but Demmy wasn't there. Have you tried Jimmy?'

'Just about to; did you see Jimmy in the pub?'

'No, Jimmy wasn't there either. I'm sure she'll be alright, you know. They're probably both crashed out somewhere.'

Gemma's voice faltered. She didn't really know what to say and was frightened she might have said the wrong thing. It was a well-known fact that Mr Harper hated his daughter dating Jimmy Bransdale.

'I need to get back to work now, Mr Harper. Would you get Demmy to ring me when she returns?' Gemma worked at a café in Whitby. Gemma's voice had lost some of its youthful chippiness. She was beginning to worry now. Where was Demmy? After the phone call she shrugged off her anxiety. Mr Harper was bound to be worried; he was Demmy's dad after all; and it had barely been two years or so since he had lost his wife to cancer. He was bound to be over-protective of Demmy. She was sure Demmy was just fine. She'd probably lost her phone again and crashed out at Jimmy's.

Mick rang Jimmy's phone again. No reply – he was probably avoiding his call. He slammed the phone down. He was beginning to get angry. He hated Demmy going out with Jimmy Bransdale who was into all this damn Goth business; dressing up and wearing strange make up seemed to be the only thing Jimmy was any good at. And Demmy always seemed to be at his place.

Jimmy called his dressing up 'art'. 'Art!' scoffed Mick, 'Art! That kid wouldn't know art if it kicked him up his backside – the daft prat!' Mick was a tough businessman who had been brought up to believe that keeping your feet on the ground and good hard work made for the only valid reality. And that was that.

He turned on his laptop to distract his angry thoughts. He was a member of a local community group on Facebook and someone was reporting the body of a young woman found washed up on the beach at Robin Hood's Bay.

Within an hour his world would crumble as he discovered that his worst suspicions were true: the body of the girl washed up on the beach was his own precious Demmy.

CHAPTER 3

Sunday 12th September 2018 - Scarborough Police Headquarters.

In the Investigation Room at Scarborough Police Headquarters, Elsie pinned up the photograph of the dead young woman she had found on the beach before looking at the silent expectant faces of her team.

'Thanks everyone, for coming in on a Sunday and at such short notice. Demeris Harper – twenty years old; lived in Robin Hood's Bay; worked in Whitby. Suniya has just confirmed that the girl's death was caused by a fatal blow to the head...prior to her body being placed into the sea.' Elsie's voice imperceptibly shook but she managed to disguise it with a cough.

Shannon Cafferty, one of her junior detectives, interrupted, 'And then the bastard dumped her at sea. What was it - hot date gone wrong so he clobbered her one?'

Else sighed inwardly, she'd exhorted Shannon, both publicly and privately, to modify her language. At least the Super wasn't in today.

'Shannon!' she said in a warning tone.

But it was like telling a hungry dog to stop chewing a bone.

'Apart from anything else, Shannon, that kind of talk could be misleading. At this stage it is best to keep an open mind about the culprit and his or her motivations – otherwise we could all go off on wild goose chases.' Elsie's recognised that her tone sounded prim and her words didactic and cliched – but it was true, and she felt duty bound to guide Shannon's responses correctly.

Shannon farted and Elsie sighed. At least Shannon had the decency to look a bit mortified. It wasn't a loud and especially forced one, but even so Elsie couldn't help wondering if a little more physical restraint would have kept everyone from hearing it. She couldn't help from tutting rather loudly in what she thought justified retaliation.

'Sorry, Ma'am, wasn't being disrespectful, honest: curry night last night.' Shannon had the grace to continue to look grave when she said this. Gus and Sim (the other two members of the team) hardly noticed Shannon's unorthodox behaviour anymore and just patiently waited for Elsie to continue. Within seconds Shannon's capricious smile had returned and her wide green eyes darted around the room – beacons of her barely contained energy.

For now all had to be focused on the case. Elsie had found that murder cases brought out the puckish nature of Shannon's personality. Elsie knew that her exhortations rarely had much effect. Shannon found it difficult to conform to work mores. She had recently tried to guide Shannon toward a more conservative dress code and more in line with what was expected of a plain clothes police officer. It had failed abysmally. Today Shannon's fringe was blue and her doc martins were more scuffed than usual. Elsie recognised that her own management skills were also probably lacking. Although, to be fair to Shannon she always seemed to recognise when she had gone too far and was ready with an apology for her rather aggravating ways. Her pretty face with its snub nose and catlike expression often let her get away with far more than usual. Elsie sniffed in disapproval and continued.

'You know the drill, we need to question everyone involved with Demeris – or Demmy, as she was known. Find out if she had any enemies; if there was anyone with a grievance.'

'Is there anyone on the radar yet, Ma'am?' asked Gus timorously. Gus Lambert was the complete opposite of Shannon: polite; nervous; quiet and fastidiously neat. Whereas Shannon's desk was always a tip, Gus' was always in scrupulous order – even his paper clips were in tiny, colour coded compartments. Fine featured and rather diminutive in size, he was always impeccably dressed. He had a habit of perpetually smoothing down his side parting with one hand. He blinked profusely when agitated, or whenever Shannon was at her most verbally inappropriate – he blinked a lot of the time.

Gus was bizarrely obsessed with crystals and believed in their healing and spiritual powers; with a fervour which bordered, quite frankly to Elsie, on the insane. He had presented Elsie with a sizable but exquisite piece of rose quartz for her last birthday and Elsie had been touched until Shannon had spilt the beans and told her that it was meant to draw love into her life. She had wondered if Gus had taken a shine to her but, on reflection, strongly doubted it. The whole thing had been quite unnerving – she determinedly pushed the memory away.

'No Gus, according to her father, Demmy was a popular girl. Time of death, we think, was yesterday afternoon until early evening. We then believe Demmy's body was taken out to sea and disposed of there. But for the storm bringing the body back onto shore, she would probably never have been found.'

'Demmy might have been out at sea already, before she was attacked,' pointed out Gus.

'Good point, Gus,' added Shannon. Gus smiled back at her. Against all the laws in the social universe, Gus and Shannon actually got on very well and were often teamed together.

Elsie gave a smile and nod of acknowledgement in Gus' direction. 'That might have been the case but she wasn't dressed for sailing and a storm was brewing which makes me think that the boat journey was not some kind of pleasurable jaunt. I don't think anyone, in their right minds, would have put to sea in a storm unless they had to and needing to dispose of a body 'would' be a 'had to' reason, I expect. I'm more of the mind that she was killed and then her body was put onto a boat before being taken out and dumped at sea. I'm keeping all options open at the moment, however. There are no traces of alcohol or substance abuse or of an attack of a sexual nature. And there is only the one blow to the head which killed her outright. Suniya has confirmed that she was dead before her body was dumped at sea. It was likely that she was in the water for no more than fifteen hours. I found her at nine this morning so her body was likely put in the sea after about six o clock yesterday evening.'

Sim, the final member of her team put his hand up. 'Is there any information as to where along the coast her body was likely to have been put out at sea?'

'We're unsure, Sim. Her body could have been put in the sea far out in the Bay with the storm bringing it back in. Or equally possibly, it could have been put in as far up as Whitby where Demmy was last seen. The timescale could fit either scenario.'

Elsie had later on that morning, managed to catch Charley France, a local coastguard, who she had known since school. He'd told her about the tidal streams which ran along the North East coast. It would have taken about ten hours for the tidal stream from the nearby coastal town of Whitby to carry a body down as far as Robin Hood's Bay, about five miles down the coast from Whitby. If not for the freak storm the night before, the body might never have been washed ashore. He had also confirmed that last night had been high tide all along the coast so a boat could easily have been used to take the body out to sea. Elsie informed the team about her chat with Charley.

Sim nodded and proceeded to make notes on the ipad he always carried around with him. Sim Howard had joined the team six months ago. He'd been drafted out of the army into a civilian post after having served in the Middle East. Elsie had tried to find out more but his file was brief and Sim never talked of his army career. It seemed he was a man of mystery and she'd always been thwarted when she had asked questions. She trusted the Super, Ian Lansdowne, to the extent that if he felt the need to respect the privacy surrounding Sim, then she would too. She had never been part of Sim's interview, she wasn't even sure he had had a formal one as Ian often asked her to sit in on interviews for new staff. She still kept a close eye on Sim but so far he had proved to be a conscientious and able detective who, surprisingly, fitted in well with the team.

His hand shook as he put down his pad but he gazed steadily at Elsie out of piercing blue eyes which were set in a rugged but handsome face. He was a large man and powerfully built and in his mid-forties. His clothes were casual in style but always clean and well pressed. Like his neat haircut, they echoed his once military past. It was common knowledge that he spent much of his spare time in a gym or the dojo. One of the few things that Elsie did know about Sim was that he was a black belt in Shotokan karate.

'Lastly, for now,' concluded Elsie, 'Demmy was dating a young man called James Bransdale; also twenty years of age, who works as a chef at a restaurant called, 'The Mariner' on Whitby harbour. He lives in a flat in Silver Street and is very much into Whitby's Goth scene.'

Whitby was something of a draw for the Goth movement due to its association with Dracula and there were biannual Goth festivals attracting Goths from far and wide. There was already a number of home-grown Goths in the old port town. In her few meetings with members of the Goth community, Elsie had generally found them to be untroublesome on the whole; and they added to the character of the place with their outlandish style of dress. Personally, she found them rather romantic with their flowing shadowy semi-Victorian clothes and love of moody music; their awareness of beauty in the shadows and of the dark ephemeral. She was aware that she was indulging her sensibilities and moved on.

'So, what do we know about Demmy? Elsie wrote the information on the board as she spoke. 'Demmy worked at 'The Jet Miners', a jewellery shop in Whitby, which specialises in jewellery made from jet. And she helped out sometimes with the family business. The Harpers have a portfolio of holiday homes in the area. Right Gus, what do you know about jet?' Elsie knew the question was irrelevant but Gus was the shyest member of the team and he lacked confidence. She tried, wherever possible, to encourage him to speak out in the group meetings.

After a pause Gus, in a measured tone began, 'Jet's a semi-precious ebony black stone which has been found in and around Whitby for several centuries. Whitby jet is of a particularly high quality and used to make jewellery. Queen Victoria made the wearing of jet popular as she wore it when in mourning for her husband Prince Albert.'

'Wiki-Gus!' punctuated Shannon.

'Thank you, Gus. Demmy was an apprentice learning how to fashion jet jewellery. I'll be interviewing the owners imminently to see if they can shed any light on what's happened,' said Elsie.

'OK, I want Shannon and Gus to ask questions around Robin Hood's Bay, especially the fishermen. See if they heard or saw anything last night. Knock on doors and see if anyone witnessed anything. Sim, you can come with me. We'll get hold of some of the fishermen at Whitby and see if anyone spotted any unusual activity with boats going in or out, but we'll start with the Harpers and of course, we'll pay a visit to Jimmy Bransdale – the boyfriend. Alright, you know the drill: back here tomorrow morning to put together what we have.' Elsie took a deep breath. It was going to be a busy Sunday.

<u>MY OLD FISHING-BOAT (Writer unknown)</u>

Yes, there she lies,

The lass that we prize,

There she rests from her work awhile,

Hauled high on the beach

Where no waves can reach,

Where at storms she can smile.

And she should be blest

With her turn of rest,

Unvexed by the waves.

CHAPTER 4

Stoupe Brow Moor (The Butts) Overlooking the
Bay, North Yorkshire, July 1797

Jeb's muscles rippled as he dug further down into
ground. He was fifty five years old but his physique
and strength was more like that of a much younger man. Robin Hood's Bay, where he lived, was a
fishing village but it was also a smuggling port and
many a dark night involved the lugging of contraband that the boats from France secretly brought to
English shores. The smuggling trade was constant
and hauling the bolts of silk, chests of tea and cas-
kets of brandy onto shore, and then stowing them
into the myriad hiding places in the village kept Jeb
in peak condition. Not to mention the fishing.

Jeb had dug about three foot down now, into this
secluded little spot on the moor near to the ancient

raised burial barrows, locally known as 'The Butts'. These barrows had existed for several thousand years and were set up high on the cliffs overlooking the bay toward the village of Ravenscar which was situated on the far southern cheek of the bay. The village of Robin Hood's Bay nestled into the northern cheek of the bay.

He reckoned that he had dug down far enough now. The first two feet hadn't been too bad as the top lying earth had been quite peaty, but in the last foot down the earth had been more compact and clay-like. Despite the cooling mist on the moor, sweat poured down Jeb's face and back. He was getting a bit weary of all this, he thought, as he took a brief rest leaning against his spade.

The smuggling cutter last week had only just managed to get away from the excise lugger. They had hardly smuggled the contraband into the secret beck tunnel, underneath the village, before the excise dragoons on shore had turned up. There had been a few near misses of late: the government were cracking down on smuggling operations because they needed the revenue to fight all these damn wars with France.

Jeb glanced with a smile at the wooden casket to the side of him. He was satisfied that he had dug down far enough by now. He lifted the lid of the box for one last time and glanced into its reinforced lead innards. It was full of jewels and guineas that sparkled and gleamed in the newly emerging morning sun. The treasures within the box had been selected, collected and put away over many runs and contained items from many distant lands overseas. The best things always travel far he had found.

Jeb was prosperous enough, but he liked the idea of his little nest eggs put by just in case. Who knew what the future held? Next time, he could be caught by the increasingly wily duties men, or he could lose his life at sea, even though he was one of the best fishermen in the Bay. Not that the treacherous North Sea showed any respect or mercy despite the skills of the fishermen. Then there were the press gangs, constantly on the alert for able fishermen to kid-nap into the King's naval service. Of course, such hostiles were constantly watched out for: the alert-ed womenfolk would subsequently bang on drums which could be heard throughout the village - giving their menfolk time to hide in the various secret cup-boards, basements and tunnels which were dotted profusely throughout the village. Still, no matter how organised the village, the odd fisherman had been known to be captured and never be seen for years.

And, of course, the casket could not be stored at home. The cottages in the bay were often raided by the customs' officers.

He hammered the box closed with some nails and quickly hauled it into the hole. At least Alice, his eldest and favourite daughter would now be provided for. She was married to a wastrel: a fearless smuggler was Wilf, but he liked his brandy and cards too much. Jeb could quite easily see Alice in penury in her later years. He had made similar provisions for his other four children and his wife, Emma, of course – with their futures secured in various boxes for them hidden in holes buried around the village of Robin Hood's Bay.

The mist had practically cleared and he did not want to be spotted by some passing journeyman, or a fishwife on her way from the Whitby markets to offload her wares in the nearby towns. He took a moment to straighten his back and look around. Despite the damp start, it was promising to be a fine day. The heather was brightening to amethyst, and the azure sheet of sea melded with the blue overhang of sky; the skylarks careened overhead in their summer joy, and the smell of gorse hung heavy in the air. He covered the casket with the peaty earth and replanted the heather on top as if it had never been disturbed. He then made his way home back to Robin Hood's Bay village.

All that was left was to ensure that Alice, his precious daughter, was able to find the casket when she needed it. He glanced back at the ancient burial place, set high on the moor above the village, and smiled.

THREE SCORE AND TEN

(Shanty Traditional – Writer Unknown)

Refrain:

And it's three score and ten

Boys and men were lost from Grimsby Town

From Yarmouth down to Scarborough

Many hundreds more were drowned

Their herring craft and trawlers

Their fishing smacks as well

Alone they fight the bitter night

And battle with the swell.

Me thinks I see a host of craft,

Spreading their sails at lee

As down the Humber they do steer,

Down for the great North Sea

Me thinks I see a wee small craft

And crew with hearts so brave

They go to earn their daily bread

Upon the restless waves.

Refrain:

Me thinks I see them yet again,

As they leave this land behind

Casting their nets into the sea,

The herring shoals to find

Me thinks I see them yet again,

And they save on board a right

With their sails close-reefed, their decks moist-cleaned

And their side-lights burning bright.

Refrain:

October's night brought such a sight,

'Twas never seen before

There were masts and yards and broken spars,

Washed up upon the shore

There was many a heart of sorrow,

There was many a heart so brave

There was many a true and noble lad

To find a watery grave.

Refrain:

CHAPTER 5

Sunday 12th September 2018 - Mick Harper's
Residence, Robin Hood's Bay.

Mick Harper tried not to break down when he answered the door.

Elsie knew Mick Harper. She didn't know him enough
to say hello to, but most people at least knew each
other by sight, if not to talk to, living in this part of
the world. The Harper's were prosperous and lived
in a beautiful house at the top of the cliff, along a
narrow rural lane, overlooking the village of Robin
Hoods Bay. Mick Harper looked as if he had aged
about ten years since the last time she had seen
him. The confident, efficient, business-like air, that
she remembered, was no longer apparent in this
downbeaten man, cloaked in abject misery and his
face lined with grief.

"Mr Harper, I'm Chief Detective Inspector Elsie Storm and this is Detective Sim Howard. We're here about Demeris. It is possible to have a few minutes of your time?' Elsie stayed silent for a few minutes allowing Mr Harper to collect his thoughts. 'I appreciate this must be a very difficult time for you,' she added

Mick Harper waved them through into the kitchen and took a deep breath and met Elsie's eyes. They both knew that it would be information that would lead them to Demmy's killer and not tears. Determination crossed the poor man's face.

'Mr Harper,' she began gently, 'I'm so sorry for your loss. I can assure you that we will do everything we can to find out what happened.'

Mick Harper visibly swallowed back his tears. Elsie loathed this part of the job more than anything else. There were no right words in such situations. She paused for a few seconds and then began. 'I have to ask, did Demeris have anyone who might have wished her harm?'

'Of course not!' he snapped.

'I'm sorry, Mr Harper, I have to ask these questions. I know some of them seem a bit …direct. When did you last see or hear from Demeris, exactly?'

'Friday evening. She'd been working all day and came back here for tea before going back to her cottage, in the bay, to get ready to go out. She said she was going to a party and then staying at Gemma's. I never really believed that she stopped at Gemma's. She just didn't want to tell me she was with that feckless sod, Jimmy Bransdale. It wouldn't surprise me if he had something to do with this…I warned her about him, so many times, but she never listened.' Mr Harper struggled to contain his anger. He looked back up at Elsie.

'Had Demeris and Mr Bransdale been arguing, to your knowledge, Mr Harper? Had she said anything about not getting on well lately with him?' Sim interjected.

A variety of emotions and thoughts seemed to cross Mick Harper's face but he eventually shook his head no. 'Demmy never really told me much about her and Jimmy's relationship but I can't say she ever mentioned that she and Jimmy weren't getting along.'

'And yet you think he might have had something to do with what happened to Demeris?' Elsie gently queried.

'When you see him, you'll know what I mean. Dressing like he does and hanging around the kinds of places he goes to; shouldn't be surprised if drugs are involved.'

'Do you have evidence that he took drugs?' asked Elsie.

'Not as such, no, but he certainly seemed to hang around with the sort who would.'

'And Demeris?'

'Demmy taking drugs? I never saw any, but then she'd likely hide any evidence from me, wouldn't she?'

This was getting them nowhere, thought Elsie. And who knew if it was Harper's understandable grief and anger talking or whether his claim had substance - but it was an angle they would pursue anyway. Drugs were so prevalent, especially amongst the young that it was always investigated.

'Mr Harper, I can assure you that we will do our utmost to find out who was responsible for this. We will be closely questioning everyone involved with Demeris,' continued Elsie. 'So, you saw Demeris on Friday night. Was that the last time you spoke to her?'

'No, she rang me from The Jet Miners – the jewellery shop where she works, on Saturday morning. She knows I like her to ring or text to check everything's OK. She didn't talk for long as a customer came in. That's the very last time I spoke to her,' said Mr Harper, his eyes misting over at the memory.

'Do you live here on your own, Mr Harper?'

'No, Sam, my son...Demmy's brother lives here too. Only the two of us left now. My wife passed away two years ago...cancer.' He looked at the floor. Up until about six months ago, Demmy lived here too but she inherited a cottage down in Robin Hood's Bay from her Aunt Jess. She's been living there since then.'

'Do you have a set of spare keys for the cottage, Mr Harper. We'll really need to take a look in there.'

Mick Harper shuffled to his feet and opened a drawer in a large oak dresser and extracted a set of key. 'No 3 Sunnyside,' he said woodenly as he handed Elsie the keys.

'Thank you, Mr Harper, I live in the Bay too so I know that lane. These will be returned to you as soon as possible. Is Sam around? I need to ask him a few questions.' Elsie was really thinking it might be better to question Mr Harper with his son present for support. Mick Harper sat heavily down as if the simple act of standing up had taken every last reserve of energy.

'Sam's seeing to the…arrangements for Demmy's… body. She was just a quiet lass; never any trouble. Always creative – likes to spend time on her own but always has...had friends too. Who would harm her and then dump her in the ocean like that?" Mr Harper's voice cracked. Elsie decided to just let him speak.

She nodded in sympathy. Mr Harper's eyes rested on a wooden piece of artwork set on the mantelpiece. He reached out and picked it up and placed it lovingly on the table. With a catch in his voice he said, 'Demmy did this. She always liked to beachcomb along the Bay; made that out of some driftwood.' Elsie looked at the piece with interest. It was of a comical looking seal waving with its fin at the onlooker; the attention to detail showed artistic merit. Elsie could see that Demmy had had talent.

'It's lovely,' she commented.

'That's how she got into making jewellery out of jet. She used to love finding pieces of jet along the coast and really wanted to learn how to carve them into jewellery. That's why she got herself an apprentice-ship at 'The Jet Miners' jewellers in town. She was a hard worker and still always stepped in to help us out in the family business when she was needed. She was a good girl and not spoilt, like so many kids nowadays. My kids have had to work for their money. I've never just given it to them.' He added, his voice cracking again.

She glanced around the perfect kitchen with its tasteful décor complete with gleaming aga as the centrepiece; all leading out onto the perfectly man-icured garden with its distant views across the sea; a perfect kitchen in a perfect home. It was very dif-ficult to look at this poor miserable man; ravaged by tragedy within the pristine environment he had carefully put together for his family.

Elsie knew the jewellers as she had bought a pen-dant from there years ago. A tiny black gem of jet stone, polished to an almost mirror shine, set in a silver art deco design.

'She was a natural, according to Harry Skegwin, the owner. Many of the pieces she created sold well. She had an eye for what people wanted to buy as well as having a natural skill in her work. She'd been there two years and was already talking about setting up her own workshop one day. Skegwin thought the world of her.' His eyes teemed with unshed tears and then rolled down his cheeks as he picked up the little figure of the seal and held it lovingly in his hand.

The front door slammed and firm footsteps were heard. A young man in his mid twenties entered the room. He was good looking, blond and tall with a capable and frank expression. Elsie presumed that this must be Demmy's brother, Sam. She introduced herself and Sim.

The young man went to his father put his arms round his shoulder and gave him a brief hug.

'Cup of tea, dad? Officers?' He directed a look of concern at his father. Elsie and Sim politely refused the offer of tea.

'No thanks, son, I might just go and have a lie down,' said Mr Harper, 'if that's alright.' He added wearily, looking at Elsie. His face had taken on even more of an ashen hue. Mick Harper went to stand up but as he did so he suddenly keened over bent double and emitted a low animal like moan. Sam rushed to his side and propped him up. Mick Harper seemed to straighten as his son touched him and he raised his face – a little strengthened. He got to his feet. Elsie looked away.

'Come on, Dad, let's take you upstairs.' Mick Harper shuffled away, half supported by his son. Elsie glanced at Sim, whose face had taken on a look of sympathy at the sadly desperate scene they had just witnessed: of Mick Harper, clearly a proud and dignified man being subject to such debilitating pain. There were no words and the two were silent until Sam Harper's return.

Sam returned with a stricken look and the two detectives allowed him a few minutes to compose himself as he absently made himself a cup of tea. Elsie got the impression that he was keeping himself busy with routine tasks in an understandable effort to keep the shock of the situation under some kind of control.

'Can you tell me a little bit more about the family business, Mr Harper?' asked Sim.

The young man considered the question. 'We've interests in a number of projects: our main interest lies in holiday property ownership. Dad began the business when he was very young. We rent out holiday homes. He acquired one cottage and used the rent to fund another and then another. We're now the major holiday home provider in this part of Yorkshire. Dad and I have expanded the business from Runswick Bay down to Scarborough.'

Sam said all this in rote fashion as if it were the standard missive given to usually, business associates. Despite the words, it was said without pride or arrogance. He glanced at a pen portrait, of Demmy and himself when they were children in pride of place on a wall adjacent to the dining table. He gave an imperceptible sigh.

'Could anyone have harboured ill feeling toward you and your father, do you think, Mr Harper. You have clearly both been very successful and some people can resent that kind of success.'

'And got back at us by killing Demmy you mean?' asked Sam in a puzzled tone. 'I very much doubt it. That kind of thing doesn't happen around here really does it?'

Elsie kept quiet – there had been a case with exactly that kind of scenario, solved by a colleague of hers near Leeds a couple of years earlier. Who knew what kind of offences our quietest actions and words could cause as we blustered our way through our individual lives? And the success of others often inspired resentment in others no matter how modest or unassuming the demeanour of the successful.

'And no,' he calmly continued, 'I can't think of anything we might have said or done in our business dealings, or otherwise, that might have caused that kind of attack. We've always just been a quiet kind of family who have just worked hard and have had a bit of luck along the way.'

Sim interjected, 'What do you know about James Bransdale, Mr Harper? I believe he was Demeris' boyfriend.'

Sam responded immediately, 'Dad hated him, mainly because he's into the Goth lifestyle. Dad always says, 'If he put as much effort into a hard day's work, as he puts into his dressing up, he'd be a roaring success.' I always thought that was a bit unfair as I think Jimmy does work hard. I suppose he just doesn't make much money. Dad's not a snob though,' he hastily added, 'it's just that he wanted the best for Demmy. Dad just didn't like him. He's...he was, very protective of Demmy.

'And you, Mr Harper, what did you think of James Bransdale?' asked Sim.

Sam considered his response. 'I just thought Demmy was going through a bit of a phase in going out with him, I guess; with them both being creative arty types. I told Dad it wasn't likely to last but Jimmy just really riled him for some reason.'

'Do you like Jimmy? Mr Harper?' asked Elsie.

'I didn't really think of him to be honest. We're opposites. Bit like me and Demmy, I suppose.' He paused, 'Then something like this happens you wish…'

'When something like this happens, in fact when anyone loses a loved one, the ones who love them most often feel regret, Mr Harper; things you wish you'd said or done.' Sam didn't say anything for a moment and then he nodded in agreement at her.

Elsie paused and then continue, 'Did they get on as a couple, Jimmy and Demeris?'

'I suppose. They seemed to spend a lot of time together. Dad was often annoyed that she didn't see more of her own friends on her own but their friends all seemed to hang around together. To be fair, Jimmy and Demmy were just part of the crowd. Part of the Goth crowd. They all dress up and hang out in the same places; listen to the same music. Demmy loved it. I suppose she found me and Dad a bit dry…'

'Did she often stay out late, when she lived here?'

'Yeah. Dad was always having a go at her about it. Sometimes she stayed out all night; mostly at Jimmy's. That's why she was so keen to move into Aunt Jess' old cottage down in the village – she left it to Demmy. Demmy and she were very alike. Dem used to spend a lot of time with Aunt Jess; both were of an artistic temperament.

'Could you give us the names of any of Demmy's friends, Mr Harper, please and places she tended to frequent, do you think.'

'Of course, Demmy is…was popular but particularly, friendly with Gemma, Gemma Leyburn. Here, I'll give you her address. I gave Demmy a lift there a few times. In fact, I'll write some of her friends' names down, if you'll just give me a minute. She tended to meet up with her Goth friends at the pub, The Angel, and Sherlock's café in Whitby. Gemma works at Sherlock's.'

'Thank you,' said Elsie.

'So did Demeris not drive then?' asked Sim.

'She could, but not when going for a night out,' Sam's voice faded away – the strain of having to discuss this horrific situation in as normal and clear a way as possible. Elsie had seen it before in newly grieving loved ones. They wanted the culprit caught but the strain of talking about it…she would not prolong the visit.

Sam retrieved pen and paper from his briefcase, on the kitchen worktop and swiftly wrote down any names of people or places associated with Demmy. He handed the paper to Sim who was sat nearest to him.

One last question, for now, Mr Harper, would Demeris have driven her car into work?' asked Elsie.

'Yes, she did most days. She parked it in the big park near the supermarket by the harbour. I hadn't given it any thought but I guess I'll need to sort that out.'

'Leave it there for now, if it's still there, Mr Harper. We'll notify the council. We'll need to take a look at it,' advised Sim. 'What kind of car was it? I don't suppose you can remember the number plate.'

'A blue corsa, about three years old, SW24 NYD.'

'Mr Harper, I do need to ask you – I can appreciate this is a sensitive question but can you verify you and your father's whereabouts on Saturday afternoon and evening?'

Sam's face reddened, 'Me? I was with some friends - afternoon and evening; watching the local cricket team. A couple of the guys play and we usually make an event of it.' He retrieved his phone again from his inner jacket pocket and keyed in his contact list then scribbled down a couple of numbers before handing the piece of paper to Elsie. 'My friends: Jamie and Martin – they'll verify I was with them the whole time. As for dad, he had a bit of a dinner party with some family friends.' Sam thought for a few moments, 'I'll get hold of their numbers and text you them. They usually arrive quite early for these things. They take it in turns, you see, once a month. It was dad's turn on Saturday. He cheats a bit and gets one of his neighbours, an ex chef, to give him a hand. I'll text you his number too, Graham Spearfoot.'

'I think that's enough for now, Mr Harper,' said Elsie. I'm sure that you can appreciate we will need to ask similar questions of all Demmy's friends and acquaintances.

'It's fine; you're just doing your job. Just glad we've got people to confirm where me and dad were. I'd hate for you to waste time investigating us instead of the person who did this.' He added shortly.

We'll let you tend to your father. We do have a family liaison officer who'll be in touch, I really think it might be a good idea to let her help. Please assure your Dad we'll be doing everything we can to find out what happened to Demeris. I may need to call by with some more questions, OK?'

'Yes, of course.' Sam's eyes lifted to the portrait again and it was with a visible effort that he managed to blink back the tears.

CHAPTER 6

Robin Hood's Bay 1797 (Based on a true story)

Jeb Whittaker looked out across the Bay. It was a fine sunset and the waves lazily lapped the cobbled landing area of the dock. Several gulls swooped and darted amongst the waves excited by a shoal of herrings meandering along the depths of the high tide. The beauty drew his eyes for a moment before he turned and entered the Fisherman's Arms which overlooked the dock.

The tavern was packed with the fishermen of the bay and some of the citizens who serviced the residents of Baytown: chandlers, grocers, ironmongers etc. The dense fug of the open fire; close body odours; the heady aroma of hops from the ale and smoke from the pipesmoke was in direct contrast to the fresh briny air outside its walls.

A once wrecked ship had been stripped and used to supply the interior panelling, floors and beams of the inn. The dark honey glow of oak and elm infused the interior of the bar with an elegant air of sparse solidity. As they had done when they had belonged to the officers' quarters of some long-forgotten, ocean-bound vessel.

Many of the men greeted Jeb as he walked into the inn - as becoming his status in the village as the head of the most powerful smuggling family in the bay.

Jeb made his way to the bar and Mercy Tindale, the landlady of the tavern immediately pulled down his tankard from the hook from the beam overlying the bar area. She smiled when she placed the freshly pulled ale in front of him.

'I'll have some bread and cheese with that, Mercy,' said Jeb, 'and one of your tasty beef pies. I've been looking forward to one of those the best part of the afternoon.'

A day's work fixing the cobles had worked up his appetite. Of course, he was a man of some means and could quite easily have paid other men to fix his boats but he liked working outside in the fresh sea air and it paid to be in close contact with his fellow baymen. As the lead man of the smuggling operation it always paid to know what was going on in the town which might affect the free trade of the town in any way: any illnesses; anyone who was loose tongued; grievances between the men. Constant vigilance was paid to anything which could result in Jeb (or any of the others) being deported, forced into service or even dangling at the end of a rope. Jeb's attention to detail and personable ways inspired trust in the villagers and in turn, Jeb valued that trust for the gold that it was.

The food was brought to him almost as soon as he seated himself at one of the small tables by the window: Jeb's preferred seating place so he could observe interactions between the other men and of course, anyone who entered the tavern. The Customs officers often frequented it just to make their presence felt.

The food was of an excellent quality – the finest to be found anywhere in England as Robin Hood's Bay was one of the wealthiest villages in the country due to both its free trade and fishing enterprises. Jeb knew that he was a fortunate man having been born and raised in Baytown.

John Tindale, the owner of the tavern, spotted Jeb and came over to the table. He pulled a chair from a nearside table and sat down and leaned in conspiratorially. 'That brandy is still down in my cellar, Jeb. I thought Wilf was to have shifted it by now.'

Wilf was Jeb's son in law, married to his eldest daughter Alice. As a member of the Whittaker family,

Wilf was expected to take a responsible role within the free trade operations.

Jeb bristled at Wilf's name. No contraband was meant to stay in the village; it was meant to be moved to one of the safe hiding places beyond the village eg. in secret hiding places in nearby farmhouses or homesteads. That was the rule. Any goods not despatched immediately across the moors to nearby towns was meant to be stored in a nearby safe dwelling until its buyer was able to claim it. A disruption in the supply chain had led to the unusual situation of ten casks of brandy having to be stored temporarily in the Fisherman's Arms.

'He's a lazy rascal, John. I was given assurances that he would move it out of Baytown within a couple of days. And it was a buyer of his that let us down which led to it still being here.'

'He was in last night, Jeb, and said it would be moved today – it's still here.'

Jeb's anger grew. Wilf had whined about how he wanted more responsibility within the operation and this was the result.

'I'll be honest with you, John. I rue the day our Alice met Wilf. He's nowt but trouble with his cardplaying, sodden ways. He arrived here in rags and smiles and set his hat at our Alice. She should have had more sense.'

'I know, Jeb. But you can't choose who are young uns set their hearts on - but that brandy has to be moved.'

'I'll see to it now, John. A couple of the lads will move it into the tunnel. Leave it with me.'

'Thanks, Jeb'.

'I'll make sure Wilf doesn't get the chance to put us all in danger again, that's for sure,' simmered Jeb as John stood up to tend to the bar. Jeb nodded to a couple of young brawny men at a nearby table and they approached. He whispered his instructions into their ears. The pub cellar lay directly above one of the smuggling tunnels beneath village. He told them to move the casks into the tunnel and then return to their table.

Jeb's meal was ruined. The pie felt like sawdust in his mouth. He shouldn't have trusted Wilf despite the assurances that the goods would be safe in his hands. Jeb usually oversaw whatever Wilf did but Wilf had noticed and complained - had demanded Jeb's trust and respect. Angry more at himself for putting family etiquette before his instincts, Jeb made mental calculations as to how and where the brandy needed to be shifted to. A captain he knew in Whitby was sailing a cutter up to Newcastle and he would welcome the brandy to sell on, he thought. The captain was sailing in several days' time.

Jeb didn't rest easy until the young men, who had shifted the brandy into the secret tunnel below the inn, had returned. The brandy would be taken from the tunnel entrance later on that evening under disguise of the dark.

Jeb pushed his half-eaten food away from him and begun to drink the last of his ale when the door to the inn was flung open and in strode the local customs officer, Captain Lucas, followed by two of his dragoons.

Adrenaline surged through Jeb but long used to worrying situations he pulled his plate back toward him and began to eat again so as not to arouse suspicion. With his relaxed demeanour he looked for all the world as if he was a hard working fisherman who, after an honest day's work, was relishing his well-earned repast and respite…

CHAPTER 7

Sunday 12th September 2018 – Demmy's Cottage, Robin Hood's Bay

Elsie turned the key in the lock and opened the front door of Demmy's cottage. Donning latex gloves, she and Sim stepped gingerly inside. They took a few paces in and looked around.. It was a typical Robin Hood's Bay Cottage: there was only one downstairs room and it was the sitting room and kitchen combined. In the centre of the room was a large original range which showed signs of recent use as there were traces of black cinders on the hearthstone. There was a cooker in the kitchen corner of the room so presumably the range was just used for heating.

'That range must be over two hundred years old,' thought Elsie to herself. She could see why it still remained. It was charming; she had known other owners, of older houses in the area, keep them too. They were brilliant at kicking out heat for the size of the houses they inhabited. Sometimes they were just kept for their decoration and ability to enhance the character of the old cottages. No wonder.

'What are you thinking, Sim?' asked Elsie.

'Probably the same as you, Ma'am: ashes in the grate; seems well kept. No immediate signs of anything untoward.' He stepped over to the kitchen area. 'Washing up cloth looks fairly recently used – no sign of mould. Cooker clean and the surfaces all look like they've been wiped down fairly recently.' He opened the fridge: 'Milk, eggs, cheese and bread; eggs and cheese within date.

On the kitchen worktop were a couple of bottles of wine – one half drunk. Sim peered at them. 'Chateau Des Bardes Saint Emilion. These are quite

expensive, Ma'am. The type more of a connois-
seur would drink. Around fifty pounds a bottle.'

Elsie took a picture of them with her phone and
made a note to herself to ask Mick Harper if his
daughter had an interest in wine.

The furniture was old but comfortable and the colours of the curtains and carpet a neutral light colour – they were obviously new. If Demmy was responsible for the décor she had done a good job as
the combination of old and new had given the place
a pleasant uplift whilst still retaining the cosy charm
of the cottage. There were a few accomplished
paintings, of local scenes, placed on various walls.
Closer scrutiny showed them to be signed by Jessie Whittaker – presumably Demmy's great aunt.
Mick Harper had mentioned how his Aunt Jess had
been creative. One picture by the front door was
not really a picture at all. Elsie looked at it: it was

a finely drawn family tree showing a prominent line of Jess's forebears. Demmy and Sam were at the bottom of the tree, tracing upwards through their parents then Jess and her siblings and so on, right up to a man called Jeb Whittaker in the eighteenth century – a name Elsie had heard of as he had been a famous smuggler in Robin Hood's Bay.

Many people in the village were interested in tracing family trees. Old families were often shown to be interrelated, at some point, over the past two or three hundred years or so. Elsie herself was descended from a prominent Bay family. In fact some of the outer branches of Jess's family tree showed links between the Storm and Whittaker families. She didn't have time now to pursue the family links but she couldn't resist taking a picture on her phone to enlarge at some point on her computer and investigate the links more closely. Elsie too had always been interested in Bay ancestry and how her forebears had spent their lives. Nowadays was so different to then, but as she glanced at the pull of the timeless North Sea beyond the window she realised that in some ways her visceral feelings were probably just the same as those who had gone before. Like many before and probably after her, Elsie felt as if the North Sea would always anchor her to the Bay.

She noted that the prominent line, Jess had drawn up through her family tree showed a list of captains, sea merchants, doctors and wealthy farmers in the area. Fortune had smiled on Jeb's descendents she mused momentarily to herself. She felt a gust of air on her neck and felt as if someone was looking at her. She turned quickly expecting Sim to be behind her but all her eyes met was a photograph of Demmy, standing with an old lady outside the door of the cottage, on the mantelpiece. Demmy was a few years younger but her arm was casually placed around the shoulders of the old lady who was also beaming into the camera. Anger fought pity in Elsie's heart and neither won as she gazed at the reflection of the fresh faced young girl. With a wrench she tore her eyes from the photo and carried on appraising the rest of the cottage.

Sim's gaze rested on something on the kitchen work-surface and he looked at it for a few seconds. 'Ma'am?'

Elsie walked over to look at his find. It was a leaflet advertising an arts and crafts fair in York which had taken place over a week ago. Written in neat letters across it were the words, 'Perhaps we could find the time to visit this on Friday afternoon. What do you think? Love xxx.'

Elsie took a picture of it to add to her collection of the umpteen ones she had taken around the cottage.

The rest of the cottage didn't reveal anything of particular note – except for the fabulous views across the bay from what looked to be the guest bedroom on the second floor. On the first floor were the main bedroom and a bathroom.

The main bedroom was a large cluttered room (contrasting with the neat décor of the rest of the cottage) with a double bed and deep red velvet curtains at the window. There was a dressing table with a large bevelled looking glass – its surface was covered with make up: dark lipsticks, pale make up, dark pencils. The dark cream walls were covered in a variety of posters depicting current Goth bands or moody Goth inspired scenarios. A heavy walnut wardrobe took up practically one side of the room.

Sim started at one end of the room and Elsie the other and they sifted through the innumerable bits and pieces that had made up Demmy's life. Elsie

tried to switch off her feelings but it was hard –
sifting through the childhood keepsakes was the
worst. Those and the various pieces of sculpture
which lay casually placed around the room. Elsie
was particularly struck by a sculpture of an octo-
pus, again made from a piece of driftwood. One
tentacle slightly raised as if waving – it seemed to
be a characteristic trademark of Demmy's work. It
seemed so animated Elsie felt it was capable of
moving, such was its lifelike representation. She
sighed at the wasted talent. Determination drove
her on.

After about half an hour, Sim quietly murmured,
'Ma'am'. Elsie turned to see him holding a card depicting a beach with some writing in it.

'Love you and thank you for wine xxx.'

'The same writing as the other note,' commented
Elsie.

'Both don't state a name either,' added Sim.

'We'll compare it to Jimmy's writing. It could just be a rendezvous message from him,' said Elsie cautiously.

'When we were at Jimmy's flat he had some notebooks open on the coffee table – about Goth events in the town from what I could make out. His handwriting is large and sprawling,' answered Sim. 'And it seems a bit odd that both of these notes don't leave an actual name'.

They both looked at the small neat handwriting on both pieces of paper.

'Ok, let's see if we can find anything else.'

Despite a thorough search, nothing else of particular interest was found.

Being unable to glean anything of obvious significance, Elsie and Sim left the little house in Sunnyside Lane. This little old cottage, with its probable history of smuggling secrets, possibly held secrets of a more modern, gristly nature. Hopefully, a full investigation by the forensic team might discover some of them.

CHAPTER 8

Sunday 12th September 2018 - Whitby

Elsie drove a small fiat which was perfect for small country roads. She'd specifically asked for a vintage green colour when she had bought it as it was one of her favourite colours. She watched Sim as he drew on his cigarette before he climbed back into the car. She found it unusual that Sim smoked as he was such a fitness fanatic. It wasn't her place to comment.

Elsie pulled out of the layby. Sim was already tapping away on his ipad. He was often to be found typing on some device or other. It crossed her mind, more than once, that he had been in some kind of intelligence service in the army. She'd even known the police force techies to consult him about particularly tricky problems - such was his expertise.

'Sounds like Demmy was the odd one out in the family,' said Elsie. 'Do you think Sam Harper was telling the truth about his dad and him having no enemies?'

'I do to be honest. I've ran some preliminary checks and there's nothing in their backgrounds to suggest trouble. Some of their business associates need to be contacted to see if they know anything. There were no signs of fear or anxiety when you asked the question.'

Sim spoke in a well-educated, modulated tone. His observances of human body language, facial expression and tone of voice usually turned out to be dead on accurate. Elsie turned her thoughts to Jimmy Bransdale and as if reading her mind Sim looked up from his screen and said, 'James Bransdale has form.'

Elsie hid a smile. It sounded odd: such an expression coming from someone with a cut glass English accent. 'Go on,' she urged.

'He spent time in a youth correctional facility when he was fifteen. Up to then he was in and out of a number of care homes. He had two incidents in correctional care where he was accused of violence. General feral behaviour led to his time in correctional care.'

Elsie's hated these kinds of situations. Too many kids from care homes got into bother. Without the anchor of regular people in their lives, many ran adrift and, too often, their lives just lurched from one bad situation to another in an ever downward spiral. But the question had to be asked: was Jimmy a hardened individual who resented his girlfriend's wealth and family security and had hit back when given the opportunity?

'It goes without saying that we need to focus on Mick Harper until we've discounted him from the enquiries. Like you, Sim, I don't expect to find anything there, or with Sam.' She sighed. Sim nodded. Mick

Harper's shock and grief did not exactly make him a lead suspect, in Elsie's eyes, but sadly, it wouldn't be the first time that a parent had been responsible for harming their own child. Mick Harper couldn't be discounted. And perhaps Sam too could have been involved. Her mind ran unwillingly to grim scenarios: Mick rowing with Demmy and it resulting in her being killed; Sam helping his father to dispose of the body. There were obviously tensions in the family. She hated how this job forced her to suspect everyone – even the grief stricken: their grief not exculpating them necessarily from guilt. She was glad that both Sam and his father seemed to have clear alibis – which obviously needed to be confirmed. The numbers Sam had given them were already being investigated back at the station.

As they tipped the last hillock of the moors, the Esk valley dropped below to the river which ran into the old harbour of Whitby bisecting the town on its journey to the sea. On the other side of the harbour, the valley rose again, through the oldest cottages of Whitby, to be crowned by the wonderful sight of Whitby Abbey with its lace-like stonework against a blue backdrop of sky. Elsie never grew tired of this view.

It was an unusual kind of light in this part of the world. There were often days that were as grey as steel, but there were also days like this, when everything seemed suffused with an alluring, blue gold light as if it were a prism through which could be glimpsed a sense of an ethereal timelessness. Elsie wondered if this was what had first attracted the Christian monks, in the 7th Century, to this little part of the coast for the building of their monastery. She wondered at the technical expertise and other worldly aestheticism which had built this wonderful edifice later on in the early part of the 13th Century - several centuries after the

Danes had laid waste to the monastery on one of their many raids of the coast. The old Abbey completely belied such communities as being somehow primitive and backward. What buildings built today, or in recent years, drew such equal reverence, affection and awe as this ancient Abbey – even in its present ruined state? She wondered to herself.

Sim stopped tapping for a moment and looked at the view. 'I used to live in Whitby…well boarded at Ampleforth for most of the time,' he added. Elsie was amazed. Sim never spoke about himself. She waited quietly for him to continue but infuriatingly he went back to tapping on his computer. She already knew he had attended Ampleforth: it was a public school in the heart of the North Yorkshire countryside. Sim's accent betrayed wealth anyway but his schooling had been one piece of information included in his rather sketchy CV.

Meanwhile, Sim had stopped tapping on his ipad for information, 'Apparently, Jimmy Bransdale is quite a fixture of the Goth world. He's contributed lots of articles to a prominent Goth website; his face has been in the papers several times at local and national Goth events.'

'Have you managed to find out any more about his early background?' asked Elsie.

'Will let you know when I do,' he said as he went back to tapping on his computer.

By now they were dropping into the town with its suburban houses and winding roads leading down to the old town and its harbour. A quick check in the car park, near the supermarket, confirmed that Demmy's car was still there. A SOCO team was already on its way to meticulously check it over. Elsie drew up and gave a cursory inspection but there was nothing to suggest that anything was amiss.

They waited for the SOCO to arrive and then she and Sim left to find Jimmy's street.

Elsie and Sim drove to Mariner's Parade, one of the main parts of the tourist thoroughfare filled with shops and restaurants – many having flats above them. Jimmy lived in a flat of one of them - above a tourist shop selling seaside sweets and souvenirs.

Elsie peered at Sim's computer screen which he drew to her attention when she had parked the car. It displayed a photograph from the Whitby Gazette of Jimmy Bransdale at a Goth event in the town a couple of months previously. Jimmy looked like some kind of distinguished Edwardian gentleman in a black suit. His thick black eyeliner accentuating his pale handsome features. 'He's certainly an attractive looking young man,' Elsie commented before getting out of the car

It took a few rings of the bell before a bedraggled young man answered. He was dressed in on old wrinkled track suit that looked as if it had been slept in and his hair was unkempt. Sartorially he was as unlike the perfectly groomed young man in the photo as it was possible to be. Despite that he was exceptionally handsome, even more so in real life, with his dark hair; violet eyes and pleasing features enhanced by the firm jawline – despite its unshaved dusting.

'Mr Bransdale? I'm Detective Chief Inspector Storm, and this is my colleague, Detective Inspector Howard. Can we ask you a few questions?'

Without a word and with a defeated air, Jimmy motioned for them to follow him through and up the unpainted and poorly carpeted hall and stairwell. His flat seemed better cared for and quite cosy but it was untidy. Elsie looked out of the sitting room

window through which could be spotted the harbour. Some fishing boats were returning from their
morning forages whilst gulls wheeled overhead.
The ancient Norman church of St Mary's, with its
square crenelated tower, clung to the rise which
swept up from the opposite side of the harbour,
above the dwellings of the oldest part of the town
which skirted it. The squat owlish church, which
gazed down on the town, proved the perfect con-
trapuntal to the dramatic sweeping arches of the
old Gothic abbey soaring into the sky behind it.

'This is a lovely view, Mr Bransdale.' Probably the
wrong thing to say, given the circumstances but
she just wanted to break the ice in a non-threat-
ening way.

'Whatever,' replied the young man, as he sat in
a battered armchair and stared moodily at the
unlit fire.

'You'll have heard about Demeris Harper?' Elsie asked. She decided to sit down uninvited. It was better that she was on Jimmy's level she thought. Sim remained standing by the door but facing Jimmy.

The young man's fierce red rimmed eyes blinked but he made no answer. Elsie wasn't surprised at Jimmy's uncommunicative responses. He didn't seem either defiant or cooperative. It was the standard response of young people who had regular dealings with the authorities. Give nothing away and try not to do anything to bring more trouble to the door.

'We'd like to offer our condolences,' said Elsie.

'Before you bang me up,' muttered Jimmy under his breath; his self-control breaking in spite of himself.

'Sorry,' asked Elsie. The young man didn't reply. Elsie thought she saw a rim of tear line the lower curve of his eye but in a blink it was gone. 'Why did you say that? Is there something you want to tell us?'

Jimmy tried to swallow back his anger but it got the better of him and he burst out, 'You won't look much further than me will you? Ex kid in care; been in trouble with the police before; out of my league with Demmy? Yeah, you've got it all wrapped up haven't you! Well, I didn't do it and I want you to find out who did. That's the only reason I'm talking to you now so you can get on with finding the bastard that did do it.'

Jimmy was intelligent. He was right. This is how it would look on paper. He was a prime suspect and clever enough to know it.

Elsie tried again. 'Where were you on Saturday night, Jimmy?'

'Here.' He said succinctly.

'Here, the whole night?'

Jimmy nodded in reply. 'Mostly'.

'Were you on your own, Jimmy?' interjected Sim.

'Yeah,' he replied in a monotone as if he hardly registered Sim's presence.

'When did you last see Demeris?' asked Sim.

Jimmy nodded, still staring into the fireplace, 'Yesterday about two. If you must know we had a row. You'll probably find that out anyway.'

'What was the row about?' asked Elsie softly.

'Stupid stuff,' he shrugged miserably. 'Then she said she was going home and that was the last time I saw her.' He looked down at his feet.

'What time was that, Mr Bransdale?'

'About one-thirty, she'd just finished work.'

'Have you got any idea who might have wanted to harm Demmy?' asked Sim. Elsie and Sim watched Jimmy closely.

'No-one!' said Jimmy angrily, 'No-one could have any reason to hurt Demmy. I can't think of anyone she knows who would have a reason to do this.' His face was tight with fury. Elsie detected tears in his eyes again.

'What exactly did you row about, Mr Bransdale?' persisted Elsie.

'I wanted to go out that night, but Demmy didn't, again. I couldn't understand why. She used to love meeting up at the Angel with everyone. It was the highlight of our week.'

'There had been other times when she hadn't wanted to go out, then?' asked Elsie, tentatively. She knew that they were fortunate that Jimmy was being forthcoming and she didn't want to stem the flow of his words.

'If you must know, yes,' he said resignedly.

'Why do you think that was?' asked Sim gently.

'Don't know,' said Jimmy with a barely perceptible gulp. 'She'd changed, seemed to be getting tired of me. It didn't help that her fucking stupid father hated me. Maybe she was beginning to think she could do better for herself than...me. Can't blame her I suppose. But one thing's for sure, if I'd been with her nothing would have happened to her. No one would have dared come near her. She probably was too good for me - I always thought she was; couldn't believe my luck that she was with me. But nothing would have happened to her if she had been with me - that's for fucking sure.'

A look of fury had again crossed the young man's face as he spoke but as he finished the words were replaced by two dry sobs. The young man tried to hide his face by leaping up and going to look out of the window. He stared at the Abbey perched on its lofty cliff opposite the harbour, its 199 steps tracing up to the top and its old lamps studded alongside; leading the way to a place of perceived salvation at its top. Jimmy Bransdale brushed his sleeve against his eyes in a swift movement.

They gave him a few moments. 'Can you recall what you said to her, Jimmy; what she said to you?' asked Elsie.

Jimmy took a deep breath and turned around to face them. 'I asked her why she couldn't make the Angel. I asked her if she was starting to listen to her fucking old man and thought I wasn't good enough for her anymore. I wish I hadn't asked her that. We were different. I could see she was moving away from me. I can't hold that against her but I was shouting and I wish I hadn't shouted at her.

Not her fault if she didn't feel the same anymore. Not her bastard father's fault neither. I'd be wary if my kid took up with someone like me - still hate him though: gave Demmy nothing but grief; she was like a shackled dog. I wouldn't have shouted at her if I knew they would be the last words I ever said to her though.' He turned to face the window again and took deep breaths.

'And how did Demmy respond?' asked Elsie quietly.

'Like she always does, she just shut down; went all quiet. Said she'd try to ring later; and then she just turned and walked away. I wanted to say more, but I knew it was no use. She'd just stay quiet. So I turned and walked away. What else could I do? Didn't know it would be the last time I'd ever see her.' He gave up all pretence at hiding his grief at this point, and turned back to the window and lowered his head onto his sleeve and quietly sobbed.

'Were, you worried perhaps that she was seeing somebody else, Jimmy?' asked Sim.

'Dunno,' he replied morosely. He went to the armchair and slumped down onto it. His eyes filling with tears once again, 'I suppose the signs were there but she never said anything. Mebbe she was building up to telling me.'

'Do you think she would have been worried to tell you, something like that?' asked Sim again.

'What, in case I hit her or something, do you mean?' Jimmy's voice was raised and he began to pace the room.

'You tell me,' said Sim.

'She knew I would never hit her...ever.' He abruptly sat down into an old armchair and slumped there miserably. 'I guess, she might have felt...sorry for me. That's the truth of it. Sorry that she couldn't give me the relationship I wanted, I guess.' He looked up and stared Sim defiantly in the eye. 'That's the 'only' reason she wouldn't have told me.'

'Can you give us an idea of your whereabouts yesterday afternoon and evening, Jimmy?' asked Elsie.

'After Demmy left me on the quayside, I came back here for a couple of hours, messed about on the computer for a bit; trying to take my mind off her. Then I went out with a couple of mates – got back about nine. Didn't feel like staying out.'

'You went on the computer?' asked Sim. 'What for?'

'I help organise the Goth festival in late Autumn. Just organising gigs and events, why?'

'Just asking,' said Sim.

'Just asking,' mimicked Jimmy. 'Asking to see if there is any online evidence of me being hooked up to the computer, you mean? Well, feel free to look, mate. There's plenty on there to show me talking to the others at the time I said I was. I'm telling the truth and you're wasting time dragging me in.'

'Jimmy, we want to find the reasons for Demmy's death, as much as you seem to. If we didn't investigate everything fully you'd want to know why, wouldn't you?' said Elsie. He gave a begrudging nod.

'And I would like you to come to the station to help us further with our enquiries,' she added.

'Of course you would,' he said bitterly. 'What are we waiting for and don't forget to bring the computer,' he added sarcastically. He stood up. Elsie stood up too - a little shame-faced, in spite of herself.

The Fish

By William Butler Yeats

Although you hide in the ebb and flow

Of the pale tide when the moon has set,

The people of coming days will know

About the casting out of my net,

And how you have leaped times out of mind

Over the little silver cords,

And think that you were hard and unkind,

And blame you with many bitter words.

CHAPTER 9

Robin Hood's Bay 1797 (Based on a true story)

John Tindale glanced across at Jeb calmly eating his food and was reassured by Jeb's unruffled appearance at the entrance of the customs dragoons into the inn.

'What can I get you, gentlemen? Mercy has just finished baking a few of her pies, if you'd like me to call her to bring some through. Or maybe just a well-earned tankard of ale?'

Captain Lucas, the custom officer's eyes gleamed at the mention of the ale, he was well known for his regular presence in the local taverns. Tindale passed a tankard of yeasty frothing ale under Lucas's nose and across the bar to a waiting customer. Lucas inhaled – he couldn't help himself.

'Not today, Tindale. We're here on the King's business,' replied Captain Lucas, with a touch of regret in his voice as he eyed the customer quaffing the ale thirstily.

'Oh?' queried Tindale with a look of surprise. 'And what business would that be? You know I run an honest trade, Captain Lucas? '

'We've heard rumour that there are unaccounted for goods on your premises, Mr Tindale. From a recent smuggling run; from a cutter bound from France. We're here to inspect your premises, including your cellar.'

'As you wish, Captain Lucas, but you've inspected these premises before and found nothing untoward. The person who has directed you here is up to mischief and I hope you deal swiftly with them after your inspection.'

Captain Lucas gave an irritated look around the bar and spotted Jeb. Lucas glowered. He'd had his suspicions about Jeb for a long time but had never managed to catch him out. It didn't help that he had wooed Emma, Jeb's wife, many years ago, only to be cast aside when Jeb began to take an interest in her. Aware of the Captain's glares, Jeb calmly continued eating his meal.

If Lucas could only find some of the contraband, he was sure that pinning the blame on one of the villagers would smoke Jeb out. As if reading Lucas's thoughts, Jeb calmly turned his head to face him. Jeb raised his tankard in greeting, smiled at Lucas and then placidly proceeded to drink the last of the ale. Lucas scowled at him. 'I'll catch you one of these days,' he muttered to himself.

The government was alarmed at the success of the smuggling operations along this coast and

Captain Lucas had been recently reprimanded for not making enough progress in seizing the contraband, never mind catching the smugglers involved. Revenue was needed for the wars in France and much of it was lost through smuggling. Of the 13 million pounds (weight) of tea consumed by Britain, only 5.5 million, it was said, was brought in legally. Not to mention the gin, brandy, silk and other luxury items.

John Tindale waved the dragoons through the bar and down the stairs to the cellar with a much aggrieved look on his face.

…………………………...

The sudden appearance of the dragoons in the tavern had unnerved Jeb so he decided to oversee the removal of the casks of brandy from the tunnel later that night.

Leading the two young men (Reuben and Tom) who had mover the brandy to the underground tunnel earlier at the inn, he led the way into the tunnel to retrieve the casks. Shoulder type panniers ensured that only one journey was necessary. Jeb would carry two of the ten casks and the two younger men would carry four each, across a short stretch of the beach into a wooded cleft in the cliff called Boggle Hole - through which a track led up onto the moors. Charlie, Jeb's eldest son was acting as lookout. Another of his sons, Sam, would be waiting at Boggle Hole with some horses. Jeb planned to move the casks to a hiding place, in a nearby cottage just outside of the village. The cottage had a hidden cavity behind its fire place.

The tunnel below the Fisherman's Arms was actually formed from a beck which ran under many of the cottages in Robin Hood's Bay. Many of these cottages had access to the tunnel which made the dragoons' job more difficult when attempting to intercept contraband which had recently landed ashore.

As usual the men were primed as to what to do beforehand so that they could carry out their task silently and efficiently. The men gathered the casks and exited the tunnel - after hearing Charlie's low whistle. They set off along the beach staying as near to the cliffs as possible to escape detection. Luckily, it was a moonless night, so far, and the men knew the path well so swift progress was made. They were halfway to the Boggle Hole cleft when Charlie's whistle was heard once again. It was a low whistle timed to the crash of the waves. The men's hearing was attuned to the sound of the secret sounds which the smugglers used between themselves. This time the whistle sound was broken into a series of five whistles. Charlie had spotted something.

Jeb whipped round. The moon came out from behind a cloud at that very moment. The dragoons were at the base of the dock area about a couple of hundred yards away and had spotted them. The shape of their hats gave them away as did the dark shape of the long rifles which they carried slung over their shoulders. In the next moment they were taking the rifles from their shoulders to load up and fire at them.

'Jeb?' whispered Reuben in a panic, when he too glanced behind.

'We can't run carrying these,' said Jeb. 'We won't make it to the horses. Leave the casks!' he commanded.

A shot rang out as sharp as a thunder crack with the light from the powder lighting up the determined face of Captain Lucas.

'Don't worry lads, he likely won't be accurate from that way back. Drop the casks and run for the horses. I'll catch you up.'

'What…?' Tom began to ask but remembering the protocol of the smuggler operations he jettisoned his question. There was no time to question. Jeb had to be obeyed and trusted in his decisions. Unnecessary talk wasted life-saving seconds.

Reuben and Tom untied the casks from their shoulder panniers and began to run. The three dragoons were running toward them now. Jeb kept an eye on the dragoons in case they stopped to take aim again. He bent down to one of the casks, he had dropped on the sand, and swiftly loosened its stopper. The sweet smell of a high quality French cognac assailed his nostrils. He propped the cask against another so that the brandy dripped out but didn't pour out. He glanced up. The dragoons were fifty yards away or so and all three had stopped to aim their rifles at him.

Jeb turned and ran alongside the cliff base. A shot from a rifle whistled past his shoulder. Another above his head – so close that he felt its heat pass the top of his head. He ran hard then, leaping over rockpools and across the scars of rock the bay was known for. He knew this beach as sure as he knew the lanes and ginnels of the Bay. He'd played on the beach since he was a small child chasing the gulls from the landed herring boats. Adrenaline though, made his feet skitter at one point but he leapt up and forward again. Another shot whistled past him just as he turned into the cleft of Boggle Hole. He was safe. The dense wood in the chasm would hide him. He ran up the path of the chasm until he found Sam waiting for him. Reuben and Tom were poised to leave. Seeing that Jeb was safe, they kicked their horses with their shins and galloped away up the path of the cleft to the moors. Sam, his son, waited until his father was mounted before kicking his heels against the sides of his horse. Within seconds, Jeb and Sam had disappeared into the darkness of the wooded track.

The three dragoons knew that once out of their sight it would be impossible to catch the smugglers. Still, Captain Lucas' eyes gleamed when he spotted the mound of casks that the smugglers had been forced to leave behind. The dense fragrance of the brandy hit his nostrils.

'Willis, set off at once to alert the militia. We'll need some help getting these under lock and key. Roberts and I will guard the brandy until they arrive. We're lucky it's a mild night. Hurry now!'

Sergeant Willis immediately turned and jogged back up the beach toward the dock. He would be a little while as the militia were based just outside

Whitby. Still, he would likely return before the night was over.

'Roberts' gather some driftwood. We need a fire.'

Soon a small fire was roaring lighting up the two men's faces against the dark embrace of the cliff.

The two men huddled against the fire whilst they waited for the return of Willis and the militia. Despite the warmth from the flames, a sea breeze had sprung up. All was quiet so they laid aside their rifles and moved closer to the fire. They could see in all directions from the low glow of the moon.

The breeze sharpened and Captain Lucas wished for Willis's swift return. He had noticed earlier that one of the casks, in the nearby mound, had a loose stopper so had quickly tightened it. By doing so he had spilt a small amount of the liquor on his overcoat. The aroma of brandy heightened as the patch of brandy on his coat dried out.

'Roberts, what do you say to a little brandy just to keep the cold at bay, whilst we wait?'

Roberts too had noticed the increasing warm woody aroma of the brandy. He hadn't eaten since dinner-time (with Captain Lucas' exhortations to search for the brandy, 'until it was found'). The warm fug of brandy would help to dampen his hunger.

'Just here to obey orders, sir,' and then he added for clarity, 'whatever you think best, sir.'

'Well, here we are on a cold night, risking life and limb for our betters. It seems only right that we avail ourselves of a tincture to keep us warm, don't you think?'

'Well, it would help to warm us up, sir'.

As if in cosmic agreement, a gust of wind wrapped itself around the flames funnelling the heat away in another direction completely allowing the damp chill to descend on them once again. The two men glanced as one at the inviting mound of casks.

'Now, don't go getting ideas, Roberts, just a tincture is all that we will partake. No-one will even miss it, I warrant.'

'Most certainly, sir.'

'I mean, this fine beverage is bound for the dinner of a fine lord and his lady, I'm sure that they wouldn't begrudge a sip or two in order ensure its smooth passage to their table.'

'If they were here now,' said Roberts warming to the tone of the conversation and its likely outcome, 'I'm certain they would insist on a glass as a reward for risking…'

'Life and limb. Exactly, concluded Captain Lucas. 'Fetch one of the tubs over here, Roberts,' he commanded. 'We'll only have a little, mind – just warm ourselves with a little tot. No harm in it. It's foolish to sit in the cold,'

'Risking life and limb, sir.'

'Hmm,' said Lucas, wondering if Roberts' enthusiasm for the idea had tilted into mockery. But that was by the by. Roberts had, by this time, hefted himself up to fetch one of the casks. Captain Lucas's eyes gleamed in the orange firelight.

Meanwhile, the smugglers had gathered on the moor in order to receive instruction from Jeb. By this time, Charlie had joined them too.

'Shame about that brandy; one of the finer types – it would have fetched a fair bit of silver,' said Reuben.

'Not a great haul though. We'll just have to let it go, won't we, father?' asked Sam.

Tom just snorted his annoyance at the dragoons having caught them with the brandy and now having ownership of it. A shilling was a shilling in his eyes and though the haul was small it was worth a pretty penny.

Charlie said nothing. He could read his father and had noted the expression of mischief on his father's face. 'Father?' he said warily?

'I'd usually agree with Sam,' said Jeb, as his natural caution had avoided many a dangerous outcome, 'but Captain Lucas likes a drink, doesn't he? I venture we go back and see if he's managed to withstand the temptation of one of the finest cognacs in France. I warrant he has not. And Roberts, is his regular drinking companion. As for Willis, he's the youngest of them and always does Lucas' bidding. I reckon he'll have been sent to fetch the militia. That will take several hours.'

Now the smuggling men of Robin Hood's Bay were a pragmatic and canny bunch. They were used to taking considered risks and this was not quite in that category but Captain Lucas was a bully. He had become more belligerent as the years had passed. He was easy to outwit and his successive failures at reducing smuggling in the bay had increased his sense of grievance toward the villagers. He had recently held young George Farthing overnight in a cell, for not being able to account for his presence on the moors at night – George had repeatedly told Lucas that he was fetching the midwife for his sister in law, Lil. Not to mention Lucas' untoward behaviour toward the younger women of the village. Captain Lucas had become a grim kind of sport to the villagers as a consequence.

'Who's in?' asked Jeb. Any man who'd rather get home to the hearth can leave, no bad feelings, lads.'

The men looked at each other and smiles broke all round…

…………………………..

Within twenty minutes or so, Charlie was once again at his lookout, Sam was waiting by the horses at Boggle Hole and Jeb, Reuben and Tom were at the base of the Boggle Hole chasm listening to the waves gently breaking on the shore.

After about another hour or so, Jeb crept toward the dying embers of the fire. Captain Lucas and Sergeant Roberts were both snoring gently, unused to the richness and high alcoholic content of the brandy. The mere sips of the 'tincture' had soon turned into more generous slurps from the cask. Such is brandy: impossible to resist once its warm greeting has met the lips.

Jeb quietly approached the two snoring dragoons and picked up their rifles which he placed behind a rock in the unlikely event that they woke too soon. With the quiet stealth of men used to such doings the three men loaded up their shoulder panniers and as silent as moonlight were soon on their way back to the horses and speeding away with their precious cargo.

By the time the militia arrived, the smugglers were back by their own hearths, toasting themselves, with a tot of brandy…after all, they were risking life and limb to bring it to the tables of the fine lords and ladies.

CHAPTER 10

Sunday 12th September 2018 – Scarborough Police Headquarters

'Where did you go in the evening? asked Sim.

Elsie, Sim and Jimmy Bransdale were seated in the Interview Room at Scarborough Police Station. They had been through all the questions that they had posed in Jimmy's flat for corroboration and for the benefit of the recorder in the interview room. Jimmy had answered all of the questions with exactly the same answers as before. Jimmy's demeanour had hardened during the quiet journey from Whitby and now he sat sullen and pale-faced before them. An emotionless husk of the person he had been in his flat. His flat eyes stared resolutely down at the cup of tea which he had been given and which he had barely sipped.

'Didn't fancy it after Demmy and I had had a row. We always used to go there together. Some mates and me, Arnie and Marcus, just went to a few of the other pubs around town. They went onto the Angel but I came home about nine.' He stared uncomprehendingly at the cup. His thoughts etched onto his misery savaged face – furrows of grief already ploughed there.

'Do we have your permission to search your property?' asked Elsie

'As if I have a choice.' He uttered tersely after a moment. 'I suppose the sooner you realise I didn't have anything to do with this, the sooner you'll be off my back and be able to catch the bastard that did this to Demmy. Anyway, I know you'll search the flat if you arrested me. And you would arrest me if I didn't give my permission. Just like you'd arrest me anyway if I didn't agree to come with you now to the station. I know all your tricks. Just hope your tricks are good enough to catch the evil scum that did do it.'

The sound of the interview room door opening with a loud squeak made him jump. Shannon popped her head around the door, 'Ma'am?'

'Interview suspended at 7.40pm, Sunday, 25th September 2018,' Elsie said before clicking off the recording machine. She stepped out of the room, closing the door behind her. Shannon was slouched against the wall, outside the door of the interview room. 'Well?' enquired Elsie.

'The techies have checked out Jimmy's computer. Between two and four he used it quite extensively discussing and helping to organise the forthcoming Goth festival in Whitby – this November. Apparently, he's one of the chief organisers.'

'So it's unlikely that he was somehow involved with Demmy at that time. Although I suppose she might have come to his flat to maybe make up. Still doesn't gel though, does it?'

'It's not impossible that she was there at the same time he was on his computer.' Shannon said. 'Anyway, forensics should be able to verify if anything untoward happened at the flat on that afternoon.'

Elsie thought for a minute, 'He might not have actually been at the flat when he used the computer. It's a laptop. We know he used it at those times – but he could have used it in other places. Even used it as a means of creating an alibi.'

'Nipping off to clock Demmy between posts, you mean?' asked Shannon.

'Yes, I suppose that is what I mean. Maybe he and Demmy drove somewhere, or even walked somewhere, and the murder was committed there.'

'Likely to have used a car then, as you wouldn't cart a laptop around if you were going for a walk. It wouldn't make sense. And what would he have done with the body? Stuffed it under a bush?'

'Could have,' said Sim, 'maybe they carried on their row and he hid the body until he could collect it later – for which he is likely to have used his car.'

'We need to check Jimmy's car, if he has one, and we need to check with his neighbours to see if they saw Demmy arriving or them both leaving or returning to the flat yesterday.'

'On it, Ma'am. Gus and I haven't found any relevant information from the people we've questioned at Robin Hood's Bay. There's no sighting of her there yesterday, at all. We'll mosey over to Whitby and check out Jimmy's neighbours. Sunday evening's a good time to catch everyone – most will be in.'

'Excellent, Shannon. Keep me informed.'

'Yup.'

Irritating though Shannon was, she seemed inde-
fatigable and never seemed to show any objection
to the long days and nights that murder cases always seemed to create. She did her job and she did
it very well, Elsie was the first to admit. She went
back into the interview room where Jimmy and Sim
sat in silence; Jimmy still seemingly absorbed with
his own thoughts, oblivious to his surroundings.
He didn't even look up when Elsie re-entered and
clicked the recording machine back on.

'Interview with James Bransdale, Sunday 25th September 2018, 7.45pm. DCI Storm and DI Howard
present.'

'Jimmy, do you have a car?' asked Elsie.

'No,' he answered succinctly.

'You say you used the computer between two and four yesterday. Did you use it in your flat or take it somewhere else to be used?'

'In the flat, why would I bother lugging it around? Oh I see, Use it to cover my tracks you mean? Well done, you, for thinking that. I used it at the flat and never saw Demmy again after speaking to her at 1.30. You won't find any evidence that I saw her or did anything to her after that time because there isn't any evidence to find.'

His voice rose. 'You're wasting your time with these questions.' He placed a clenched fist agitatedly onto the table. He grabbed the cup of tea as if to distract his temper and seemed to force himself to take a sip. He put his hand down by his side and forced his gaze onto the cup holding the liquid which swirled lazily around from the movement a few moments before – seemingly at odds with the tension in the room.

'Jimmy, we're going to keep you in overnight. Do you understand? We'll check out your flat and take things from there.'

'You're wasting good time, I wish you could understand that. Whoever did that to Demmy is walking free and probably covering up any evidence,' he replied tersely. His face looked taut, as if it were made of wood, and as if every word had to be forcibly and painfully expelled from its fixed features.

CHAPTER 11

Robin Hood's Bay 1797

The seagulls cawked from their chimney top perches and the sound ricocheted around the red pantiled roofs of the fishermen's cottages in Robin Hood's Bay. Old Tom Harrison was sat outside his cottage on Sunnyside Lane and was busy repairing his lobster nets, singing an old sea shanty as he did so. A clutch of sea shells hung from a piece of string over his door: clack, clack, clacking as the sea breeze caught them. Emma Whittaker was stood chatting to Jen Robinson, and their kids, too numerous to mention, spilled in and out of the doorways on Sunnyside Lane. After the long hard grey winter, it was as if the energy from the breaking sunshine had woken something in their souls. As Billy, the eldest of Jen Robinson's brood, barged into his mum, Jen bawled at all the kids to clear off and go and play on the beach, 'Go and help your fathers with the herrings. Tide's out for another couple of hours, so don't come back till then.'

Almost as one, the twelve children or so, hurtled out of the little cobbled alleyway; almost tipping into one another as they scuttled down the steps onto the Dock. The children's happy cries faded away into the brine-washed air.

'This one is going to be full of tea, I've heard,' said Jen quietly.

'So it is,' confided Emma, 'and thank goodness, I was getting low on tea. 'Tea always makes a tidy profit, so that'll put a smile on Jeb's face.'

'Hope it goes well, there's a rumour that they're going to draft in more dragoons to catch the us.' Jen always worried about the customs men and dragoons. It was just her way. Emma did too, if she was honest, but she tried to put out of her mind such apprehension. Smuggling – or free-trading, as she preferred to call it, was their way and she more saw the dragoons as just a hazard of the job. At the same time prudent caution was a way of life.

Emma was married to Jeb, the chief lynchpin of the smuggling enterprise in the village. She, as his wife, was jointly responsible for ensuring that smuggling in the Bay was as efficient and coordinated as possible. Baytown folk were meticulous at taking precautions to ensure that news of a run was kept secret; nothing untoward was spotted during the run and that they left no traces of the contraband.

Every village had to fight for itself in these times and what would the Government do with the revenue anyway? Keep it for the rich or for these never-ending wars with Napoleon. Not that she wanted Napoleon to win but enough taxes were paid from the herring trade - fishing being another lucrative industry in the village. The village earned its keep as well as ensuring that it looked after its own and repaid the villagers for their enterprise and hard work, she thought. No, Emma refused to be worried about any aspect of the free-trading enterprises in her village and the part she and her family played in it (as generations of Bay families had done before them). She would go to Church each Sunday; gut, pack and take the herrings to market; tend her family and like a cog in an ever-ticking clock, play her part when the smuggling luggers stole into the Bay.

And there were smugglers and smugglers. She hated as much as others, those swindlers that would take good folks' money and leave them with a box of tea filled mostly with sawdust, or who would sell their friends to the customs officers in exchange for a bit of leniency, or special favours - not to mention the fighting and drinking which some smugglers spent their time and money on. The folk of Baytown did not hold with such ways. Their smuggling was a business – a free-trading enterprise, between those bringing the goods to English shores and those in the Bay who would ensure their swift passage to the towns and parishes in the shires for a fair price. What good folk paid for, good folk got – and without the heavy hand of the government syphoning off profits to spend on its never-ending wars.

In addition, their village was a God fearing one. Every Sunday the services in the chapel at Baytown were packed to the brim - as was St. Stephens at the top of Baytown. John Wesley, the famous Methodist preacher, himself had visited the village, some years ago - to lay the foundation stone for the new chapel. The villagers took their religious duties seriously. Wesley had seemed to have a liking for the old village and its people, and had often ensured he visited after preaching to the great and good of York. And he had always been received warmly by all the citizens of Robin Hood's Bay. His chapel sermons had always been packed and he'd even been known to preach on the dock in the open air with a throng of villagers in attendance. No, Baytown free-trading was a lucrative business that repaid the hard work the villagers invested in it.

Baytown had many secret tunnels and the houses had many secret rooms and cupboards leading to other cottages - and so many narrow ginnels and alleys, that it was said that contraband could be smuggled from the dock at Baytown, up through the houses that cascaded down the cliffs, right to the top of the cliff without ever seeing the light of day. This was true. The village had grown with the smuggling and every brick which had been laid had been laid with the objective of furthering its hidden industry.

The families had grown together over generations and everyone had their part to play. From the men and women who would haul the contraband to shore and transport it through the village to the moors at the top of the cliff and beyond; to the children who acted as lookouts so that their kinfolk could thwart the beady eyes of the customs men. Even the grandparents and great grandparents played their crucial parts: the grandmothers by knitting and chatting in the alleys, with their husbands tending to the lobster baskets outside the little cottages, or standing outside the inns, to create the illusion of normal, everyday, unruffled village life whilst a run was taking place or contraband was being shifted. Secret signs and knocks; candles in windows and a myriad other codes ensured that the villagers were in a full orchestra of communication with one another. The free-traders would have long disappeared and their booty hidden by the time the dragoons had stepped even five paces or so into the village.

Emma was not too worried about more dragoons. Jeb made sure that Captain Mead, who led the Bay-town dragoons, was amply provided for. It was for this reason that the Dragoons always arrived just a little too late, or happened to be at the South Peak end of the Bay when they should have been at the North Peak - usually just after the luggers (no longer packed with tea, brandy, silk or lace) had swept silently and lightlessly out of the bay.

And Charlie, Emma's eldest lad, had already come back to tell that the second part of the smuggling chain (those folk that helped transport the goods across the moor and onto such places as the lucra-tive markets of York) were in place and in hiding on the moor awaiting their delivery. This was to be a straightforward run.

She heard Jeb before she saw him. He was shar-ing a joke with Tom - the usual joke about some lobster nets being luckier than others - but only if Tom had made them. Jeb then sauntered toward them. 'Have you seen our Alice today, Emma? She said she'd be calling this morning.'

'Haven't seen her, Jeb, I was going to call on her later this morning.'

Jen gave an embarrassed cough, 'Our Peter saw Wilf out last night – a bit worse for wear he was,' she said with downcast eyes.

Emma and Jeb exchanged glances.

'Back in a minute, Emma.' Jeb strode off toward Main Street, in the direction of Wilf's and Alice's cottage. Emma closed the door and scurried after him. 'Why hadn't Jen said something before?' But she knew the answer: Jen didn't want to make it look like she were sticking her nose into other people's business - but she was quick enough to pick up that

Alice had not turned up as expected and had the wit to remark upon it, thank goodness. The villagers had for generations learnt to tread the fine line between kinship and interference. Besides, Wilf getting drunk was usual and didn't usually result in Alice getting a hiding. Alice said he usually passed out as soon as he got home. Emma hoped to God this was another one of those times.

Smugglers

Traditional Shanty

The boat rides off frae Ailsa Craig in the waning o'
the light

There's thirty men in Lendalfoot tae mak' our bur-
den bright

And there's thirty horse in Hazel Home, either ha'
turns on her e'e

Or sit this night upon yon high if wind or waters be

And when at last the dawn comes up and the cargo's safely stored

Like sinless saints to church we'll go God's mercy
to afford

It's champagne fine for communion wine, and the
parson drinks it too

With a sly wink prays, Forgive these men, they
know not what they do

Oh lads ye hae a cosy bed, and cattle ye hae ten

Can ye no live a lawful life and live like lawful men

What must I live with homely food when there's for-

eign gear so fine

Must I drink at the waterside and France sae full

of wine

CHAPTER 12

MONDAY 13th September 2018 - Whitby

The Jet Miner's jewellery shop was towards the top of Church Street in Whitby - an ancient thoroughfare leading to the 199 steps up to the ruins of Whitby Abbey. The salt basted breath of the breeze whipped keenly down the old cobbled street as Elsie and Sim ducked their heads and made their entrance into the glittering little shop. It was early Monday morning and the area was not yet thronging with the tourist crowd. Low lights picked up the gleam from the assorted gold and silver pieces which studded the interior of the shop. Bracelets, necklaces, earrings, brooches, set in silver or gold and all united in the fact that they were inset with highly polished, black as night jet; the stone for which the area had been famed since high Victorian times and which was harvested locally.

Almost like a ghost, a small pale man in his mid-fifties appeared as soon as the doorbell chimed through the shop. He was balding with wispy grey hairs tucked neatly behind his ears. He had sharp bright eyes like a bird and was dressed tidily in an expensive blue, neatly pressed shirt with small jet cufflinks. His black pressed trousers ended in shoes as black and shiny as his jet wares. The lights of his spectacles gleamed in the low lighting of the shop as he peered at Elsie and Sim.

'Hello, can I help you?' he enquired, with the practised smile of welcome habitual to the seasoned shopkeeper.

'Mr Skegwin?' asked Elsie.

'That would be me,' replied the man. His smile slipped. He'd guessed that Elsie and Sim were police officers.

'I believe Demeris Harper worked here,' began Elsie, flashing her ID card after she had introduced themselves and their reason for the visit.

'Poor, poor Demmy,' said Mr Skegwin. Her name sparked tears in his eyes. 'If there's anything I can do to help. But I don't think I can tell you anything of much use. Sam rang me this morning, poor lad.'

'I believe, Demmy was working here on Saturday, is that right?' Mr Skegwin nodded affirmatively.

'That's right. Such a shock when my wife told me. Demmy had worked for us for over two years. She was my apprentice and so talented; such a creative young woman. People were already coming into the shop to commission pieces from her. This is a selection of her work.' Mr Skegwin came out from behind the counter and pointed to a cabinet full of jet jewellery. All of the pieces were modern in design. Elsie's eyes were particularly drawn to a small jet black figurine of a mermaid dangling from a delicate gold chain: its fish tale covered in tiny scales and its face cast down, smiling demurely to itself as if in possession of some mystical secret. It was exquisite.

Mr Skegwin pulled out a handkerchief and blew noisily into it. 'I was expecting her to leave us within a year or so and set up her own shop. I would have missed her of course. She was like a member of the family but you can't stifle that kind of talent, can you?'

'Her work is beautiful.' Elsie agreed. 'We need to ask you a few questions, Mr Skegwin.' Skegwin nodded still looking sadly down at Demmy's work in the tray on the counter. 'Was Demmy working with yourself, on Saturday?' asked Elsie after a suitable pause.

'Demmy stayed late on Saturday, to try and finish a pendant she had been working on. She left about one, I think, Anna said. She's only supposed to work up to twelve but often stays a bit later.'

'Did you see her go, Mr Skegwin?' asked Sim.

'No, I wasn't at work on Saturday. Anna, my wife was here. Why don't you come into the office and talk to her - she's in here.'

Mr Skegwin replaced the tray and pressed the buzzer to lock the shop door and then led them through to the workshop behind the shop into the office area at the back of the building. A woman in her late forties or early fifties, with kindly features, was sat busily polishing some finished pieces of jewellery. The woman had neatly coiffed, short, dark blonde hair and soft features. She was an attractive woman and dressed in a lovely summer dress of pink and green with a green cashmere cardigan slung around her shoulders. The open trays of jewels in front of her gleamed and glittered and Elsie longed to peer closer at the beautiful objects. The woman put down the piece of dark raw jet stone she had been looking at and gave them a sad smile.

'It's the police, Anna. They need to ask us some questions about Demmy.'

Mrs Skegwin's chin quivered, replacing the stone on a tray and then pushing the tray away from her on the desk in front of her with a shaky hand. 'Such a shame; such a wonderful girl; I still can't believe it,' she began tremulously.

'Who could have wanted to harm her?' said Mr Skegwin incredulously.

'She didn't have any enemies to your knowledge?' asked Elsie.

'She never said anything about anyone disliking her and I can't really imagine why anyone would,' he replied.

'Mind, she didn't really talk about her social life too much,' added Mrs Skegwin. 'And we didn't like to pry. She did good work here and that was enough for us.' She added staunchly, adopting the tone of the non-gossip.

'So you don't know if she was seeing anyone else apart from Jimmy?' asked Sim.

'We have no idea how she spent her social life and we never pried,' said Mrs Skegwin primly. 'We knew she was into all this Goth business and she sometimes mentioned Jimmy and her best friend, Gemma - and occasionally they came into the shop, but that was it.'

'She was a wonderful employee,' added Mr Skegwin mistily,

'And she worked here full-time?' asked Sim.

'Four and a half days, actually. She liked to have Monday free to help with her father's business,' clarified Mr Skegwin.

'And her hours on Saturday were, what, nine till twelve?' asked Elsie.

'That's right and she worked every Saturday morning.' Mr Skegwin clarified. Anna and I come in most Saturdays together as it's our busiest day so we can see to the shop. Demmy liked to come in to finish off bits she'd been working on during the week as well as serving in the shop too - she liked talking to the customers; to see what kinds of things they liked and to help give her ideas for new designs. Being a small business means that we can be quite fluid in our working arrangements. I wasn't in the shop this Saturday, though – it was just Anna and Demmy. It was one of my friend's birthdays – we spent the day in Scarborough. I didn't get back until around ten that night.'

'Did you go anywhere special?' asked Sim.

'I'm a member of a local photography group and we took some shots supervised by the tutor, Jim

McKerry – it was his birthday. Then we went for a late lunch at the Ox Pasture Hall – just outside Scarborough; we just stayed chatting and what have you, before I got a taxi home about nine-thirty. We've all known each other for years; Jim's birthday has turned into a bit of a tradition.'

'It would be helpful if you could give us Mr McKerry's number, Mr Skegwin. Sorry to ask but we need to verify the whereabouts of everyone who was in some kind of close contact with Demeris Harper. I'm sure you understand,' said Sim.

'Oh, absolutely, one minute, please.' Mr Skegwin seemed a little disconcerted at the thought that his movements would be checked but he ferreted about in his jacket pocket which was draped over a nearby chair and withdrew his mobile phone. He retrieved McKerry's number, wrote it down and gave it to Sim with a shaky hand.

'Thank you, Mr Skegwin.'

'So Demmy left about what time?' asked Elsie.

'She left just after one,' said Mrs Skegwin.

'And how did she seem?' asked Sim.

Mrs Skegwin took a moment to think and then replied, 'A bit quieter than usual but I think she'd been out on Friday night so perhaps may have been...a little worse for wear.'

'Did she say where she'd been the night before,' queried Elsie.

'No, but she often does...did go out on Friday night. You'll often see the Goth crowd around the town on a Friday and Saturday night. And then she usually went to Jimmy's after work on a Saturday, I think - he sometimes came to the shop to meet her.'

'Jimmy Bransdale?' asked Elsie. Anna Skegwin nodded in confirmation.

'And did Jimmy come to meet her on Saturday?'

'No, I don't think so, but she might have met him in town.'

'So, that was the last time you saw her?'

'Yes,' concluded Mrs Skegwin sadly, her eyes flickering down to the tray in front of her.

'Do you have CCTV for the shop?' asked Sim.

'Yes, yes of course. We keep the tapes, wait a moment. She turned to a monitor and clicked it on and rewound it to the time that Demmy was last in the shop. It was strange seeing a living, breathing Demmy leaving the shop and turning to say goodbye to Anna Skegwin who was serving in the shop at the time. Demmy seemed tranquil and composed; it was dreadful to be aware of the fate she was walking toward in this everyday, inconsequential little scene. Demmy left the shop and Elsie and Sim scrutinised the scene for any sign of anyone waiting for her outside the shop, but Demmy simply turned right and began walking in the direction of the street leading to the harbour – presumably toward Jimmy.

'I can upload a copy of the scene for your records if you would like,' offered Anna Skegwin.'

'Thank you, Mrs Skegwin but we will need to take this tape. Policy, I'm afraid.'

'Yes, yes of course. I understand.' She slid out the tape and handed it to them, deftly inserting another into its place.

'So, presumably security is quite tight in the shop,' said Sim.

'Well, we've been targeted by thieves before. As have many owners of jewellery shops in the town – it's a well-known downside to the trade,' said Mr Skegwin. 'We have a full alarm system and panic buttons. CCTV in the shop and over the front and back doors; all doors are fully secured – a pass code system is in operation over the back door so only we can enter and customers can only enter the front door by pressing a buzzer to alert us to letting them in. We have to keep our insurers happy.' He concluded.

'Is there anyone else who works here apart from yourselves?' asked Elsie.

'No, just me and Anna, we couldn't really afford another assistant. Demmy was a great saleswoman and talented apprentice - I don't know how we'll manage without her.'

Anna Skegwin appeared lost in thought. She held up a piece of jewellery from the tray in front of her, it looked like one of Demmy's distinctive designs - a finely carved, little, black crab dangling off a silver chain-link bracelet. Her husband gently touched his wife's shoulder and they both stared at the piece, locked together in their joint valediction.

....

The sea-breeze blew straight into Elsie and Sim faces as they stood at the top of the cliff on which the ancient Abbey ruins were placed – positioned slightly, as it was, behind the square, brown, Norman church of St. Mary's. It had been Sim's idea to take a walk up the 199 stone steps to the Abbey. Elsie had readily agreed. Murder cases always felt claustrophobic and dirty. It was good to spend a short while away from the grimy, hidden corners of life and let the sea breeze freshen the mind.

A jig- jag of old, wind-slanted gravestones, many commemorating sailors lost at sea from centuries long ago added to the dramatic atmosphere. They grimly greeted the out of breath visitors who had struggled to the top of the 199 steps - to this strange, eerie, ravishing place where the limitless vaulting sky and the proximity of the vast ocean seemed more real than the tiny aspect of the town below on the inland side of the cliff.

This was a place of wild natural and ancient sanctity; a place to remind you that greater things existed than the paltry present lives and concerns of everyday men and women. It was a place where Elsie had often come in the past to think. She found it inspired her to ponder higher things than the tangled tragic cases which polluted her spirit. A sense of grace and history seemed embedded here. She could see why so many visitors were drawn to climb the steps to the remains of this Benedictine Abbey which had been here, in its present form, since the 13th Century. And before that, the monastery which had been ravaged by the Vikings.

It was clear why the Goth community made regular pilgrimages, up to the Abbey: the combination of the sublime and gloomily ethereal must draw them like moths to a candle, Elsie thought to herself.

Its great Gothic arches and distinctive classical columns had withstood the ravages of time - and the exquisite ancient Rose window of the Abbey, like some celestial cobweb, still remained pane-less but intact at its eastern transept.

'A talented popular girl, loved by everyone; adored by family, friends, boyfriends and employers... killed for no apparent reason,' muttered Elsie, a rush of anger shooting through her. A seagull suddenly squealed loudly above them and Elsie jumped. She watched as it wheeled in the clear blue sky overhead before heading out to a fishing trawler chugging toward the harbour below.

'I wonder if the forensic team will find anything at Jimmy's?' mused Sim.

'Mmm,' replied Elsie. It had to be acknowledged, that at this moment Jimmy seemed the most likely suspect. Was his seemingly obvious grief a cover for guilt? Had he become violent because Demmy wanted to discontinue the relationship? Was she seeing someone else? Was that his motive? Maybe Demmy was at the end of a long line of personal rejections for Jimmy – the final straw.

She looked out at the blue calm of the North Sea; such a glittering blue vastness of controlled calm - today anyway. The weather was perfect. The fishing trawler pulled into the harbour; a frill of white splash following in its wake. She looked out across the ocean and remembered a line from Bram Stoker's 'Dracula':

'There's a legend here that a mysterious bell is heard to toll when a dead soul is lost at sea.' She murmured.

'It's based on a true story. I remember learning about it at school,' replied Sim. It came from the Dissolution of the Abbeys during the time of Henry the VIII. The ring of bells of Whitby Abbey were dismantled and were to be sent to London; the bells were placed on a ship and when it embarked, a fierce storm blew up and the ship sank, barely after leaving the harbour. Myth has it that the toll of the bells can still be heard when a fisherman or sailor from the town is lost at sea.' Sim lit a cigarette as he gazed distantly out to sea.

Elsie wondered if the ghostly bells were somewhere out there ringing for Demmy. She could almost hear them.

Asleep in the Deep

(Traditional Shanty)

Stormy the night and the waves roll high,

Bravely the ship doth ride,

Hark! while the lighthouse bell's solemn cry

Rings over the sullen tide

There on the deck see two lovers stand,

Heart to heart beating, and hand to hand;

Though death be near, she knows no fear

While at her side is one of all most dear

CHORUS

Loudly the bell in the old tower rings,

Bidding us list to the warning it brings

sailor, take care - sailor, take care

Danger is near thee, beware, beware, beware, beware

Many brave hearts are asleep in the deep,

so beware, beware

Many brave hearts are asleep in the deep,

so beware, beware

What of the storm when the night is over

There is no trace or sign.

Save where the wreckage hath strewn the shore

Peaceful the sun doth shine.

But when the wild raging storm did cease,

Under the billows two hearts found peace

No more to part no more of pain

The bell may now tell its warning in vain.

CHAPTER 13

Monday 13th September 2018 – Scarborough Police Headquarters

'Ok, let's see what we have so far.' Elsie stood in front of the investigation board and looked expectantly at her team.

'Door to door enquiries in Robin Hood's Bay didn't yield much, quite frankly,' said Shannon. 'No-one saw Demmy in the timeframe we investigated - none of the fishermen, or inhabitants of the cottages overlooking the Bay, saw her and no-one saw any boats out during the storm.

'She was last seen in the Bay, by accounts so far, on 24th August at about three-ish, Mrs Kettlewell, a neighbour at number 11 Sunnyside, thinks. She remembers because she was on her way to getting her barnet done,' added Shannon.

'Nothing else?' asked Elsie.

'Demmy has fairly recently moved into 3 Sunnyside - apparently a relative, who recently died, left her the cottage. She hasn't seen that much of Demmy around the village though.'

Elsie had gone to school with Debbie, Linda Kettlewell's daughter so she knew Linda already. She would call on Linda Kettlewell: it was always worth using personal contacts to have a chat.

'Sim and I spoke to Mr Harper and his son, Sam, yesterday and Mr and Mrs Skegwin, Demmy's employers at the Jetminers. None of them know of anyone with a grudge against Demmy; which is what Jimmy Bransdale, her boyfriend, also said. You've seen the two unsigned notes from Demmy's home but as yet we don't know who they came from. Samples are being collected from her friends and acquaintances to check against. It might be something or nothing.'

'But some git took the time and trouble to kill her and dump her body at sea,' said Shannon.

'And it would have to be someone with access to a boat,' said Sim.

'But like Shannon said, we talked to all the fishermen in the Bay: no-one saw a thing. The fisherfolk knew there was a storm on its way too, so admittedly, not many of them were about then. A couple of them had been out on the dock though, securing their boats,' said Gus.

'Right, Gus, Shannon, let's focus on Whitby fisherfolk. The body could have been taken out at Whitby with the tide stream bringing it back down to the Bay, with the storm bringing it to shore. We've released Jimmy Bransdale pending further enquiries - his alibis seem to check out and none of his neighbours recall seeing either him or Demmy arrive or leave the flat on Saturday afternoon - bar one, who saw Jimmy leave about 5pm with some friends.

Forensics did a full search of his flat last night but they have found nothing untoward. There is some evidence that Demmy has been in the flat recently but that's to be expected. We can't hold him unless something else turns up. I also want to speak to some of Demmy's friends.' Elsie almost added that she believed Jimmy's account of his whereabouts but she did not want to encourage the idea to her team that intuition should be relied upon. In any case, if he had been clever and had somehow murdered Demmy then she would look a fool. 'The town's CCTV street cameras are being scanned to look out for sightings of Jimmy as well as Demmy. Although CCTV in Whitby is notoriously bad and only covers part of the town and even then, some of them are usually found not to be working, of course. But then we all know that. It might give us something, though. In other words, Jimmy is by no means off the hook completely.'

'Everything's possible...yep, we know,' added Shannon.

'And I checked with the taxi drivers and the owners of the firms. No one recalls anyone of Demmy's description using the rank on Saturday afternoon - just in case she decided to leave her car in the car park, for whatever reason. There's no trace of any fares to any of the addresses we have: Demmy's home, her father's, friends or Jimmy Bransdale's. It drew a complete blank,' added Gus.

'Looks likely that she was murdered in Whitby then, or somewhere near,' said Sim. 'And forensics have verified that there is nothing suspicious about her car.'

'Maybe she was bundled off by someone else in their own car and murdered out of town,' contributed Shannon.

'Unlikely, in broad daylight and in a small busy town, though,' said Gus.

'Maybe it was someone she knew and they took her somewhere quiet, maybe back to their own gaff,' added Shannon.

'We can't discount it. Looks like we're going to have to scrutinise those town CCTV street cameras. There must a trace of her somewhere,' said an exasperated Elsie. 'Bodies don't just disappear; especially, as Gus has pointed out, in a small busy tourist town on a sunny Saturday afternoon in September'.

CHAPTER 14

Robin Hood's Bay 1797

Jeb rapped loudly on Wilf and Alice's door. The cottage was at odds with the other cottages on the street. Baytown folk took great pride in their dwellings: everything had its place. All was kept spotlessly clean and even the fishing nets and lobster baskets outside the cottages were neatly mended and stacked. In contrast, Wilf and Alice's cottage showed signs of neglect with chipped marks on the door where Wilf had hammered it in with his fists after coming home steeped in rum again. There were no lobster pots or fishing nets stacked outside their front door as Wilf did not have his own boat. He worked as a hand for the other fishermen on the few mornings he wasn't hungover.

There was no reply for several minutes and then Jeb angrily shouted out, 'If you've hurt our Alice it'll be me you'll have to answer to, Wilf Seamer, do you hear me? Now answer this door before I break it down!' Emma frantically peered through the grimy window but could see nothing as an old grey rag of a curtain was draped across it.

After another minute or so of Jeb's increasingly loud rapping, there was a shuffling noise behind the door and it slowly creaked open. Emma took an inward gasp of disbelief. Alice's face was a mass of bruises and swellings.

Jeb took one look at his daughter's swollen face and then pushed past her into the cottage and charged up the narrow winding stairs. A heart-lurching series of banging and shouting was heard overhead; more terrifying even than the lashing of the North Sea wind against the sea-ward cottages on stormy nights.

Within minutes the sound of a body being dragged down the bare wooden stairs was heard. Jeb held Wilf by the leg and the still drunk man tried in vain to hold onto the flimsy stair rails but to no avail. Wilf's head clunked nastily as it hit the final step.

Jeb leant down and gripped Wilf's face, 'Now, yer listen to me, Wilf Seamer. Yer leaving Baytown this very minute; yer to speak to no-one and yer will never see Alice again, do yer understand, yer rancid dog? Because of Alice, I've tried to help and straighten yer and turn yer into some semblance of a man but you're rotten and you'll always carry the stench of rot, like the vermin yer are. Yer turned up here ten years ago but you'll not stay another day longer. Yer can crawl back to whatever slimy hell-hole spat you out! Now get out, yer filthy god-forsaken bastard!'

Wilf's rat-like features stared at Jeb as if he was frozen and his eyes flickered in abject terror. Then he twisted his face to look at Alice, 'What is it wife, that you don't stop yer kin from attacking me? No man should interfere between a man and his wife – tell him Alice.'

With that, Jeb hauled Wilf to his feet. Wilf mewled again, 'But where am I to go? Alice is with child - she needs a husband by her side else she'll be taken for a...' Alice never heard the rest as Jeb threw Wilf through the open door and kicked him all the way down the narrow lane they called 'The Bolts', before hauling him to his feet once again and throwing him onto Bay Bank: the main thoroughfare of the village.

For good measure, Jeb watched the halting sway-ing steps of Wilf Seamer as he made his way up Bay Bank on his way out of Baytown. After about thirty yards, Wilf turned and scowled at Jeb but shuffled away hastily as Jeb made a step as if to follow him. 'Cowardly bastard!' snarled Jeb. 'And make sure yer never cross my path again!' Jeb's enraged shouts were carried on the sharp wind to their target. Wilf hurried his steps and turned the corner of Bay Bank as it wound its way up the cliff, to the top of the village - and onto the moorland beyond.

Sailor's Prayer

Tom Lewis

This dirty town has been my home since last time I was sailing
But I'll not stay another day; I'd sooner be out whaling.

Chorus:

Oh Lord above; send down a dove,

With beak as sharp as razors

To cut the throat of them there blokes

Who sells bad beer to sailors.

2. Paid off me score and them ashore, me money soon was flying
With Judy Lee upon my knee in my ear a lying,
Chorus:

3. With my new-found friends, my money spent just as fast as winking

But when I make to clean the slate, the landlord says, "Keep Drinking".

Chorus:

4. With me money gone and clothes in pawn and Judy set for leaving

Six months of pay gone in three days, but Judy isn't grieving.

Chorus:

5. When the crimp comes round, I'll take his pound and his hand I'll be shaking

Tomorrow morn sail for the Horn just as dawn is breaking.

Chorus:

CHAPTER 15

Monday 13th September 2018 – Elsie's Cottage,
Robin Hood's Bay

Elsie was weary on the Monday night but her version
of weary sometimes meant being hyper and unable
to relax even though she knew that she wanted to.
So many things were going through her mind. Murder cases did this to her. She knew that she would
not relax until the murder was solved and the culprit
brought to justice. It was, of course, a possibility
that it might never be solved. A discomfiting thought
that she instantly pushed away. She had a 'ping'
meal - what she called a microwave ready meal:
spaghetti bolognaise this time; it tasted more or less
the same as the ready meal of carbonara the night
before. She watched a bit of telly (an acclaimed
drama series which was about half way through
its run of episodes) and which last week she had

enjoyed immensely. She had looked forward to this week's instalment, but she just couldn't relax. She kept rerunning her conversations with the Harpers; Jimmy Bransdale and the Skegwins.

All seemed distraught at the loss of Demmy; all seemed innocent of any wrongdoing although Elsie knew that it was too early in the investigation to come to firm conclusions as of yet. The Harper's alibies had checked out. Despite intensive questioning of Jimmy Bransdale their enquiries had come to nothing - just a reiteration of what he said in his flat. More importantly, his alibi that he had been with his friends for most of the late afternoon and evening, had checked out as had the time he said he had spent on his computer. The techies had found continuous interaction between Jimmy and some other local Goth members on his laptop during the time that Demmy was known to have initially disappeared. The security cameras at the Jetminer's shop verified Demmy's entrance and exit to the shop. There were no leads at all.

Most of all what kept running through Elsie's mind was Demmy's pale lifeless face after her body had been washed up on the shore. She tried very hard to dismiss the image of the apparition which had stood behind her after she saw the body. She knew it was a symptom of her anxiety. Similar things had happened before but she had not dared to speak to anyone about it, fearing that her mental health would make her be considered unfit for her job - and her job was everything to her.

She'd thought about having a family, over the years, but for some reason it had never happened. Relationships had come and gone and she'd never fancied raising a child on her own. And she'd always been too busy with work to give it too much consideration. And if she was honest, she was quite content to live on her own without her daily routines having to be compromised and subjected to someone else's needs and wants. She reflected that this must mean she was selfish; all the more reason that it was the right decision then, she usually concluded.

Elsie decided that she would do what she had always done and try to firmly put out of her mind any memory of the apparition. She knew that the image would fade after a couple of days, if she could just harden her resolve. *'I shouldn't be here, should I?'* No, she refused to think of it.

Elsie opened a bottle of wine, hoping that a couple of glasses would help to ease the nerves which stiffened her whole body and made lounging on the sofa impossible. After one glass of wine she still felt as if her nerves were ratched up to full scale. She heard every sound as if life was turned up in full volume. The light steps of someone on the cobbles passing by her cottage sounded like the rapping of a gun; the voices on the television sounded strident and cacophonous; if she turned the light on it startled her senses – hence the one candle, which segued the light into dark in a more soothing way. She turned the television off and decided to see if a bath would help. Her bath was one of her favourite places. The back of her cottage, with its small garden, was perched on the cliff, just above the sea wall and she could hear the sea thrash or plash against the sea wall, depending upon its mood, through the open window of her bathroom.

She filled the bath with warm water and sprinkled in a couple of drops of lavender essential oil and then lit the candle placed by the window. With an exhalation of pleasure she sank herself into it. She placed another glass of wine on the shelf on the wall next to the bath. She glanced at it. Her face appeared bulbous and swollen in the curve of the glass. She reached for it and took a large sip. The golden flame of the candle flickered its light around the walls whilst the sea-breeze sighed intermittently through the slightly open window. Her mind stilled as the water cossetted her body.

She took another sip and she felt her eyelids creep downwards as the warm steam caressed her face.

Slowly, slowly she fell asleep. She was dreaming of walking along a forest path where the leaves were unfurling into full spring green, and the friend-ly sounds of insects thrummed in the undergrowth. Small unseen paws rustled the undergrowth as they foraged the woodland bounty and bluebells cast their magical blue haze and melded with the mollifying green of the forest.

She dreamt that she came to a cave but it was blocked by a large wooden door. She felt compelled to know what was on the other side but could see no door handle. Reaching out she pushed it but knew it would not move. She raised a hand and curling it into a fist she knocked upon the door. It wasn't a random knock. She knew that it had to be a very precise kind of series of knocks, with specific pauses in-between: Knock, knock, knock…knock, knock…knock, knock. Nothing happened and yet she knew that the knock-ing code was correct, so tried it again…nothing. Frustrated she knocked in the same way again and again, crying with frustration, she knocked again.

Her eyes flew open. The path was gone, the cave, the door…all of it; just the warm candle glow flickering along the walls and reflected in the half full glass which twinked and gleamed in the half light. She heard it softly at first. She knew she would; she almost expect-ed it: the same series of knocks she had heard in the dream. It came from the wooden wainscoting along the far end of the bathroom wall toward the window where the wind breathed in. She knew that the knocking would get louder. And it did. 'Knock, knock, knock…knock, knock…knock, knock.' She closed her eyes willing it to stop. She took deep breaths. Gradually the sound of knocking faded until the intermittent sounds of waves sweeping the sea walls, and the rising moan of the breeze, brushed them away.

She had heard many stories of how smugglers in the village had employed secret knocking signs to alert their fellow neighbours to the imminent passage of goods to their property - or to the imminent arrival of the custom's men, or press gangs. She knew that the knocking could not be real; she knew that it was just her nerves trying to untangle themselves from the crush of anxiety in her mind. She knew that she would get slowly out of the bath, dry herself with the towel and then drape herself in her favourite rose coloured bathrobe and then leave the bathroom and tread downstairs to make a sensible cup of tea. She knew that these series of mundane acts would serve to ground her back to reality and force her to dismiss that knocking on the wooden wainscoting, which she had heard, at the end of the bathroom wall.

And after a time it would work because the mind is a curious thing: it craves reality and it craves routine and does not like to dwell on shadows and will always try to beat them mercilessly back with mundanity, and sometimes it worked. Within ten or so minutes she had made her cup of tea - not too strong and with not too much milk - just as she liked it. And then she gingerly carried it to the sofa with a barely shaking hand and reached for the remote and forced herself to watch and engage with the first programme which illuminated the screen. She would force her mind to engage with the programme and she would not, she definitely would not, think about the knocking on the wooden wainscoting, at the end of the bathroom wall.

CHAPTER 16

TUESDAY 14th September 2018 Scarborough Police Headquarters

Elsie knocked on her boss's door. Superintendent Ian Lansdowne was in his mid- sixties and resembled a toad. He just did. His face was large and warty and his demeanour ponderous. It belied the fact that he was the possessor of an extremely agile mind. He had a very wide girth and Elsie sometimes wondered how he actually managed to fit into his tiny but scruffy office. He was one of the best people that Elsie knew. His eyes were an incisive green and missed nothing, despite their sleepy appearance.

Invariably, he would put little concerns aside in pursuit of the bigger picture. And pursuit of the bigger picture had inevitably reaped success in criminal cases which, within a more exacting and pedantic structure, might not have been achieved.

'Elsie, hear you had an interesting day yesterday?'

Elsie apprised Ian of what had been done so far.

'Forensics are searching James Bransdale's property (he doesn't have a car) but so far nothing untoward has shown up. His last sighting of Demeris was about half past one on Saturday afternoon; the last known sighting of her. Apparently they had a row.'

'Doesn't look good for him, then.'

'It doesn't but he's been quite upfront about the fact that they argued. He comes across as not having anything to hide.'

'He would though, wouldn't he, if guilty, that is?'

'Suppose so.'

'But you don't suspect him at this stage?'

'Forensics found nothing untoward at his flat. Jimmy says that he was on his computer from two and then with two other friends on the late afternoon until about nine that evening. His alibi checks out; we brought him in for questioning but have had to let him go.'

'And the next steps?'

'We're reviewing CCTV footage of the town. What we've managed to find is patchy but it shows Demmy leaving work, walking toward the swing bridge, crossing it and then walking toward the harbour, to meet Jimmy Bransdale. Harbour CCTV confirms that meeting and her setting off back alone, presumably to her car in the car park. The CCTV in the car park does not show her arriving at her car though and she does not go back the same route. That is the last sighting of her.'

'She might have gone into town, maybe met up with Jimmy again?'

'Jimmy said he was on his computer from two until four and the las time there is evidence of him being with her is from the Harbour camera. She left him at 1.45pm. It's like she vanished into thin air after meeting with him.'

'Interview everyone else: friends; neighbours. The usual: butcher, baker, candle stick maker - of Whitby, where she worked - and in Robin Hood's Bay, where she lived. Perhaps she met someone and they had a car. I'll assign you DS Gianelli and DS Thomas; sounds like you might need an extra couple of house callers.'

'That'd be great, thanks Ian. They could start today by collecting samples of handwriting on their travels.' Elsie then apprised Ian of of the two notes found in Demmy's cottage.

Elsie supposed that her relationship with her boss was nothing like the films where the Super was usually fractious; Ian Lansdowne was an exceptional Superintendent. Scarborough Police Force had a very good success rate and that was largely due to Ian's supportive and knowledgeable supervision. He knew however, when to allow Elsie and her team full rein of their competences. If that meant giving full rein to their idiosyncrasies, so be it. And they were idiosyncratic: Elsie with her buttoned up ways; Shannon with her barely curbed puckishness; Gus with his rather bizarre sense of the mystical; his baffling crystals, for goodness sake, and Sim, well who knows what went on with Sim?

'Gianelli and Thomas would be good, once again, thanks.' Reiterated Elsie, Both fledgling detectives were conscientious and enthusiastic and would complement her team with their quiet assiduity, Elsie thought.

'Ok then.'

'Ok then.' And that was that. As long as Ian was kept up to date and on cases like this, regularly up to date, Elsie and her team were just unleashed to track the case – what they did best. No drama, no conflict, no silent screams, no tears running down the inside of cheeks.

But Ian looked like he wanted to say something else, and continued looking at her whilst fiddling with his pen. She waited for him to continue. 'Was there something else, Sir?'

'No, well maybe yes,'

Elsie looked even more curiously at him. Prevarication wasn't his thing.

'I'm retiring soon, Elsie. It's time for me to start looking to do new things. And as you know, Maggie has been suffering with her health.' Maggie was Ian's wife and had multiple sclerosis which was gradually worsening. He'd mentioned retirement a couple of times lately but Elsie had just blanked it out. She couldn't imagine Scarborough Police Force without Ian in it. It literally didn't bear thinking about so she didn't. She'd cross that distant and forbidding bridge when she had to.

Elsie sighed, 'I can see understand you and Maggie might want to spend some nice times together. Just can't imagine you retired, Ian.'

'Did you put that application in for Superintendent, like I suggested? There's a good chance you might take over here.'

Elsie looked down at her feet and shuffled, 'No, I can't see me moving up at this stage.'

'Why not, you have the experience, the skills and you know my reference would be brighter than Filey lighthouse?'

Elsie didn't want this conversation. Her anxiety levels were worsening and yet she felt awkward talking to anyone about it. Even with Ian - especially with Ian, after all he was her boss and had always had high expectations of her.

'I'm happy where I am for the moment, Sir,' she said firmly and further explanation was fortunately interrupted by Ian's phone ringing. He answered it with a note of irritation and Elsie held up her hand as a goodbye. Her wave was not energetic and more like a flag flapping listlessly on an overheated day. She didn't want Ian to retire and she did not want to apply for the post of Superintendent. She was happier with the way things were.

CHAPTER 17

TUESDAY 14th September 2018. The Drunken Sailor, Whitby

The aroma of freshly baked bread and a thousand other delicious smells emanated from the kitchen behind the dining part of the restaurant, 'The Drunken Sailor', which was situated on the front of Whitby harbour. It was early Tuesday morning, so there were only a couple of breakfast diners in the restaurant. A smartly dressed woman of middle years approached them. She had a hangdog expression and dark rings under her eyes - probably from too many late nights tending to the restaurant. She looked like the owner and her sharp eyes continuously moved around as if on a permanent prowl for misplaced cutlery, or glasses which were guilty of being less than gleaming.

So as not to alarm the diners, Elsie introduced herself and Sim discreetly. The woman, Mrs Glaisdale it transpired, hurriedly led them to an office at the back of the restaurant and motioned for them to sit down. The rattle and clank of pans could be heard from the adjacent kitchen.

'I believe a James Bransdale works for you, Mrs Glaisdale. We're investigating the death of a young woman who was a friend of Mr Bransdale's.' Elsie began.

'Demmy Harper wasn't it,' asked Mrs Glaisdale. 'Jimmy rang in this morning saying he wouldn't be in,' she sighed.

'Has Jimmy been working for you long,' began Sim.

'About a year, he's a good worker; reliable and keen to learn. He's one of our best chefs. Demmy came in sometimes, had a coffee whilst she waited for him to finish his shift. I can't believe the news. Such a pleasant young woman: always polite. She and Jimmy got on well. He's devastated, of course.'

'Does he tend to work Saturdays?' asked Elsie.

'Not the Saturday just gone. The chefs work five shift days a week but take it in turns to have a Saturday off - our busiest day. It was Jimmy's turn to be off last Saturday. He worked Friday afternoon though, and was as hard-working as ever. I remember complimenting him on his fish casserole.'

'Do you know if he'd been having any personal problems lately, any changes of mood; any words he said about any problems he might have been having?'

Mrs Glaisdale paused to think. 'No, I don't think so, although I don't get too involved with the personal lives of the staff.' She paused and then added, 'I like Jimmy, you know. He shows an attention to detail, like me. I think he'll go far as a chef. You probably know about the problems when he was younger, being in care and such, but I've never regretted for one moment having him working for me. I think he likes working here too. He puts his heart and soul into his cooking.'

'When did you last see him with Demmy?'

'I haven't seen Demmy for a while. I was wondering if they had problems but then again, it's not unusual for break ups in relationships at that age. I suppose he's been a bit quieter lately and not talked about Demmy so much, thinking about it but nothing particular made me think that things might have finished between them.' She paused again and Elsie was about to ask another question but then Mrs Glaisdale continued:

'Jimmy's a kind lad, if anything his past has developed that kindness: like he wants to make pain better. The other staff love Jimmy, and he's the first one they go to with any personal problems. He's a model employee and a good person, I honestly believe.'

She had obviously been expecting their call and had been readying herself to say her piece. In spite of trying to remain objective, Elsie was quite touched at Jimmy's employer's determination to present him in such a positive light.

'Did Jimmy have any particular friends here, you know, who he is particularly pally with?' asked Sim.

'Well, he's friendly, like I say, with all the staff. They all like him, but he's particularly good friends with Liam. He's also one of the chefs here. Jimmy rang Liam and told him the dreadful news last night. You can talk to him now if you like; he's on the lunch shift - covering for Jimmy, as it happens. He's in the kitchen next door. I could call him in if you want.'

'That would be very helpful,' replied Elsie.

Mrs Glaisdale left and soon there was a timorous knock at the door. Liam was a friendly looking, rather lanky man, of about twenty-five, and he gave them a quick but nervous smile as he sat down at Elsie's invitation.

'You've obviously heard the terrible news about Demeris Harper's death, Mr…' began Elsie.

'Timbrell, Liam Timbrell. Jimmy rang me last night. He was in complete shock, we all were when we found out,' said Liam quietly.

'What can you tell us about their relationship,' asked Sim.

'I don't know if I know that much really. Jimmy was smitten, he would never have harmed Demmy, I know that.' It was obvious that the restaurant staff had a consensus on this view, but it did say something for Jimmy's character nevertheless. Workmates often do see a different side to someone but this could be a good or bad thing. Jimmy could be good at obfuscation and at promoting a character he wanted others to see; alternately, he could be exactly as the staff seemed to think him to be.

'And did Demmy think of him in the same way, do you think, Mr Timbrell?'

'I honestly don't know. I know Jimmy had been worried about them breaking up lately but he can be a bit insecure like that. Always thinking Demmy might be too good for him. They both loved the Goth scene - always going to different gigs and parties. Goths around here tend to meet up a lot - 'The Angel' pub or Sherlock's caf.'

'Did Jimmy say when he had last seen, Demmy?' asked Elsie.

'Saturday lunchtime by the harbour. She met him after work.'

'Had they been arguing, are you aware, Mr Timbrell?'

Liam paused, 'Jimmy mentioned that they had had words, but who hasn't in a relationship? Me and our lass are always having barneys.'

'What had they been arguing about? Did he tell you?' persisted Elsie

'Jimmy was looking forward to his night off, we don't get every Saturday night off - it's our busiest time. But yes, he said they had been arguing because Demmy had told him she didn't feel like going out that night. She wanted to head off home and he thought she wasn't telling him the truth: not telling him that she didn't want to be with him anymore. He was upset.'

'Do you think the argument got out of hand, Mr Timbrell? Was Jimmy suspicious that she was seeing someone else, for example?' asked Elsie.

'It was just an argument. Jimmy's never mentioned being worried about her dating someone else.'

'And was the argument just words, shouting, you know?' queried Sim.

'Do you mean, did he hit her? No, of course not. He's not like that. He'd never hit Demmy anyway. Jimmy can get upset about things, but I've never known him to lose it.'

But unfortunately, Jimmy had 'lost it' before. Sim had informed Elsie during their drive to Whitby that there had been two previous occasions when Jimmy had had violence recorded against him: one of the incidents had involved an altercation with one of his care workers, when he had been fifteen, and one with another man in a pub a couple of years ago.

CHAPTER 18

Moor above Robin Hood's Bay 1797

'T'aint right. Alice should've taken 'er man's side. Curse 'em all…That's a bastard keen wind' Wilf muttered to himself as a sharp wind cut across the top of the moor and pierced his threadbare shirt. Jeb hadn't even given him time to don his gansey before throwing him out of his own home. 'Suppose I'll ave to sleep on the moors tonight.' Full of rage and still half-drunk, Wilf rambled and ranted as he made his way across the moor.

'Little bitch running to 'er da. Tis none of 'is concern what takes place between a man and 'is wife. I'll 'ead to Whitby - there's always work on t' whaling ships - I dunt mind a bit o sea. Aye that's what I'll do. With no wife or kin my money's me own. I hated Baytown, anyways - everyone knowing t'other's business; everyone listening at walls. Glad to be shifted o' em. Thoughts they were better than me. Well they ain't. And that da of hers. Despite 'is airs and graces - 'e ain't nought but a thief, what deserves to be at t' end o' the gallows. That's where 'e belongs an that's where e'll be, damn im, if I ave ought to do wi it. Asked for it and n' they's gonna get it!'

After a while, Wilf stopped and mumbled to himself. 'Aye, there it is and it looks busy – almost like they're expectin me.'

Wilf had reached the top cliff of Baytown and was now walking south toward a large squat building with several horses tethered outside of it. He laughed grimly to himself, 'My last little gift to t' fine upstanding folk of Baytown. Besides tis only right I pay me respects to the fine Dragoons before I take me leave.' Wilf gave another mirthless chuckle which turned into a racking cough. A dragoon came out of the house and blinked at Wilf. The brass buckles on his heavy red military coat gleamed in the weak sunshine. Wilf had never seen this dragoon before and judging by the shape of helmet and epaulettes on his shoulder, it looked like the dragoons had a new, higher ranking commander. Wilf didn't recognise the horses either: four of them. It looked like the Customs Officers had increased their numbers.

From his newly pressed cravat to his newly shined boots, this commander looked as stiff and proper as they came. Wilf didn't think Captain Lucas ever polished his boots and most of the time he didn't even bother to wear a cravat.

The new commander took a step toward Wilf. His demeanour was far from friendly as he surveyed Wilf's raggedy and bruised appearance.

'You there! What is it you're wanting?' The commander glared at Wilf out of unflinching eyes.

'Begging your pardon, Sir...'

'It's Captain to you, Captain Bullock, who are you and state your business!'

'They call me Wilf, Cap'n, Wilfred Seamer. And I'm here to see you, if you please. I have some news for ye. News I think ye'd be fair interested in.'

'Spit it out then, you worthless beggar, in the name of the King!'

'I'm a poor man, Sir, and it is in the King's name that I come. I'm a simple but honest man, Captain and I have some news for you,' rambled Wilf.

'Simple but honest man who reeks of drink! Get to it!' barked the impatient Dragoon.

'Well this is it, Captain, this is it. Information is all I have but it's news you'd be glad of – regarding Baytown.'

The Captain was silent for once. He looked at Wilf in a calculating manner. 'What 'news' could the likes of you have for me, yer drunken beggar?'

'Now, if we could just come to some sort of arrangement, I'd be sore wanting to share this news with you.' lisped Wilf quietly, through swollen lips. He put his face closer toward the Dragoon, who recoiled momentarily from Wilf's rum sodden breath, but as Wilf spoke he braced himself, and leant forward again to listen keenly to what he had to say.

Song of the Fishes

Come all you bold fishermen, listen to me,

While I sing to you a song of the sea.

Chorus:

Then blow ye winds westerly, westerly blow,

We're bound to the southward, so steady we go.

2. First comes the blue-fish a-wagging his tail,

He come up on the deck and yells: "All hands make sail!"

Chorus:

3. Next comes the eels, with their nimble tails,

They jumped up aloft and loosed all the sails.

Chorus:

4. Next come the herrings, with their little tails,

The manned sheets and halliards and set all the sails.

Chorus:

5. Next comes the porpoise, with his short snout,

He jumps on the bridge and yells: "Ready, about!"

Chorus:

6. Then comes the turbot, as red as a beet,

He shouts from the bridge: "Stick out that foresheet!"

Chorus:

7. Next comes the whale, the largest of all,

Singing out from the bridge: "Haul taut, mainsail, haul!"

Chorus:

8. Then comes the mackerel, with his striped back,

He flopped on the bridge and yelled: "Board the main tack!"

Chorus:

9. Next comes the sprat, the smallest of all,

He sings out: "Haul well taut, let go and haul!"

Chorus:

10. Up jumps the fisherman, stalwart and grim,

And with his big net he scooped them all in.

Chorus:

CHAPTER 19

Gemma Leyburn, Demmy's best friend, lived on an old 1930's street on the outskirts of Whitby with her parents. It was a row of modest semi-detached houses. Gemma's house was utterly unlike the polished expensive house belonging to Demmy's family. A woman in her early fifties; somewhat straight-laced with her neat short haircut and colour-coordinated cardigan and skirt answered the door. Permanent lines of tension were etched on her forehead.

'Mrs Leyburn?'

The woman nodded and Elsie introduced her and Sim.

'Thanks for your call,' said Mrs Leyburn in a tight, high voice, 'Gemma is waiting for you in the lounge.'

Mrs Leyburn led Elsie and Sim into the lounge and invited them to sit down. 'We'd just like a few moments to speak to Gemma, if that's OK, Mrs Leyburn,' said Elsie. Mrs Leyburn obviously wanted to stay and was half perched on the arm of an armchair. Mrs Leyburn glanced at Gemma who said, 'I'll be fine, mum'.

Mrs Leyburn sighed, 'I'll just be in the kitchen, then,' she said stiffly and stood up and left the room.

Elsie looked at Gemma who was dressed all in black and wearing heavy make up. Her glossy, long, raven black hair contrasting with her deep burgundy red lipstick suggested a grown up rather louche glamour which was completely at odds with her mother's conventional and plain demeanour. Sensing Elsie's scrutiny, Gemma looked up at Elsie and her chin quivered. Despite the young woman being twenty-one years old, at that moment she seemed much younger.

'I can't believe this has happened. I keep expecting Demmy to ring me. Who could have done this?' Anger flashed across Gemma's face and then her chin quivered again.

'I'm sorry for what's happened to your friend, Gemma. That's why we're here, to ask you to tell us everything you can about Demmy,' responded Elsie. A tear slid down Gemma's face.

'Listen, Gemma you're the best person to give us information about what might have happened to Demeris. You probably knew her movements better than anyone and Demmy is most likely to have confided in you about anything that was worrying her.'

'But I don't know anything,' cried Gemma. 'The last time I saw Demmy was in the Angel on Friday night. She left early. She said she had to be in work the next day. That's why she wasn't staying long...'

'What time did she leave?' asked Sim.

'Very early - about six. She said she was just having a quick drink before heading home. We sometimes met up for a drink after work. I got the feeling that she was in a rush to be someplace else.'

'Was it usual for her to leave at that time?' he asked.

'It was getting to be a habit. She used to stay until the end of the night. It's just lately she hasn't been doing that. She'd say she was tired.'

'And did she seem her usual self on Friday evening?' asked Sim.

'She seemed a bit quiet, I suppose. She and Jimmy had had a bit of a fall out.'

'Do you know what it was about?' questioned Elsie.

'Nothing heavy, Jimmy thinks, thought, the world of her.'

'What were they arguing about, Gemma?' persisted Elsie.

'I think Jimmy thought Demmy fancied someone else. He thought Demmy wanted to end their relationship.'

'And did she?' persisted Elsie.

Gemma took a deep breath. 'I think she did.'

'You think?' prompted Sim.

'I just feel like I'm betraying her confidence. It feels like the last thing I could do for her ends in her betrayal. I know I'm being stupid...'

'You're not,' Elsie insisted, 'you're not being stupid. Did Demmy ask you to keep a secret of some kind? Circumstances have changed, if you know anything at all, Gemma...'

Gemma took a deep sigh, 'I think Demmy had begun to see someone else. But she wouldn't tell me who.

She seemed a bit distant lately. I tried to get it out of her but she's been acting different, preoccupied with something. I think Jimmy had picked up on it too. That's why he kept picking fights with her all the time. I think she didn't want to say anything in case Jimmy found out. She could be quiet like that, she didn't say much when her mum was dying of cancer. She was quiet and withdrawn, I knew something had to be going on. It was just the way she was.'

Sim looked at Gemma searchingly, 'So why do you think she was seeing someone else; especially if she wasn't telling you anything?'

'There were a couple of clues. If she came in the 'Angel' or 'The Tavern', to meet up with me and our mates, she sometimes wouldn't stop long; making up excuses for having to go elsewhere. I sometimes wondered if she came in just to throw Jimmy off track - or maybe she was waiting with us until she was meeting up with, whoever. She'd often be checking her phone for messages. I used to joke with her about checking her phone hoping she'd confide, but she never would.'

'A couple of times Jimmy came in after she'd gone and he didn't know where she was either. Jimmy tried to hide it but he was mad with her. And the biggest clue was that she was always done up...you know, like she was going somewhere special...for someone special, I guess. It didn't really chime with her being tired. And she looked excited. I could tell knowing her so well.'

'The Tavern?' asked Sim.

'Yeah, 'The Middle Earth Tavern'. It's a Goth hang-out in town.'

'And you never saw her with anyone else? And she never told you who she was seeing? Gemma, remember Demmy has been murdered. You need to tell us everything you know,' prompted Sim.

Gemma looked up simply at Sim - her face open and her eyes direct. 'I don't know who he was. I wish now I'd pressed Demmy about it but she didn't seem the same. I mean, our friendship wasn't the same.' It annoyed me sometimes,' she concluded with an expression of pain in her eyes. 'It seemed like she was growing away from us all.'

Sim seemed content with her response and glanced at Elsie who picked up the questions again.

'Do you know anyone who did not like Demmy, Gemma?'

Gemma thought for a moment and then looked down at the carpet again. 'Not really,'

'Not really,' echoed Elsie. 'If there was someone please tell us, Gemma. It doesn't mean they are guilty but we need to investigate. At the moment we only have what her friends can tell us.'

'Demmy was inoffensive, really quite quiet. She didn't go out of her way to upset anyone,' said Gemma.

'But?' asked Elsie.

'One of the Goth crowd didn't like her, I suppose, but I really can't see that she hated her enough to... kill her,' said Gemma.

'What's her name, Gemma? We just need to ask her a few questions, that's all.'

'Tia,' said Gemma quietly and then more robustly, 'Tia Stanton. I can't see her being to blame, though, she just was jealous of Demmy because she likes Jimmy herself. She used to go out with Jimmy before he met Demmy.'

'Are you quite friendly with Tia Stanton?'

'She's a Goth but goes round in a separate crowd to us. I haven't spoken to her since we had a row in the Angel a couple of months ago. She'd been saying some really nasty things about Demmy so I would overhear them. And she kept talking to Jimmy when Demmy was there, saying bitchy things. She became really upset when Jimmy got angry with her and told her to pack it in.'

'Do you know where Tia lives, Gemma?' asked Sim.

'Tia? I don't know exactly where she lives – toward Sandsend, I think, but I'm not sure.'

'Did she ever physically harm Demmy in any way?' he asked.

'Never hit her if that's what you mean. She knew it would anger Jimmy. But she often made snide comments when Demmy passed her at a pub or club; you know, things like 'stuck up bitch'. Stuff like that.'

'Does Jimmy still like Tia, do you think?' asked Elsie

'I don't think he likes her in the way he liked Demmy. But, yeah, they are, kind of, friends. Tia comes from quite a tough background. I think he feels sorry for her, if anything. That's what I think anyway. I really can't see her doing anything to hurt Demmy properly though. She knows it would upset Jimmy too much, for a start.'

'And there's no-one else you know who disliked Demmy?' asked Sim.

'There weren't many people who could have had a grudge against her. Everyone liked her. I miss her.' Gemma's resolve seemed to evaporate and she tried to blink back the tears.

'Thanks, Gemma. I know this is a difficult time for you. We haven't really got any more questions for now.'

A few minutes later, in Elsie's car; Sim and Elsie compared notes. 'Do you think she knows who Demmy's new boyfriend was, Sim?'

'I don't think so. She showed no sign of nervousness from lying. Nothing about her body language made me think otherwise: her manner was still and open. I could be wrong, though. But no, personally, I think she was telling the truth.'

'Are you beginning to think that this mystery lover had a reason for wanting to keep the relationship quiet?' asked Elsie. 'He didn't even put his or maybe her, name to the notes left for Demmy.'

'The obvious conclusion, of course, is that he was married. It might explain why Demmy didn't want to advertise his name as her new boyfriend,' said Sim.

'So, we need to find who the mysterious man is and find Tia Stanton and see what she has to say,' said Elsie.

'If she was seeing someone else, I wonder why she didn't confide in Gemma,' commented Sim.

'Indeed, it's strange. Maybe she was trying to spare Jimmy's feelings.'

'It would've been better to tell him straight,'

'Yes, it would but maybe she wasn't sure about the new relationship; maybe she was leading up to ending it with Jimmy; maybe she felt sorry for him, having been in care and all that. I guess, we'll never know,' sighed Elsie. 'But yes, it seems deceitful but who knows what was going through her mind.'

'She was obviously hiding something - and from her friends too. I can understand her being cagey with her father; he does seem over-protective, but with her friends?'

'Early twenties can be a funny age, Sim, though: when new doors open resulting in old friends being left behind and forming new ones. Maybe she felt as if she had outgrown her old crowd. Maybe she wanted to be part of it but at the same time, didn't. Maybe she had to keep the new relationship secret, for some reason. If he's married that might explain why.'

'Who'd want to be young again?' commented Sim, 'Mind if I have a cigarette?'

CHAPTER 20

WEDNESDAY 15th September 2018 Whitby moors

Sandsend is a wide cove with a sandy beach extending for about a mile or so and is situated just north of Whitby. Its traditional seascape, with its grassy dunes and therapeutic rolling waves across the vast expanse of its beach attracts visitors from across the county and beyond and is a very popular destination in the summer season.

Tia, it transpired, lived in a dilapidated homestead a couple of miles inland from Sandsend. It had taken some finding and though its setting was bleak but beautiful, the small farmhouse had seen better days. Slates had fallen off the roof and some even lay underfoot as they walked up the muddy pathway toward the house. Paint on the old windows and door was peeling and a thin dog, chained to a post at the front, barked non-stop and rather disconsolately as Elsie and Sim approached the house. The frayed rope tethering the dog to a holding post only just kept it at bay from them as they approached the door. Elsie didn't really mind dogs and she felt sorry for this one tied up like that. Its fur was matted and tufts of it were tipped with dry mud. She kept her eyes averted as it growled when she walked past. It triggered mild feelings of anxiety but no more or less than routine interactions with some of the humans she had to deal with on a day to day basis.

Elsie knocked on the door which sent the dog into a frenzy. She hoped that the rope would not give way. A keen wind blew from across the moors and pushed its cold fingers into her unzipped jacket. It would soon be time to dress for winter. She wouldn't like to experience winter in this ex[psed place she thought to herself.

The door was wrenched open and a man in his mid-fifties stood before them dressed in a vest (which did little to hide his protruding pot belly) and a pair of ill-fitting trousers.

'Afternoon, I'm DCI Storm and this is DI Howard. Is Tia Stanton here, please?'

He glanced disinterestedly at Sim and Elsie and then asked in a belligerent tone, 'You coppers?'

'Might be; then again we might not be, but the clue's in the name,' answered Sim. Elsie tried not to smile.

'Thought so, can always smell a copper. So can the dog so I'd watch your step,' added the man stepping outside and slamming the door behind him before lighting up his cigarette. The dun fug of stale alcohol emanated from the man as he blew a puff of smoke in their direction. A sharp breeze swiftly carried the bloom of smoke away.

'Are you, Mr Stanton?' asked Elsie.

The man looked at her, 'Yeah.'

'So Tia is your daughter?'

'Do you wanna tell me what this is all about? What's the silly cow done now?'

'Nothing as far as we can tell, we're conducting an investigation into an acquaintance of hers, that's all. Is she here?' Elsie tried hard to keep a friendly tone and expression as the man blew another puff of smoke in her direction.

'Or maybe you'd like to come down the station and help us with our enquiries,' said Sim warningly.

'What for?' scoffed the man.

'How about keeping a dog in cruel conditions?' said Sim.

The man looked at Sim for a moment or two and then spun on his heel. 'Come in then,' he said tersely. They followed him through a dark narrow hallway to a door which led into the kitchen area which, though shabby and old-fashioned, was surprisingly clean. An appetising smell of a casserole emanated from an old cooker which must have been at least thirty years old. Mr Stanton left the kitchen momentarily to shout Tia downstairs.

A few moments later Tia was ushered into the room. She sat down wordlessly without making eye contact. Disinterested, her father disappeared off outside again. If nothing else, Elsie admired his fortitude at braving the keen early autumnal wind wearing only his vest.

Tia was a stumpy looking girl dressed all in grey. She had long mousy hair tied back in a ponytail which hung over her right shoulder. Her most notable feature was her numerous ear piercings. Above her top lip she also had a piercing: the stud was of a small skull shape. She looked as if a scowl rather than a smile was more habitual to her.

Elsie introduced her and Sim and proceeded straight to business.

'We'd like to ask you some questions about Demeris Harper, Tia. I've reason to believe that you knew her quite well.'

'I knew her,' replied Tia tersely.

'You'll have heard about her death, Tia,' said Sim.

Tia nodded without a trace of emotion crossing her features.

'Rumour has it you weren't friends,' said Elsie.

'We weren't,' replied the girl. She caught Sim looking at her. 'Well there's no point telling lies; just cos someone's dead, is there?' Her voice rose an octave.

'I suppose not. Although it is sad that someone so young has had their life taken away like that, isn't it Tia' Elsie responded gently.

Tia looked toward the window as if irritated.

'I didn't like her, but yeah.' Tia fell quiet and waited for the police officers' next words.

'Do you know of anyone who wanted to harm Demmy, Tia?'

'I know it wasn't me, if that's what you're getting at,' responded the girl with a hostile glare. 'And I want a ciggie, so…' She stood up and reached for the front door.

'Just a minute, Tia,'

'You can't stop me,' said the girl with shrillness to her voice, 'Anyway, if you want to ask me questions, like that, I want my brief. I'm not talking to you again unless I've got my brief with me, got it?'

It was obvious that Tia had run into trouble before. They'd checked her out before the visit. There'd been some minor stuff but nothing to cause undue interest - and not particularly recently.

'We're not accusing you of anything, Tia, really. But the more information we get from those who knew her and were in her life, the better. That's all.' Elsie tried her hardest to placate the girl.

'I made it my business not to be in her life. Stuck up bitch, always thought she was better than me. Don't know what Jimmy saw in her…'

'Just a few questions, that's all, Tia.'

'It's the kind of questions that's the problem,' said the young woman sharply, raising herself as if to stand up from the table.

'Do you really want to accompany us to the station, Tia? If you want a solicitor we'll need to head down to the station to do it properly,' said Elsie making her meaning quite clear.

'I was just about to put our tea on.'

Elsie looked at Sim.

'I think this might be more important, Tia,' said Elsie.

'Why should I have to come with you to the station? It wasn't me. And I've got to put tea on for our Paulie. He's due back from school anytime soon.'

'Paulie?' asked Sim.

'Me younger brother: I like to give him his tea when he gets in, can't rely on that bastard out there to lift a finger.'

'Your dad, you mean?' asked Tia.

You can call him that if you want to. We don't if we can help it. Our Paulie needs his tea. He's not going to grow up running about all over the shop eating at any old time of day, going to bed when he wants. I've seen plenty who've lived like that and how they've turned out. If it was up to that bastard, out there, that's exactly how Paulie would turn out.'

'Why don't you answer a few questions now, Tia and see how we get on?' asked Elsie gently.

Reluctantly, Tia sat down.

'I should have a brief with me. This is fucking inconvenient. Go on ask, but if I don't like how it's going - that's it.'

According to records Tia was nineteen and it was hard to see how any young woman would choose to live in this draughty, decrepit, old house on the edge of the moors when she presumably had some kind of life in Whitby. The inside of the house was shabby but scrupulously clean. Elsie guessed that the cleanliness wasn't due to Mr Stanton - in his multi stained vest, and trousers with holes in both knees.

'Paulie's your little brother, yes?' Elsie began.

Tia sighed. 'He's the only reason I haven't moved out. Want to but he won't let me take Paulie. He couldn't give a shit about Paulie: just likes me to clean up and cook and likes the child benefit - old bastard. If it wasn't for Paulie…'

'How old is your brother, Tia?' asked Sim.

'Ten. And he's a good kid. That's why I keep out of trouble now. Don't want him to copy my ways. I wasn't a good kid at school. He's a good kid, does his homework and all that, straight after his tea; every night. Why should I have to go down the station? It wasn't anything to do with me.' She demanded angrily.'

'You've got a job as a cleaner, in Whitby. Is that right?' persisted Elsie.

'Yeah, in a hotel. Pays me a bit - keeps us in food and clothes and that: can fit the hours around Paulie's school times. The old git out there can't be relied on.'

'Is he abusive to Paulie?' Elsie asked.

'He wouldn't dare!' said Tia angrily looking Elsie straight in the eye. 'He knows I wouldn't stand for that.'

Elsie knew that Stanton had been done a couple of times for assault in the pubs he had frequented and for being drunk and disorderly. She was beginning to feel a bit of admiration for this determined young woman before her. Her concern for her younger brother seemed sincere. Still, she had to ask her about Demmy.

'When did you last see Demmy, Tia?'

'Dunno, couple of weeks ago, I think. We're not exactly in the same crowd.'

'You're both Goths, right?' asked Elsie.

'Yeah, but we don't all hang around in the same group.'

'So what does being a Goth involve?'

'Funny question. What do you want to know for?

'Just curious, that'all.' Elsie was interested in why Tia was drawn to the Goth movement, although she expected that part of the attraction was Tia seeking an interest away from her otherwise dreary existence. Also Elsie was trying to break the rather brittle ice which Tia had formed around herself. It was always easier to get information if relations were friendlier.

Tia paused for a bit and then answered, 'We're a bit into the dark, I suppose.' Tia screwed up her forehead in concentration as she thought more about the question. Sim, wisely, kept quiet and just listened and let Elsie do her thing. Neither Elsie nor Sim wanted Tia to become more hostile and less forthcoming. There was no real reason to take her down to the station, as yet.

'A lot of people think it's some kind of escapism but that's not really true. It's a choice to live another way of life completely: the music, the clothes, the feeling that you're creating a whole different world with others like us. I don't expect you to get it,' she said with a sneer.

'I kind of do,' said Elsie. 'We all wander around in our own worlds. Who's to say one world is more acceptable than another's and if you join with other people, to share a particular world, that's OK.'

Tia listened to Elsie's words and watched her expression for any sign of cynicism. Elsie guessed that Tia was used to people laughing at her beliefs. It didn't take much imagination to guess that Mr Stanton scoffed at his daughter's choice of clothing and music. Tia seemed though, to accept Elsie's words as genuine and shrugged before continuing.

'It's a bit more than a club though. It's a way of looking at life. Folk try to clean life up and package it neatly away from death: cushion themselves with shopping, a new house or car. Goths don't do that: we know death and life are intertwined. That's why we dress…' Tia stopped speaking. She hadn't meant to say so much to the police.

Elsie looked at the drably dressed young woman in front of her. She liked her explanation of her beliefs

'Can you remember exactly when you last saw Demmy, Tia?'

'As I told you, a couple of weeks ago. In the Middle Earth Tavern, I think it was. She was with Jimmy.' She paused to think, 'Two weeks ago, last Friday – early on, about 7 or 8, I think it was.'

'Did you see her around town much?'

'Not really. There are others who were more friendly with her who you should be asking all this.' Tia's voice adopted a shrill tone once again.

'We are asking around - all those who knew her, Tia. Did you ever see Demeris with anyone who wasn't part of the usual crowd?

'Hardly ever saw her, unless she was in one of the usual pubs - and then she was always with Jimmy, or that wet little mate of hers, Gemma. And the places we all hang out are that busy that you don't really notice anyone else in there unless they are the mates you especially meet up with.'

'Right, but Jimmy is your friend too, isn't he?'

Tia nodded.

'How did you and Jimmy meet?'

'Known him for a few years. He had a foster place-ment in Whitby a good few years back but that broke down and he was in a care home after that. Knew him from a youth club and then, later on, he got into the Goth scene about the time that I did. We went out together a few times, on and off.' Her voice tailed away, as she remembered. She rested her chin on her hand and looked out of the window at the swirling grey sky which was threatening rain. 'I hope you catch whoever did it. Jimmy must be in bits. He worshipped her.'

'Did it bother you, him worshipping her?' asked Elsie.

Tia reared up as if suddenly back on guard. She dropped her hand back onto the table; back on full alert. 'Oh here we go - the killer question. Was I jealous of her? Did I have a motive? Well, I've got nothing to hide. I told you: I certainly didn't like her. It was only a matter of time before she'd ditch him. Out of her league, he was. And no, I didn't hate her enough to kill her. Jimmy's me mate. He'd never have forgive me for a start - and what would happen to Paulie if I was found out?'

'Can you tell us what you were doing last Saturday, into Sunday morning, Tia?'

Tia puckered her brow as she tried to remember. 'At work till three; came back got Paulie's tea - and his,' she nodded her head in a hostile manner toward the window at her father's looming shape outside the window as he threw his cigarette butt into the wind. 'Then Kelly picked me up and we went out with our mates. We were at The Angel all night - then I crashed at Kelly's' Got a lift back here early Sunday afternoon.'

'Kelly picked you up? What time was that?'

'About six.'

'And you work, where?'

'The Spyglass Hotel', Whitby.

Sim scribbled it down. 'So after work, you got here at what time?' he asked.

'The usual, about half three. Maxi lives out this way too and gives me a lift on a Saturday – our shifts match on weekends.'

'Maxi?'

Maxi Tierney - she's a cleaner too.'

'She's a cleaner at The Spyglass?'

Tia nodded grumpily in assent.

'And can you give us Kelly's full name and both her and Maxi's addresses?'

'Kelly Thomas, 14 Sycamore Street,' she uttered sullenly. 'And Maxi lives at Grouse Cottage, a few cottages further on from us.'

The door slammed and Tia's father entered the room, holding a beer can.

'You still here? We'll be wanting our tea, soon. The kid'll be back anytime now, just seen his bus. Ain't she answered enough of yer questions?'

'Yes, well I think we've wrapped up here, Tia. We'll possibly be in touch again. Of course, if you remember anything, even if you don't think it's that relevant I'd appreciate it if you could give us a ring. Here's my card. By the way, have you heard of Demmy seeing someone else, apart from Jimmy, I mean,' asked Elsie.

'Seeing someone else? Wouldn't put it past her. Always seemed a bit too good to be true, she did,' responded Tia, a small note of glee in her voice.

'Had you heard anything like that?'

'No,' replied Tia grudgingly. 'Not likely to have spread news like that around though, was she? Why'd you ask?'

'Just covering all bases - standard questions when a couple have been known to row,' said Elsie

'Whatever's goin on, it won't be her, she ain't got time to mess about. I see to that.' interjected Stanton belligerently. 'And you just said you were goin.'

'Ok, thanks for your time, we'll see ourselves out.' Elsie said, wanting to avoid pointless conflict. As she and Sim made their way out Elsie turned and asked Stanton, 'Can you verify Tia was here with you on Saturday afternoon between three and six pm, Mr Stanton?'

'Got here soon after work and made tea. Before she went off Gothin or whatever she does. Long as I get me tea, don't care what she does. You goin, now?'

As she and Sim made their way back across the muddy path to their car, they saw a slight young boy of about ten wandering up the track toward the house, the school bus trundled away in the distance. He looked askance at them as he passed.

'Hello, Paul,' said Sim. The boy gave a half-hearted smile before stroking the excited dog and then entering the house.

'I think a call to the RSPCA is in order, don't you, Sim?'

'I do indeed, Ma'am,' said Sim, reaching into his jacket pocket for his mobile phone.

'And to social services. Wouldn't do any harm to keep an eye on that family. Tia does her best, but that father of theirs…a bit of an unknown quantity.'

'Yes, Ma'am.'

The rest of that afternoon was spent on putting some kind of timeline together with everyone contributing the various pieces of information which tracked Demmy's last few days. Alibis were checked and double-checked and time was taken to keep on top of other less prominent cases which inevitably stacked up when a big case was being investigated. Elsie planned to leave a little earlier though as she planned to pay a visit to Linda Kettlewell. As Demmy's neighbour she might have valuable information.

CHAPTER 21

WEDNESDAY 15TH September 2018 Robin
Hood's Bay

She looked out across the expanse of the Bay and
took a sip of coffee and for the first time that day she
felt peaceful. Linda had rang leaving a message
on Elsie's mobile that she was being held up and
could Elsie please call half an hour later. No problem; it was a lovely afternoon and Elsie was glad to
have the opportunity of a quick coffee on her deck.
As Elsie gazed at some flotsam recently brought
onto shore, she remembered Demmy's beautiful
driftwood carvings and how the young woman had
made something so fine out of the detritus of life.

The waves were silver-blue and there were only a
few skeins of cloud in the sky. It was so clear she
could see the yellow patchwork of gorse that edged

the cliffs out to Ravenscar in the distance. Not for the first time she felt lucky to live here. The Storm family had lived here for generations and she felt herself rooted to this little village; perilously perched as it was on a cliff that swept down into the primal honesty of the North Sea.

It wasn't hard to imagine smugglers hiding round the corners in the labyrinthine ginnels and lanes of the village, especially on a twilit night; waiting for their secret knocks and whistles to alert them to a smuggling lugger having just entered the bay. And it wasn't hard to imagine the sound of heavy rustling skirts brushing along the cobbles, laden with unseen packets of tea or bolts of silk, to be exchanged in quick hands along the little alleys and lanes. The narrow steep road down the bank into the heart of the village forbade much traffic and it was generally only delivery vans which rumbled occasionally up and down it. Buses used to come down the bank but one got stuck and had to be hauled back up with two tractors - so that was the end of that. And that was Ok, Robin Hood's Bay felt timeless and a little otherworldy, which, in Elsie's opinion, was enhanced by its escape from the march of modernity.

The cottage, 26 Chapel Street, which she had inherited, had been in various branches of the Storm family for over three hundred years. It was not one of the biggest cottages but its location was perfect for Elsie; just beyond the reach of the sea wall which had been built in recent years. All that stood between Elsie's cottage and the sea was a short white picket fence, on the other side of which was about fifty foot of scrambly cliff which led onto the sea wall and then the shoreline below.

Elsie took a bite of her cheese sandwich and pondered the facts of the case. They were meagre. Mick Harper and his son Sam's alibis had checked out. All the times regarding Demmy's whereabouts had been verified; Demmy's friends and acquaintances had been investigated and not flagged anything in particular. There were two suspects so far: Jimmy and Tia, even though their alibis were yet to be completely substantiated. Had Jimmy found out what Gemma strongly suspected: that Demmy had another lover. Had Tia murdered Demmy in a fit of jealous rage? But how would Tia, despite her sturdy physique, have managed to put Demmy's body into a boat and put it out at sea during a storm? Perhaps Jimmy and Tia were in it together? But where would they get a boat from? The fishermen around Whitby and the Bay had been questioned extensively and no-one had seen anything suspicious on the night in question. Possibly the culprit had their own boat. Many people in the area owned private dinghies which could be put to sea at a moment's notice. There was no indication that Jimmy or Tia had their own boats – or the expertise to put to sea in an incoming storm.

Tia and Jimmy could have borrowed, or even stolen for a few hours, a small seaworthy dinghy, she supposed. A small wooden coble would have done the job. Heck, the Bay fishermen of yesteryear used to fish practically up to Norwegian waters in their little wooden cobles: those little boats being so hardy and seaworthy. Their design was, after all, based in smaller scale, on the tough Viking boats of old. Even so, the oncoming storm would have made the waters treacherous. Tia and Jimmy might have been desperate and foolish enough to try their hand though, possibly. But Jimmy's alibis so far checked out. And Tia's might very well too. She had stated her whereabouts in a very confident tone.

Elsie was aware that she was making easy assumptions and she didn't entirely trust easy assumptions; although sometimes the simplest explanations were the correct ones. A lot more work needed to be done. Elsie gazed absent-mindedly into her cup of tea. A small piece of sugar swirled to the surface before disintegrating. She just had to keep stirring this case until something appeared, she thought absent-mindedly to herself.

A breeze picked up and Elsie could have sworn that she could hear the rise of children's laughter and chatter. It seemed to be coming from the old chapel a few doors along from her cottage. Perhaps there was a coffee morning in progress - with a play group, she thought. The children began to recite the alphabet in a collective sing-song voice. The Chapel was used for all kinds of community projects. Of course the wind whipped around the coves on this part of the coastline and threw all kinds of noise up into the air and carried it elsewhere on the breeze. Maybe it was coming from the beach. Maybe the playgroup leaders had taken the children for a walk on the beach. It had become chillier. Time to go; there were things to do.

The Sailor's Alphabet

A is the anchor that holds a bold ship,

B is the bowsprit that often does dip,

C is the capstan on which we do wind, and

D is the davits on which the jolly boat hangs.

Chorus:

Oh, hi derry, hey derry, ho derry down,

Give sailors their grog and there's nothing goes wrong,

So merry, so merry, so merry are we,

No matter who's laughing at sailors at sea.

2. E is the ensign, the red, white, and blue,

F is the fo'c'sle, holds the ship's crew,

G is the gangway on which the mate takes his stand,

H is the hawser that seldom does strand.

Chorus:

3. I is the irons where the stuns'l boom sits,

J is the jib-boom that often does dip,

246

K are the keelsons of which you've told, and

L are the lanyards that always will hold.

Chorus:

4. M is the main mast, so stout and so strong,

N is the north point that never points wrong,

O are the orders of which we must be'ware, and

P are the pumps that cause sailors to swear.

Chorus:

5. Q is the quadrant, the sun for to take,

R is the riggin' that always does shake,

S is the starboard side of our bold ship, and

T are the topmasts that often do split.

Chorus:

6. U is the ugliest old Captain of all,

V are the vapours that come with the squall,

W is the windlass on which we do wind, and

X, Y, and Z, well, I can't put in rhyme!

Chorus:

CHAPTER 22

WEDNESDAY 15th September 2018 Robin
Hood's Bay

Elsie headed for the dock of the bay, turned sharp
left and mounted a few steep steps, which brought
her onto the little alley called Sunnyside. She rapped
loudly on Linda Kettlewell's door: No.11 Sunnyside.
As she knocked on the door she heard that strange
clack, clack, clack sound which she always heard
when taking a stroll through Sunnyside Lane; as if
something loose was being buffeted by the wind.
She never had been able to trace the noise. She
glanced around but as usual could see nothing.
Just as Elsie lifted her hand to rap again the door
opened and Linda Kettlewell stood before her. Elsie
had gone to the same school as Linda Kettlewell's
daughter, Caryn. Caryn now lived in Canada. Many
of the inhabitants of Baytown, and local environs,

were connected in some way - some things hadn't changed over the years.

'Elsie, Elsie Storm. How lovely to see you. Come in.' Linda's little cottage had no hallway and the front door led straight into the sitting room. The old lady motioned Elsie to sit down in one of the two deep armchairs by the coal fire with its glowing embers. 'I expect this might be to do with Demmy Harper,' she said; her face assuming a sombre expression.

'Good to see you too, Linda and yes, it is.'

'Let me just see about getting some tea first.' She disappeared into the snug kitchen and busied herself with the kettle and some cups.

Elsie knew better than to refuse the tea offered by Linda. Visitors in Baytown were expected to accept tea and offer friendly chat in return. A large ginger cat snoozed peacefully on the deep windowsill. These cottages had thick walls to keep out the robust elements in this part of the world. The furnishings in the rest of the room were equally old but all of a high quality and very well-kept. It was a beautiful room with its old fireplace and low ceilings with its scattering of tasteful ornaments. A few pictures on the walls showed old Baytown characters of fishermen and their hardy wives and sturdy children. One wall was a gallery of Linda's grandchildren. An old clock on the mantelpiece cosily and audibly ticked away the time.

A sail of sunlight cascaded through the glass onto the wide planked, old oak floors. Elsie idly wondered if the wood from the floor was taken from some old shipwreck or dismantled boat. It wouldn't be the first time some of the old boats had been used in this way in the Baytown houses. A former old inn, in the village, had had its whole interior supplied by an old shipwreck; its beams, wainscoting, flooring and shelving all testified to its original nautical provenance. It was now a holiday cottage.

Linda bustled in with some tea and biscuits. After the expected exchange of pleasantries and news (Caryn now had teenage children and Linda was going over to visit her daughter's family within the month), Elsie began,

'Linda, I know that two officers recently visited but could you please tell me a little more about the last time you saw Demmy. I just want to know for myself exactly what you saw. It might be important.'

'Well, Elsie, there isn't much to tell, really.' Linda took a sip of tea as she gathered her thoughts.

'It was the 24th of August, just before three. The date's in my calendar because I was on the way to the hairdressers. That's why I'm so sure of the date and time. The appointment was at two and it only takes me a few minutes to walk up the hill to the hairdressers at the top of the bank.'

Most of the Bay folk were fit, Elsie surmised, because the steep cliff bank on which the village was set, kept you fit as you walked up and down it during your day to day errands. The village extended to the top of the bank - with more houses and shops as well as the hotels and bus stop being situated up there.

Elsie stayed silent as Linda continued, 'I saw Demmy coming out of No.3 - four doors away, just as I was stepping out from my front door,' she clarified. 'I know Demmy's family own a few holiday cottages in the Bay and I've seen her round and about. I think she helps her dad to look after them sometimes - usually helping to clean them between visitors, you know. She lived in no. 3, though. Her aunt Jess recently left it to her so I've seen a little more of her round and about. Demmy always said 'Hello'. Nice girl.' Linda paused and then sighed. 'Some round here, laughed at her a bit, in a good natured way though, because she was often dressed oddly: black clothes; lots of make-up and heavy jewellery and what not. But I liked her. It doesn't matter how someone dresses if you've got nice manners, I think. And Demmy did have lovely manners. Her dad should be proud of who she was. He and his late wife did a good job there.' Linda's face dropped a little in sadness.

'Did Demmy speak to you, the last time she saw you?' asked Elsie gently.

'She didn't but I don't think she saw me. She looked in a rush - a bit preoccupied.'

'And was there anyone with her?'

'No, she just shut the door and locked the door behind her and then left. There was definitely no one with her.'

'Did you ever see Demmy with anyone else, around the village? A boyfriend, perhaps?'

Linda paused for a minute as she tried to remember. 'Can't say I did but when I did see her, she was helping out with one of the holiday cottages which they own. No, never saw her with anyone, you know, different…special.' This chimed with Elsie's meagre recollections of very occasionally seeing Demmy in the village. Robin Hood's Bay is perpetually busy with holidaymakers and visually everyone blends in. It was more like a small town in some respects. In a less busy environment individuals would stand out more. And it sounded as if Demmy spent much of her time in Whitby, anyway.

'Did you know Demmy's aunt, Jess Whittaker?'

'She kept herself to herself but I used to sometimes see Jess round the village - with her paints and easel usually. She was a keen artist and sold a fair few of her paintings in the local gift shop. But then she became too weak to go out. She had carers coming regularly when she got ill - until she went into a home that is. She didn't last long. I understand she passed about six months or so ago. Jess was a competent artist. A lot of folk around here have bought her paintings.' Linda looked deep in thought; probably remembering the past. 'And that's all I can tell you, I'm afraid. You've probably had a wasted journey.'

'Not at all, it helps me to build up a picture of Demmy's life - I know how difficult it is talking about Demmy like this, but thank you, you've been helpful. I'll leave my card, if that's Ok. It's got my number on if you remember anything else.' She smiled at the old lady who looked up and gave a brief smile back.

'Such a great shame, a very great shame about her though,' said the old lady softly.

'It is,' agreed Elsie. Both of the women were quiet for a moment.

'How are your grandchildren?' asked Elsie, she didn't want to leave the old lady brooding on the murder; it was probable that the old lady might be lonely living in her cottage with only her memories of the past to while away her days. It was the right question: a smile lit the old lady's face as she regaled Elsie with more of the latest antics of her two mischievous grandsons, who now lived in Whitby with her son and his wife, as well as reiterating how she was looking forward to her next visit to see Caryn and her brood of three children in Canada.

'Of course, I wish they lived in the village, Caryn too. Grandchildren are the best thing about life when you get old. I've lived here my whole life. Used to be schooled in the old chapel; lived off the fish from the fishing boats; milk and veg brought in from the nearby farms. We had everything here. It was a small little world but we were quite happy,' she mused. 'Still, the world moves on; couldn't do without central heating now to heat my old bones. And fishing's a hard life: I wouldn't want it for my grandchildren, I suppose; but even so, we were content. Sometimes the world feels safer when it's a bit smaller.'

'I heard children's voices coming from out of the old chapel earlier when I was sitting outside; must still be being used as a nursery, or something,' commented Elsie.

'Oh no, you can't have done,' said the old lady, 'There's building work going on there at the moment - they're going to make it into a café for the tourists, I heard. One of the workmen must have had a radio on, or something.'

There was a silence for a moment.

'Anything else, Elsie?' asked Linda, 'It's just that I'm afraid I need to go out shortly. Bill is due any minute, it's our weekly practise for the folk club session at The Dolphin.'

The old Dolphin Inn had been hiring out its upstairs room as a local folk singing club for years and was avidly attended by many locals in the area. Sea shanties were a particular favourite with the local folk group.

So much for Elsie feeling that she had to keep the old lady company because she was lonely. It struck her rather uncomfortably that, with her sunny disposition, the old lady probably had a better social life than she did.

There was a sharp knock at the door. 'Goodness, he's early!' exclaimed Linda springing to her feet.

'Yes, I need to make tracks, and thanks again, Linda.'

Linda opened the door to her friend. 'Hello, Bill.'

'Hello, Linda. Oh, sorry you've got company,' said a small wiry, looking man aged about seventy.'

'I'm just going, actually.' Elsie smiled good naturedly at him. She recognised him as a local from the houses at the upper end of Baytown.

'Elsie's a police-officer, she lives in the Bay too,' said Linda.

'Of course: I expect it's about Mick Harper's daughter. Terrible news. I used to go to school with Jess, her aunt. Jess was in the same year as me.'

It was no surprise to Elsie that news about Demmy had spread so quickly. She'd be surprised if any of the Bay's six hundred inhabitants didn't know the grisly news. It was probably known on many of the outlying farms and in nearby villages too.

Linda noticed the look of interest on Elsie's face, 'Bill why don't you chat to Elsie for a few minutes while I get myself ready.'

Bill was only too happy to chat about the past and was soon telling Elsie about some stories of his and Jess's schooldays. Bill was engaging but as far as the investigation went Elsie did not learn that much. 'Jess and I always got on, we both loved history,' he concluded.

'I'd say, Bill loves history?' smiled Linda, re-entering the room. 'There isn't anything about the history of the bay that's worth knowing that Bill doesn't know about, especially its smuggling years.'

'It's always has been a passion of mine. It was a whole other world, right beneath our feet; every step and stone in the bay has its own story. In fact, I helped Jess with her family tree.. She'd traced her line right back to Jeb Whittaker - one of the most successful and well known smugglers around here.'

'I wonder if you might have seen Demmy Harper recently, Bill? I know she recently moved into the village to live?' asked Elsie.

'That's right - took over Jess's old cottage, I'd heard, but no, I can't help you I'm afraid. The last time I saw her was about two months ago in the general store on the bank. She was just buying a few things. We said 'Hello' and that was it. I'm sorry I can't help you more.'

'And she was on her own?'

'As I recall, yes.'

'And there's no use asking me if I've seen any strangers around the village lately. The place is full of visitors, nowadays. It only seems like yesterday that the village was full of fishermen with their boats and lobster baskets. I don't think there's one fisher-man left that makes his living from the sea anymore. Once the big trawlers started coming to Whitby that was the end of the fishing industry in the bay.'

'He's back in his history again, Elsie, but I'm afraid we're going to have to go now or we'll be late. If I can be of any further help you know where I am. And if you need to know anything else about the history of the Bay, or Whitby actually, you'll find no-one more knowledgeable than our Bill,' she added with a smile, 'Poor Demmy though, poor poor Dem-my.'

Elsie thought about Linda's comment that there was no longer a nursery or school at the Old Chap-el, on her way home, as she passed the building again. The noisy sounds of the workmen's pack-ing up for the day and throwing their tools in a van, drowned out any other sound in the vicinity. At the time though, she had barely registered Linda's words about the current repurposing of the Chapel. She'd been so absorbed in the ambience of the cosy little living room with its smouldering, soporific fire in the grate; the sound of the clock; the sleepy cat that she hadn't really been struck by the oddness of it. Elsie had almost felt like she had been in some timeless cocoon in Linda's cottage. She had almost expected Caryn to bounce down the stairs wearing her school uniform.

The sea-breeze must have carried the sounds from elsewhere, she concluded, as she strode on by.

The Smuggler in A Sailor's Garland

O my true love's a smuggler and sails upon the sea,

And I would I were a seaman to go along with he;

To go along with he for the satins and the wine,

And run the tubs at Slapton when the stars do shine.

O Hollands is a good drink when the nights are cold,

And Brandy is a good drink for them as grows old,

There is lights in the cliff-top when the boats are home-bound,

And we run the tubs at Slapton when the word goes round.

The King he is a proud man in his grand red coat,

But I do love a smuggler in his little fishing-boat,

For he runs the Mallins lace and he spends his money free,

And I would I were a seaman to go along with he.

CHAPTER 23

THURSDAY 16th September 2018

The next morning was cloudy. Elsie and Sim were paying a visit to Mick Harper. It was heavy and still and a few gathering dark clouds looked as if it might be about to rain.

'Tia's alibi has checked out, Ma'am. Her friend Kelly confirms that Tia was with her the whole time from Saturday evening through till Sunday morning. And Maxi Tierney confirms that she gave her a lift after work and dropped her off at home about half three, Saturday afternoon. The Spyglass confirmed her attendance at work. Gemma Leyburn's movements have been accounted for too, like you asked.'

Elsie nodded in receipt of the expected information.

'All who we've investigated alibis for, have checked out.' Sim concluded'

As they drove up to the Harper property, Elsie was once more struck by its idyllic location: the vast expanse of moorland behind it and the vast expansive views of the Bay in front of it.

At first, they thought no-one was in but then the slow release of the bolt was heard on the other side of the door and it began to gradually creak open, as if unwilling to let the outside world in.

Mick Harper peered out at them: lines of grief were etched across his forehead and in the furrows of his cheeks. Mick could only have been a few years older than Elsie's forty-six years but his loss had aged him. Even his movements had become stiffened through shock.

'Mr Harper,' greeted Elsie gently.

'Have you caught the bastard yet?' asked Mr Harper without any preamble.

'I'm sorry, Mr Harper, not yet. We need to just ask you a few more questions. Is it convenient now?'

With weary steps Mick Harper showed them into the kitchen. A heavy grey pall of sky could be seen through the window. A couple of chaffinches pecked eagerly away, at a suspended nutball hanging from a nearby laburnum tree, oblivious to the approaching bad weather.

Elsie began, 'We don't have any news as yet for you, Mr Harper, but we are pursuing our enquiries relentlessly, I can assure you.'

Mr Harper looked at her. 'You don't need to relentlessly pursue your enquiries: it was that little bastard, Bransdale, who did it.'

Elsie looked taken aback.

'Have you discovered something we need to know, Mr Harper?' asked Sim.

'It's obvious isn't it? There's no way their relationship could have lasted. I've been thinking and remembering: she hadn't talking about the places she used to go to with him so much.'

'Look, Mr Harper. If it was Mr Bransdale we will do everything in our power to bring him to justice.'

'He's a slippery weasel, though isn't he? He'll likely bring up being brought up in care and all that and some liberal judge will let him off with a couple of weeks picking up litter or something.'

Elsie could understand Mick Harper's feelings of rage about what had happened to Demmy, but she didn't like the turn the conversation was taking - or the animated gleam in the distraught father's eyes.

'Mr Harper, it would be unwise to jump to conclusions until we have completed our investigation. There is no evidence to suggest it was Mr Bransdale, at the present time.' Elsie hated using standard police speak, especially to someone who had been tragically bereaved, but sometimes such language had evolved for a reason. 'You mustn't jump to conclusions.' She then added more gently. 'I've always found that it is best not to pre-judge in a case like this. Mistakes can be made too easily if you do that and you can miss lines of enquiry you should have pursued.'

Mick Harper looked at her, 'I still think it was him and that your enquiries will sooner or later show that. Who else could it have been?'

'Mr Harper, did Demmy have any other relationships with other possible boyfriends do you think?'

'No, is the answer to that. I'd have been bloody delighted to find out she was dating another lad. She never mentioned another fella. I'm sure of it, especially to me. Why, what have people been saying?' Mick Harper bristled at the thought that his daughter's reputation had been sullied in some way.

'We need to ask you, Mr Harper, did Demmy have any other friends out of her obvious circle of friends who you knew about?'

Mick Harper tried to focus and was quiet as he carefully mulled over the question, 'I don't think so. She just seemed to spend her time with Gemma and Jimmy Bransdale and her other Goth friends, I think. But then...' he was quiet again for a moment.

'Anything you remember might really help us - even the smallest thing.'

'Well,' he began, 'to be honest, she wasn't particularly forthcoming about where she was going and she wasn't mentioning her usual haunts or hangouts where she usually met up with her friends as much. You know, The Angel, Shylock's and the like. In fact, now I come to think of it, she hardly mentioned those places at all towards...' his voice faltered.

'Could she have been seeing someone else?' asked Sim, 'Someone out of that usual circle. Can you remember, had her behaviour changed, her dress, anything she might have said that was different in any way that struck you as being different? Anything at all?' Sim's voice was hypnotic and calm. Mick Harper fell quiet as he tried to remember.

'I suppose she looked a bit smarter, maybe. Less make up - and shoes sometimes, instead of boots. But no, she never mentioned any new names or places she'd been to.'

Sim held out the leaflet about the craft fair in York that he had taken from Demmy's house. It was in a

271

plastic bag. 'Have you ever seen this leaflet before, Mr Harper? I'm sorry but we can't take it out of the bag at the moment.'

Mick Harper looked puzzled for a minute. The advertising of the craft fair event in York was clearly visible.

'Demmy sometimes booked a stall at these kinds of events, to try to generate interest in her sculptures. She showed her jewellery too. Skegwin encouraged her; it brought advertising to the shop.'

'So this event was two weeks ago. Did Demmy go to it?' prompted Sim.

'Yes she did. I remember she told me that she'd been. She usually set off quite early to avoid the traffic around York.'

Sim turned the bag over so that the handwritten message was visible on the other side of it. 'Do you have any idea whose handwriting this is?'

Mick peered at it, 'No, she usually went to these things on her own, or she said she did.'

'I know this seems a bit unusual, Mr Harper, but do you recognise this bottle?' Elsie clicked on the picture taken at Aunt Jessie's house. 'No, should I?' He gazed at Elsie with a perplexed expression.

'You don't own any bottles like this?'

'I don't drink alcohol,' was his resolute reply. Mick Harper's voice quavered and he looked out of the window where the swirling sea melted into the slate grey sky.

'And Demmy didn't drink much wine either - except on special occasions. Yes, she was stopping over at Gemma's a bit more, I think she said,' he added. But that was fine by me. It was much better to see her going out with her friends, rather than wasting her time on that waster.'

Elsie decided not to react. And she remembered that Gemma had actually claimed that she had been seeing rather less of Demmy. It seemed that Demmy was hiding something.

'Can you tell me a little more about your business-es, Mr Harper. I believe you have a number of prop-erties in Robin Hood's Bay?'

Mick Harper continued looking moodily out of the window. It had begun to rain outside and the rain mist obscured the view across the bay to Raven-scar. The wind began to throw the rain half-heart-edly at the window pane. The chaffinches had flown away.

'We own seven cottages in the village. Eight now I suppose with the one Jess left to Demmy.'

'Jess adored Demmy.' Mick struggled not to cry. El-sie's heart clenched in pity for him; she gave him a few moments to gather himself.

'Demmy was living in Jess's old house, but I couldn't see that lasting for long. I thought she'd soon get bored living in the village. I'd expected her to get a flat in Whitby, near her friends at some point. A bit of a battleaxe, Jess, but a good sort, you know. She was a rock when Helen, my wife, was ill.' He added, rambling through his memories.

Elsie retrieved the note she and Sim had discovered at Demmy's cottage. 'Mr Harper, do you have any idea who wrote this - it seems to be the same handwriting as the one on the leaflet?'

'No, no idea at all. I wouldn't recognise Demmy's friends' handwriting, though. Did you find them in the cottage?'

'So you don't recognise the handwriting at all?'

'No, I'm afraid not. I could take copies and send them by mobile around her friends, if you like. See if anyone recognises them.'

'No, it's fine, our enquiries will establish if they belong to any of her friends. Thank you anyway.'

After spending a few more minutes ensuring that the family liaison officer had been in touch, Sim and Elsie left Mick staring moodily out of the window.

Elsie felt sad leaving him on his own. The big property seemed empty and there was a gloom about it even though its fittings were stylish and lovely; as if it had imbibed the sorrow of its inhabitants in some way.

'Fancy fish and chips, Sim? We could eat them back at my cottage, if you like. I don't fancy going back to the station just yet. Just want to think about where we are in this investigation.' In reality, she wasn't that hungry. She just couldn't face the station just yet; wanted to gather her thoughts and to first shake off the sadness poor Mick Harper had exuded.

'Sure' responded Sim, as Elsie turned toward the lower bay in her mini. They parked half way down the bank, in the car park in Elsie's usual spot: only foot traffic was allowed in the lower bay as the narrow streets and ginnels or vehicles for offloading. The grey skies seemed to be retreating across the bay and the sun made its fragile appearance. The silver bay lay glittering before them with the far cliffs of Ravenscar, to the south, enclosing it in its broody embrace. Elsie's thoughts though were far from the stunning scene before her.

CHAPTER 24

Robin Hood's Bay 1797

Sea mist was settling on the Bay. Emma looked out of the window and rare for her, a feeling of unease flickered through her. Her daughter, Alice was sat by the fire staring into it - all animation gone. Emma had tended her cuts and bruises as best she could but only time could heal Alice both inside and out. Alice had been a spirited and vivacious girl when she'd married Wilf. The marriage had been against all the advice of her friends and relatives. Wilf had been a newcomer who'd come looking for the work. At first, Wilf had seemed keen to be put to work on anything Jeb had asked of him but then laziness and insolence had set in. Then Wilf had begun to beat Alice.

The Bay code was to never interfere in domestic concerns. It was a rule that generally served the Robin

Hood's Bay folk well but Wilf had taken advantage of this code all too often, as he had often taken for granted the support of his wife's relations. Alice, ashamed at her situation had never spoken of her abuse to her father, although many a time she had felt like telling him. Now Jeb had the evidence which could no longer be put down to falling down the stairs or some other such clumsiness - which she had recounted with averted eyes. After all Baytown was set on the upward sweep of a cliff, skirted by a rocky shore. The villagers were renowned for being as sure-footed as goats. Their elderly tended to live long lives and few succumbed to the usual frailties of old age. He'd tried having words with Wilf but Wilf was a man who lived in the moment and his promises to be a good husband often became meaningless after he'd been at the rum. Jeb looked at his daughter as she stared blankly into the fire through swollen eyes. The once wilful Alice had seemed to fade before their very eyes since her benighted wedding to Wilf.

Emma stood up, 'Just going to check everything's ready, Jeb,' she opened the door and stepped outside. Whereas Jeb Storm was the lynchpin for getting the contraband ashore, Emma played her part in ensuring that every other villager was in place to receive the goods before passing it along the neighbourly chain from one house to the other. Closely packed houses and cottages straggled up the hill and all were full of secret rooms, trapdoors, cupboards and tunnels to make the passage of the contraband smooth and swift. Within a matter of hours, the goods (usually casks of tea; barrels of rum and/or brandy or bolts of silk) would wind their way from ship deck, onto shore, through the village, up the cliff and on their way to the markets of places such as York or Scarborough across the moors. Helped, of course, by secret knocks, candles placed in windows and clandestine whistles to ensure swift progress and to alert to any unwanted attention from the dragoons.

Jeb turned back to his daughter, 'Yer can stay here for as long as you like, lass – and the bairns too, of course.'

Alice had twin girls by Wilf: Nellie and Martha. They were about eighteen months old and were sleeping peacefully upstairs, mercifully unaware of the seismic change in their domestic circumstances.

Alice did not acknowledge her father's words; she still appeared in shock.

'Alice can you hear me?'

Jeb held out a necklace with a black moon-shaped pendant on it. Its glossy blackness showed it to be of the finest jet. He reached out for Alice's hand and wrapped it in hers. She looked down at it.

'Listen to me, Alice, this is very important. Look at the markings on the stone. Are you listening to me?'

Alice seemed to comprehend the sense of urgency in her father's voice and dutifully looked at the necklace wrapped around her palm.

At that moment Emma opened the door, 'Jeb, it's time. The mist has brought the lugger in early – probably didn't want to wait for it to get worse.' A little mist would help the smuggler's cause but a heavy fog would need stronger lights for navigation which could be spotted by the dragoons.

The light was quickly leaving the sky, chased on its way by the darkening mist. There was no time to lose. No-one wanted the lugger stranded on the rocks. 'I'll talk to you later, our Alice; when you're feeling more yourself, lass.'

Jeb and Emma closed the door. Everyone was in place: the men were on the shore ready to man the cobles to pitch out to sea toward the lugger; various village folk were stationed at the main passing points eg. the beck tunnel (a tunnel constructed as much to be used as a smuggling route as for the smooth running of the stream which ran through the village), the windows, doors and passageways along which the contraband would pass. Everyone had their place or position.

Even the elderly or infirm were stationed with candles or lanterns at the myriad little windows specially built into the houses to act as lookouts. As usual, many of the older women were sat knitting by the fire (they were to be found chatting or knitting outside their cottages on lighter evenings), with curtains opened to suggest normality to any passing unwanted eyes. The older men were stitching lobster pots or rope mats with them too, acting as stooges to promote the idea that nothing untoward was taking place. Some of the other women chatted, as they watched over the children playing in the alleys – it wasn't just their children they were watching out for.

Like many of the village families, everyone in the Whittaker family was involved: Charlie, the eldest lad, was already up on the moor acting as a look-out between the smugglers in the bay and the moor runners. The younger boys were stationed in the Bolts keeping watch out for any passing customs men, and their two other daughters were stationed at the main passing points ready to help pass the contraband from one passing place to the other.

Alice would not be taking her place with the other women of the village tonight. She barely compre-hended where she was. She had always tried to be a good wife to Wilf but somehow it had all gone wrong. She hoped he would skulk back home in the middle of the night but she knew, in her heart of hearts, that she was unlikely to see him ever again. She knew he would not change and the beatings were getting worse. Wilf had lost the respect of the other men in the village with his cards and his drinking - despite his family connections to the Whittakers who were one of the mainstay families in the Bay. And he was increasingly taking out his frustrations on Alice. Oh, how bruised she felt. She felt as if she would never have use of her sore limbs again. She felt so tired, so tired. Her eyelids drifted down and soon she was fast asleep - the pendant slipped to the floor.

'Bang, bang, bang!' Alice woke with a start and flinched as she jolted her neck in shock at the noise. Someone was banging violently upon the door. It flew open and a young lad of about sixteen years old rushed in. Alice had never seen him before. He looked as if he had been running for a while as he stood there gasping for breath; one hand on his hip as he doubled over trying to catch his breath, his cheeks bright red with exertion.

'Jeb Whittaker, I've been sent with a message for Jeb Whittaker.'

'I'm his d..daughter, Alice.'

'Where's Jeb Whittaker?' said the young lad, 'I have an urgent message for him.'

'Who are you? What do you want with me dad?' asked Alice agitatedly. She had been well taught in the ways of handling strangers in the Bay. Ask a question with a question. But still she was highly unnerved. This boy brought bad news, she could feel it.

'I've been sent by John Andrews. Jeb is not to collect the lobsters tonight. That's what he told me. You have to get the message to Jeb. The boy was becoming increasingly alarmed with every second that passed. His eyes dotted around toward the window feverishly as if he wanted to leave the house as soon as possible.

Alice stood stock still in shock at the name, John Andrews. John Andrews was the well-known smuggler from Saltburn – a small fishing community a few miles up the coast. He led one of the most successful smuggling gangs on the coast but he was also wily and dauntless enough to also have enrolled himself as a local customs officer. He worked both sides of the smuggling trade. Few people knew it but he often gave tipoffs to Jeb and Jeb often returned the favour for John Andrews. The fact that Andrews was a smuggler as well as a customs officer was not as ludicrous as it sounded. Customs officers and smugglers had a strange relationship and many of them could be paid off to turn a blind eye to, or even abet the smugglers as they carried out their precarious business. Admittedly, Andrews had taken the relationship to the extreme but he was known to be extremely wealthy as a result of his derring do and was now known to own half of Saltburn – including the Inn there, which was really the hub of his smuggling operations.

Barely had the boy's words left his lips than Alice had bolted out of the door. Adrenalin coursed through her, minimising the pain of her injuries. 'Not to collect the lobster pots' was the coded message that the run must be abandoned and that the smugglers were in grave danger. That meant that everyone that Alice cared about was in danger.

Alice skittered and limped badly along the moisture covered cobbles. Visibility was low: the mist was rapidly lessening but it still hung eerily in the air. There was some light from the windows of selected cottages with old folk sat seemingly knitting, or mending, or snoozing by their fire. For the first time in many a month Alice felt alive. Living with Wilf was only part living: the humiliations; the physical injuries; the hiding of what was really going on in her marriage; part injured pride, part shame. She had learnt to put hope and happiness away; never expecting to see them again and not wanting to; being half-alive made living with Wilf easier, somehow.

For the first time in several years she felt fear for someone other than herself or her children. Her father, the indestructible, capable hero of the Bay; the one everyone turned to for advice and direction was in danger. The militia must have got wind of tonight's run and it couldn't be the customs platoon the Bay folk knew; otherwise Jeb would have been notified of an impending raid. A new group must have been drafted in: the Bay's worst nightmare. Her family was in danger. Alice frantically made her way out of Chapel Street and down Baybank toward the dock. The tide was coming in. The run would be happening now.

Alice could see some movement through the quickly lifting mist: ghostly figures running back and forward with the contraband across the sand

She ran toward them and saw one tall figure some way out on the shore overseeing everything: her father. She ran toward him clutching her ribs which were, by now, tortuously reminding her of the vicious beating Wilf had given her.

She ran up to him. She knew better than to shout out: smugglers did as little as possible to draw attention to themselves, both in sight and sound; especially, when a run was taking place.

'Da, Da!' she cried, as she almost collapsed into Jeb's arms.

'Alice, what is it, love?' Men were running back and forward unloading the cobles, which had been used to offload the ship; a looming black presence five hundred yards away or so.

'John Andrews has sent word, father: the run must be abandoned; the customs men must be out with the militia.'

Alice felt her father tighten at the news. 'It's off, lads. Away back home!' He shouted across the sands. The men froze immediately and all turned back to shore; they knew better than to waste time questioning Jeb. Everyone knew what the message meant and fear instantly drenched the air. The race was on to get back to the Bay and hide the contraband, they had so far accumulated. They were in a race against time.

Without further ado, Jeb reached for his tinderbox and struck it. Within seconds the torch he carried on such nights was lit and he was frantically waving the lit beacon back and forth to encourage the cobles to scatter and to warn the ship to be on its way.

There was a loud crack from on shore and then further cracks as the customs officers fired at the smugglers from the dock. Their flintlocks sparked and their gunfire scored the air. Alice turned to look at them; abject fear on her face. Then she turned to look at her father who was staring at her, clutching his chest in disbelief. Then he sank to the ground and closed his eyes with his blood seeping into the sand and the gently lapping waves of the turning tide.

CHAPTER 25

THURSDAY 16th September 2018 Robin

Hood's Bay

Sim and Elsie were the first customers of the day at the bay fish shop. In fact, as they arrived the chippie was only just opening. The aroma of fish and chips hung around the shop creating an alchemy of aromas which can only occur in the briny sea air of the seaside: salt, vinegar, fried potatoes and fish basted with the seaweed which hung on the breath of the breeze. The beach lay just a few yards away from the chip shop, down the old cobbled slipway from which fishermen had launched their cobles for centuries. After purchasing their lunch they tramped the short way up to Elsie's cottage.

Elsie retrieved two cans of ice-cold cola from the fridge and took them outside to where Sim was sat at the little table. His profile was set against the vast blueness of the bay and he was deep in thought. In fact, Elsie didn't feel like talking much either. This was why she felt so comfortable in Sim's presence, she thought to herself. Shannon and Gus were able detectives but they could be exhausting company. Shannon was the direct opposite of Elsie: a flirty louder than life character who liked to crack filthy jokes. Elsie didn't consider herself to be a prude, but honestly...

Gus needed careful handling of another kind. He was so worried about causing offence; his demeanour was meek and whilst it helped witnesses or interviewees to let down their defences it was wearing in that Gus was so self-evasive and lacked confidence. Elsie had to edit everything she said and did around him in case it upset him in some way

Yes, Sim was easily the easiest of her team to be with, although he seemed to possess an underlying, vaguely defined nervous energy. He seemed to keep it under control, though, and he wasn't garrulous. He was insightful too. He often seemed to pick up on clues which the others (including Elsie) missed. And he seemed able to tune into Elsie's moods and train of thought, which always made for an easy companion. Like her need for quiet at the present time.

They unwrapped the steaming fish and chips in their heavy vinegary paper and sat for a while eating in silence. The sound of distant gulls and crashing waves was the perfect auditory backdrop to their meal. Elsie emptied her mind of all thought as she ate but then finally pushed the remnants of her food away. Sim had finished a few minutes earlier and was already smoking a cigarette. He inhaled and blew out a last plume of smoke; a slap of wind caught it, unfurled it and cast it out to sea.

'We're not getting anywhere,' commented Elsie.

'We need to find X,' said Sim.

'Mick Harper hasn't any clue at all about who the new boyfriend could have been.'

'And if he did know she was actually seeing someone else, he wouldn't have been so steamed up about Jimmy,' concluded Sim.

'I suppose she wouldn't confide in her dad, in case he got his hopes up. Maybe she didn't want Jimmy to know because she was keeping her options open. Maybe she thought she might end up going back to Jimmy.'

'Sam might know who he is,' said Sim.

'Or her other friends, or her employers; somebody, somewhere must know who this man is; or at least have seen him with Demmy.'

'X could be a girl.'

'Yes, but all we know at this stage is that, whoever it is, seems to like fancy wine - so someone with expensive tastes. Not much to go on.'

CHAPTER 26

THURSDAY 16th September 2018 Whitby

Gus and Shannon had initially felt a bit odd and stagey as they had walked the dark Whitby streets on the way to the Angel pub. Gus was wearing a dark flowing overcoat reminiscent of the Victorian era. At his neck frothed a modest frill of a white shirt. He complemented the look with dark, thigh high, leather boots. Wearing a dark wig with flowing brown locks tied in a ponytail, pirate style, he actually looked quite funky and alternative and as Shannon had said, 'quite fit', which had made him blush.

Shannon looked stunning. She was completely unrecognisable with her pale make up and deep red lipstick carefully applied over her full lips. Her resplendent red hair was piled on her head in a loose Edwardian style. Dark and dramatic purple eye make up with the contrast of the white skin make up made her look like some exquisite lead in a Gothic horror movie. She wore a tight Edwardian dress which was ankle high exposing some tightly laced ankle boots. It was an artfully put together look: a perfect combination of the prim and the louche.

'I've often seen the Goths about and wanted to have a go at dressing like this,' she commented.'

'Me too, and I've always been keen to explore the darker side of my spirituality as well,' added Gus.

'Yeah, that too,' smiled Shannon. 'Although I'm given to think that the darker side of my spirituality would involve a good rut, to be honest.'

'Kind of like the lighter side of your spirituality then.'

After some considered thought, Shannon replied, 'Suppose so.'

It had been Shannon's idea to spy on the friends of Demmy in the place where she was last seen to get more of a handle on the whole set up; although, the fun of dressing up held great appeal too.

As they walked down the cobble street toward the Angel, Gus began, 'Should I have put more make up on? Do you think they'll recognise us?' Gus and Shannon had interviewed some of Demmy's friends the day before.

'They'll never recognise you; you look completely different. And even if they do, so what? We're off duty. That eyeliner is a genius touch.'

'Yes, thanks for putting it on. I wouldn't have had the first clue.'

'I look gorgeous, don't I?' said Shannon. It was a rhetorical question but as if in some kind of cosmic answer, two slightly drunk men whistled at her as they side stepped her on the street. 'Yep, I'm defo ruttable. Friggin uncomfortable though. Now I know why corsets went out of fashion.'

Shannon pushed open the door of 'The Angel and the beat of sonorous Gothic music spilled out; the hypnotic bass made Gus's skin tingle. The bar of the Angel was heaving with a colourful mix of characters in Goth attire. Dramatic make up and unusual dark diaphanous or heavily draped clothing was commonplace. Some of the men looked very smart in their tweedy looking suits complete with hats and canes. Others sported more of a dystopian type, piratical look with boots and heavy flowing coats - not unlike the look Gus had adopted for himself. And age was clearly no barrier as all ages of folk huddled together around the tables and wide bar area.

They (very luckily) found a small table as a couple, dressed in coordinating black clothing, were just departing. Gus disappeared for drinks.

'It's like everyone's in disguise,' commented Shannon as Gus returned to the table with their drinks: double vodka and tonic for Shannon and a half cider for Gus. 'Maybe the true disguise is what people are expected to wear in their everyday lives in order to fit in with social mores,' responded Gus.

'You couldn't run after the dog in that get-up, could you?' commented Shannon eyeing a young woman wearing trousers with leather bondage straps taped to each leg.

'Mind, many of them probably dress like this every day,' said Shannon. 'If it wasn't for this corset, I might be tempted. I could do with a new more grown up look. I'm nearly thirty: doc martens and t shirts aren't really the image for an aspiring professional anymore, I guess.'

'Don't let Elsie hear you admit that. She'll soon have you in crinolines.'

'Or worse, A line skirts and flatties, like she wears,' grimaced Shannon.

Shannon didn't mind Elsie's rather straight-laced ways and found her rather benign as a boss. She more came out with the occasional comment about Elsie to wind Gus up a bit as Gus adored their boss.

'She always looks dignified…elegant, though,' said Gus in a high voice, determined to be a bit defiant in honour of Elsie, although a little bit frightened of contradicting Shannon at the same time.

'Your penchant for older birds is popping out of its box again, Gus.'

'I don't pop out of my box for older birds, as you put it. You just think I do.'

'Then why are you flirting with that woman dressed as a ghost. She must be fifty, if a day.'

The woman in question, who was sitting at the next table with a rather sombre looking crowd heard Shannon's rather strident voice and raised her eyebrows at Shannon but then smiled at Gus. Gus smiled back and then blushed deeply.

By now all the tables were taken. A young couple had claimed quite a large table: the girl had bright burgundy streaks in her hair and the boy had numerous piercings all over his face. Before long, a larger group entered the pub and greeted the couple before sitting down at the table. Amongst them was Gemma; some of Demmy's other college friends and the lamentable Jimmy who looked for all the world as if he had just been picked up by the crowd and dropped into the pub. It was clear that he didn't really want to be there - probably some of the others had wanted to take him out to cheer him up a bit. He stared moodily into his drink.

'Ey up,' said Shannon, as quietly as she was capable of being, 'It's all kicking off.'

After a while, Jimmy went to the bar, on his own, and asked for a beer. The older barman tried to talk to him but Jimmy seemed unresponsive and just stared into his pint. He seemed oblivious to everyone.

Shannon and Gus chatted meaninglessly but it was just for the sake of appearances. They were really all eyes and ears trying to check out the dynamics of Demmy's friendship group. After a while, a short but sturdy girl approached Jimmy and tentatively put her hand over his. Gus and Shannon recognised her from her photo on the investigation board: Tia. Jimmy looked up - surprised out of his reverie. The girl began to talk to him in a low voice - her head bent toward his. At first Jimmy seemed to be listening to Tia and appreciating her sympathy but after a few minutes he straightened as if startled.

'She's hardly been dead a week and you're coming on now to me. What kind of a bitch are you, Tia? No wonder she didn't fucking like you - I don't fucking like you. And don't cry. Stay out of my face!'

With that Jimmy pushed the shocked Tia out of the way and stormed out of the pub; his face a bright puce colour.

Either Tia had made a stupidly premature move on Jimmy or she had been a bit too lavish with her sympathy and the grief addled Jimmy had misinterpreted her actions. Whatever had actually happened resulted in Tia rushing to the toilets with a couple of her friends dashing after her.

The pub went silent except for some mournful Goth record playing dolorously over the speaker system. Then a furious buzz of conversation broke out. Two of Jimmy's friends from the large table got up quickly as if to run after Jimmy but the older of the two barmen stopped them and followed after Jimmy himself.

Gus leant over to Shannon, 'I'll see what's going on with those two, Ok?'

'Sure, I'll go the loos - see what I can find out about Tia.'

After the conversation broke out again, Gus got up unobtrusively and left the pub. Shannon went to the ladies toilets, after quickly downing her drink.

Jimmy was sat on the kerb sobbing into his folded arms. The older barman had his arm around him try-ing to soothe him, as if he were a child. The street was quiet, apart from the two men, with only the muffled sound of the music coming from the pub. The mourn-ful cry of a seagull, from a nearby pantiled roof-top, punctuated the mournful music every now and then. Gus wasn't spotted by the two men and he deftly slipped into a side alley running alongside the pub.

'I can't live without her,' said Jimmy his words almost inaudible through his sobbing, 'Tell me, Cal. How am I to live without her?' She was everything. What's left for me now?'

'I know you loved her, Jimmy. We all know you loved her.'

'It must be something about me, mustn't it?' sobbed Jimmy. 'I'm not meant a normal life like everyone else. My card's marked; might as well just put an end to it.'

'Sssh, mate. Course you'll have a normal life. That's what Demmy'd want. She wouldn't want you to stop trying to get what you want...what you deserve. And don't pay no mind to Tia. She doesn't know how to handle grief and things like that; she's just a bit blunt...tactless. She was probably just trying to cheer you up.'

'I suppose. I just went for her. I know she likes me. Probably glad about what happened to Demmy.'

'Doubt it, Jimmy. She looked really upset in there. Reckon she's had enough bad luck in her life. She wouldn't want it for her mates.'

Jimmy took a deep breath then shakily stood up. 'I'm off home, Cal. I knew it was a mistake to come out. Just couldn't stand looking at the walls on me own anymore.'

'Shall I get someone to come with you? They're a good lot, Jimmy. You've got good friends, you know. They'll see you through - if you let them.'

'Just want to be on me own, Cal. I miss her.' Jimmy's voice shook again and he turned abruptly to walk home on his own, head down with his hands stuffed into his pockets.

Cal took a deep breath before walking back into the pub. Shannon passed him as he entered and she stepped out into the street.

Gus stepped toward her out of the alley.

'Anything?' she asked Gus.

'Not really, he's grief-stricken, though. Felt a bit guilty spying on him, to be honest.'

'Part of the job, Gus. At least we know, I suppose, that the relations between them all seem to have a ring of truth; by what we've seen tonight anyway. Now, what's that other Goth pub? The Endeavour? Fancy a pint in there? Be a shame to waste this get-up.'

CHAPTER 27

Robin Hood's Bay 1807

Twins Martha and Nellie were squabbling about that necklace again. They were sat in front of the range whilst their grandma, Emma, kneaded the dough; her white floury hands at odds with her red flustered face. Their mother, Alice, stared absent-mindedly into the steady fire of the range. Truth to tell, Alice had never really recovered from the night her father had been killed. She had been mostly mute ever since. Many considered her to be a bit simple as she was often to be found roaming the cliffs and shoreline with a slow shambling walk. When people tried to talk to her, her speech was rambling and disconnected. She seemed to inhabit a different world entirely. Emma tried to keep an eye on her but with a houseful including Alice's twin children it was hard. Still, the villagers all looked out for Alice.

Whether it was the shock of holding her dying father in her arms or because of a blow to the head by Wilf perhaps, no-one knew or tried to guess. Emma reckoned it was a combination of the two.

In a funny way, Emma blamed herself for not protecting her daughter from Wilf. She should have seen through his initial charm and sent him on his way. That's what her own mother would have done. Her mam was always very wary of strangers to the village.

At least Charlie, her eldest, had easily taken over the reins of his father on the smuggling trade in the Bay. Thought by some at the time to be too young, Charlie had proved them wrong. He was tall and strong and had his wits about him. He'd inherited his father's knowledge, resourcefulness and quick-thinking ways. And Lizzie. her second eldest daughter was slipping easily into the role Emma played in the village when the villagers needed co-ordinating during a run.

Emma had lost Jeb but life had forced her to go on. If there was one piece of luck from that dreadful night when he'd died, it was that the dragoons had comprised mostly of new recruits and the villagers had been able to sequester the contraband to hidden quarters in record quick time. The cobles had scattered to nearby unreachable bases of cliffs and the lugger, which had already made its turning had silently and swiftly sailed away. Brock Harris had scooped up the sobbing Alice from her dead father's side and carried her away to the beck tunnel. By the time the dragoons had reached the beach all that was left was the body of poor Jeb Whittaker, lifeless and still on the shore.

'Martha, don't you dare hit your sister,' rapped Emma, grabbing and just stopping Martha's raised fist in its tracks. The twins were ten years old and like two peas in a pod to look at but as far as temperament was concerned they were oceans apart. Nellie was kind, gentle and quick to smile: Martha was cruel, noisy and quick to curse - no matter how many times Emma dragged her to the chapel to say penance.

What was it about that necklace that provoked this obsession? It was a strange looking thing anyway with its peculiar engravings. Alice often sat by the fire and played with the necklace as if in a trance. Martha had taken to prising the necklace away from her mother's hands and trying to claim it for her own. The outraged Nellie, who usually gave in to Martha's demands for the sake of a quiet life, would surprisingly, strongly object and grab it back and try to place it firmly in her mother's pocket; or run to Emma with it for safekeeping.

'It's mine, mother said I could keep it!' cried Martha who told lies as convincingly as if they were the truth.

'Grandad gave it to mum; she told me so, Martha. He said mum must always keep it close. And mum's not well. She likes to play with it. It's not yours, Martha. Give over!'

Nellie had managed to prise it from her twin's fingers, once again. Martha scowled as Nellie gently wrapped the chain around her mother's hand. Alice smiled and continued to stare as if transfixed by it.

It was a late spring day so Emma decided the girls should play outside. They had completed their morning chores; the sun had just come out so the girls could play awhile in the fresh air. The other children were on the dock, or on the beach, helping the fishermen with a few recently landed cobles of gleaming silver herrings.

At least, like the other families in the Bay, they were well provided for, Jeb had seen to that.

'Silver by day; gold by night,' was one of Emma's maxims to account for the prosperity of the village. In a few decades hence, Whitby would become the main sea faring port as the newly-invented trawlers would take over. Today, though, the little cobles held sway and the Bay hived with the activity of its main daylight harvesting – herrings.

The inhabitants of Baytown however, did not flaunt their wealth; best not to draw attention to themselves. Spare cash was often just used to build new properties or extensions to existing ones. This was why few houses had gardens in Baytown. Every precious inch of the old town was used for habitation. The sea was where the coinage was at and few wanted to live away from their tightly-knit community anyway. It was for this reason too, that the little streets and alleys were interconnected by cobbled paths rather than cart-wide streets which took up too much room. Anyway, the main street was the only wide lane needed for the carts to bring provisions from the top of the cliff down to the old cobbled dock and back up again with the herrings and lobsters.

The cottage was quiet when the children had left. Just the sound of the crackling of the fire as Alice absently stared at it, intertwining the necklace in and out of her fingers as she did so. Emma sighed and gazed helplessly at her daughter. She decided to try again.

'Alice, do you remember the secret hiding place that your father made for you. Can you remember where it might be?'

Alice continued to stare uncomprehendingly at the fire.

…………………………..

'Come on, Nellie. Race you down to the dock wall!' cried Martha as she shot through the door onto the cobbled path outside the cottage. She didn't need to be told twice to leave that cramped parlour where she never seemed to do anything right. She was still smarting at being outdone by her sister. Nellie, true to her nature, had forgotten the whole thing.

The two girls decided to race down King Street to the old sea wall by the dock - the only landing area in the whole of the Bay where the fishing cobles could be hauled in.

The children of the Bay were not unlike creatures whose natural habitat were the mountains with their dexterity and ability to bound up and down the steep walkways of the town. The girls darted through the old cobbled walkways and through the ginnels - just missing the old men mending their crab and lob- ster baskets outside their cottages and flurrying the skirts of the women, who were hauling baskets of herring up King Street which were destined for distant markets over the moors.

Martha, who was the swifter of the two, pipped Nellie to the post and the tips of her fingers were the first to touch the sea wall. She'd won, and a huge smile greeted Nellie as she came gasping up behind her.

'Slowcoach; slowcoach!' chanted Martha.

The two young girls hoisted themselves onto the roughly hewn sea wall which comprised of boulders taken from the disintegrating cliff and sat down looking at the scene below them on the apron of sand and rock which spilled out from the dock. The gloomy, bad tempered, grey face of the day they had woken up to had been replaced by a sunny blue sky. The sea wall, in this part of the town, was about five foot high but it sat atop a crumbly slope of about ten foot or so height which, at its base, melded into the beach.

A sense of purpose filled the air as they watched fifty or so men, women and children perform their various duties. Everyone had a role to play and knew exactly what was expected of them. Laughter, shouting and singing filled the air and the gulls swooped and darted onto the sand to carry off scraps of herring which had fallen from the boats or baskets.

The youngest children shrieked and roared as they chased the gulls to discourage their brazen thievery. Even the youngest villagers had their jobs to do.

In the distance, the crown of Ravenscar stretched out along the south side of the bay - full of gorse and heather and dotted with several little cottages from which plumes of smoke curled into the sky: a perfect Baytown day.

A little beetle scurried along the wall and Nellie reached out a hand to gently flick it away from them. But she was too late: Martha quickly picked up a stone and crashed it down onto the creature. Martha hated creepy crawlies and generally despatched any unfortunate enough to come her way. Often with far more relish than was warranted.

Then, with perfect balance, Martha stood upright on the wall and peered into the distance.

'Careful, Martha,' warned Nellie - the stones are still slippery from this morning's rain.'

'I can see for miles, Nellie; miles and miles. I reckon I can see France'

'Don't be daft, Mar. Yer can't see France from here. Ye'd need one of them spyglass things and even then yer probably couldn't see it.'

'Can so, Nellie. I reckon I can even see Napoleon marching up and down along the Frenchie cliffs; and his men are all marching behind him and they're all on big black horses with all their silver swords glinting in the sun.'

'Give over,' said Nellie but her voice betrayed her gullibility. 'Napoleon,' she added in a scoffing tone, trying to convince herself.

'I can though, Nell. I can see all their swords shinin in the sun - and their helmets. If you stand up here, you'll see 'em too.'

'Give over, our Martha. Napoleon!' she scoffed again.

'All their swords, pointin in the air. Stand up ere, you'll see em too.'

'I'm not standin up there. You know you've been told not to stand up there.'

'Coward, you are our Nellie. Always wantin to be good and do what everyone says. Anyway, everyone's too busy to see. Nan won't know. Oh well, you stay down there then.'

'What you doin now? Why're you waving like that? Nellie craned her neck and stood on tiptoes to see who her sister was waving at.

'Napoleon, he's waving at me, I swear. He's wavin his big silver sword at me.'

'Napoleon! Waving at you? What're you on about?' But in spite of herself, Nellie was, by now, caught in the web of belief that her sister had spun so she gingerly climbed up on the wall and carefully stood up and peered out to sea.

'Can't see nothing, Mar. There's nothing to see.'

'Over there! Look Nell!'

'Can't see nothing; yer havin me on.' Nellie stood on tiptoes, arms out to balance herself.

'And ye know Mam's necklace, Nellie? Ye know, the one she keeps playin with?'

'Forget about it, Mar - it's just she likes it. Ye shouldn't keep takin it off her.'

'And you shouldn't keep tryin to take it off me, Nell.'

Nellie felt a small push in the small of her back and despite her best (and rather comical) efforts she lost her balance and toppled forward off the five foot wall and onto the muddy slope below. She rolled rapidly down the slope to land at the feet of a small child, on the beach, who had been chasing seagulls away from the herring catch.

After a few dazed moments, the outraged Nellie sat up and turned to glare up at Martha's face gazing gleefully down at her.

'I'll ave you, Martha Whittaker! You see if I don't!'

With that she jumped angrily to her feet only to immediately fall back down to the floor, with a wail, as her broken ankle gave way beneath her.

Stand To Your Guns!

Thomas Carter-1804

Stand to your guns! my hearts of oak,

Let not a word on board be spoke,

Victory soon will crown the joke;

Be silent and be ready.

Ram home your guns and sponge them well,

Let us be sure, the balls will tell,

The cannon's roar shall sound their knell,

Be steady, boys, be steady.

Not yet, nor yet, nor yet.

Reserve your fire,

I do desire, fire!

Now, the elements do rattle,

The Gods amaz'd behold the battle

A broadside, my boys.

See the blood in purple tide,

Trickle down her batter'd side,

Wing'd with fate the bullets fly,

Conquer, boys, or bravely die!

Hurl destruction on your foes!

She sinks, Huzza! to the bottom,

To the bottom down she goes.

CHAPTER 28

FRIDAY 17th September 2018 Scarborough Police Headquarters

'We think Demmy had a mystery lover,' began Elsie. She pointed to the photograph of Gemma on the Investigation Board. 'Gemma has said that even though Demmy did not tell her explicitly, the signs were there.' And Sim and I found these notes at Demmy's cottage. Photos of the note and leaflet were enlarged on a nearby screen. We also found a half-drunk bottle of wine; expensive, at the cottage, and apparently Demmy did not like wine. Of course, the wine could be explained away by all sorts of reasons but it looks like she had a guest with expensive tastes.'

Gus put his hand up but Shannon interjected with, 'So why wouldn't she have told her best friend?'

'I think she was worried about Gemma telling Jimmy. And maybe they were growing apart as friends.' concluded Elsie.

'Or maybe Demmy's new partner was…' began Gus,

'Married - the mucky hound,' completed Shannon

Elsie smiled faintly. 'Of course, but we have to remain open to other reasons.'

Shannon thoughtfully considered this and then concluded with, 'Naah.'

'Anyway we'll keep an open mind on that one,' emphasised Elsie.

'It's likely though, as the person she was seeing would want the secrecy, I expect, if they were married and having an affair,' added Gus.

'He wouldn't want Mrs Wife to know that he was fishing for his cockles elsewhere,' paraphrased Shannon. Elsie tried not to look irritated

'Is there anything else anyone wants to add, in the expected professional manner, might I add?' requested Elsie in a peevish tone.

It was then that Shannon told Elsie and Sim about her and Gus's experience as Goths on the previous evening.

'You went to a scene connected to the murder dressed up as Goths?' blinked Elsie. 'Why?' Truth to tell, it was the kind of unorthodox wheeze Shannon was known for, although Elsie wished they had told her of their intentions beforehand.

'Why didn't you tell me what you were going to do?'

'Spur of the moment,' announced Shannon emphatically.

'Anything happen?' asked Elsie.

'Not really, all we seemed to find out is that the relationships seem as they were painted to us by the people involved,' said Gus and he proceeded to tell of the previous night's events.

'Gus was dressed as a pirate,' added Shannon. 'He looked hot. I was dressed as a raunchy Victorian slattern. I looked hot too. And the owner of The Angel is called Danny Granger - nice butt - wore a wedding ring.'

Elsie tried to keep her temper in check. 'Just run it by me first, next time you want to…be inventive with an ongoing investigation. If there'd been trouble it would have been me to blame. And look into the barman - check his whereabouts on the weekend Demmy disappeared. Let me know if anything turns up about him.'

'Ma'am,' said Gus, suitably chastened. Shannon nodded but didn't look particularly chastened.

Elsie had never known a case like this where the murderer had left no trace whatsoever with barely any clues to investigate. Either it was a fluke or the killer had been extremely lucky, or he or she was an extremely meticulous, cold character who was proving very difficult to trace and convict. No murder weapon; no witnesses; few locational clues; no enemy with a particular motive, all resulting in a murder that was seemingly impossible to solve.

'Sim and I'll pay a visit to the Skegwins and see if they remember anything about anyone new hanging around the shop; frequent quiet phonecalls etc. See if we can jog their memories. And we'll check their phone records. Her friend might have met Demmy after work. Her immediate neighbours haven't seen anything of a potentially new romantic interest. A man fitting Jimmy Bransdale's description has been seen there but that was several weeks ago. Any new boyfriend must have visited later in the evening. And a number of cottages on

Sunnyside are holiday lets so that adds another complication to finding witnesses.'

'Gus, Shannon, I need you to go to York – and to-day. There's an art fair held there, on the Friday of every month. Contact this name and number. Mrs Jarvis, the name is on the card, runs it. Demmy attended it to show off the firm's jewellery and some of her own stuff. See what you can find out. See if she ever had a man with her.'

CHAPTER 29

FRIDAY 17th September 2018 York

'First one to see the Minster gets 50p.' said Shannon as she and Gus drove along the A64 which led inland from the coast to the ancient city of York.

'Mmmph?' replied Gus, who'd been snoozing.

'It's a game we used to play as kids when the family was visiting York for the day. And I can see it, look over there. So you owe me 50p.' Shannon pointed triumphantly to the distant majestic towers of the eight hundred year old building.

'Switch the sat nav on, Gus. I think I know where the crafts fair is being held - but just to be sure.'

Gus came to and attached the sat nav to the windscreen. 'It's been a while since I last came to York. It's got a beautiful aura.'

'Mmm,' replied Shannon frowning at the car tailgating them which she had spotted in the overhead mirror. The car was flashing its lights at them unaware that the civilian car in front of it contained two police officers. 'So what does a city's aura look like?'

'Depends on how old it is,' replied Gus. 'Your newer conurbations have a pinky glow; sometimes reddish if they have a fair sprinkling of older buildings.'

'Pink?' Shannon raised an eyebrow.

'Exactly, but York has a deep crimson glow, of course.'

'Thought it was only people who had auras,' commented Shannon.

'People, animals and buildings.'

'Good to know.'

Gus was a firm believer in auras and was convinced certain kinds of criminals had certain kinds of auras.

Fraudsters apparently had double halo auras as they essentially harboured two conflicting personalities in one, so to speak. Shannon secretly thought that the whole thing was a steaming pile of guff and had intimated so on a few occasions.

'We might need you to spot the aura of Demmy Harper's murderer, Gus, if we don't pick up any leads soon,' said Shannon.

'That's a tricky one,' said Gus. 'Criminal auras tend only to be apparent when a person feels guilt: it makes their aura hazy. And murderers often believe they are justified in their actions in some twisted way or other: a jealous spouse, for example. A bad temper will manifest itself in a strong aura, of course, bright orange actually, but it will not necessarily be proof of murder.

At that moment, the car behind overtook them with a screech and then just pulled back in on time, barely missing a car coming from the opposite direction. Shannon beeped her horn angrily feeling tempted to flash the police light in their civvy car. But they didn't really have time to give chase.

'Gits who drive like that have auras covered in skiddy brown marks, I reckon,' said Shannon.

Gus gave a wan smile and started talking about crystals instead: the benefits of tanzanite to help develop conformity and diplomacy.'

'Bollocks,' thought Shannon to herself.

…………………………..

The antique and crafts venue was an old church hall adjacent to the ancient church of All Hallows on Coppergate. The attached car park was beginning to fill up already by those looking for a bargain; or collectors; or those people who just enjoy looking at sundry items from history.

Shannon and Gus wanted to get into the hall early so that the vendors would have more time to chat to them. Apparently, Mrs Jarvis didn't attend the fairs very regularly and just coordinated them. She wouldn't be there today. Demmy had had an arrangement to set up a stall once every couple of months and Mrs Jarvis had only met her the once when Demmy had initially contacted her about hiring the stall and Demmy had been on her own then. Still, the vendors themselves might have some interesting information about Demmy.

The Hall was in the very centre of York so the tourist trade would be likely to be more lucrative. There were three stalls selling individually crafted jewellery in the hall. They made the most obvious choice at which to question the vendors.

The first stall was manned by an old lady who was minding the stall today for her daughter who was on holiday so, as expected, did not recognise Dem-my's photo.

The second stall was manned by a tall amazon type lady of about fifty who looked quite stylish in a cream linen suit with a tasteful scarf knotted casually at her throat. She gave them a smile as they approached her stall which was full of beautiful silver jewellery. Amethyst, sapphire, tournamaline, turquoise gems glittered on their velvet cloths.

Shannon flashed her ID card at the woman and introduced themselves whilst Gus hung behind. He fumbled for his card and eventually found it. The woman just ignored him and coolly appraised Shannon.

'We believe a young woman had a jewellery stall here. I wonder if you ever remember seeing her.' Shannon produced a photo of Demmy from her pocket and showed it to the woman.

'I'm very sorry but I've only just started to frequent these fairs, so I really can't help you.' She said before Shannon could say anything further. She peered at the photo anyway, but confirmed, 'No, I'm very sorry. I don't recognise her.'

'Right,' replied Shannon, 'thank you for your time, anyway.'

They turned to approach the third stall, selling jewellery but as they turned Gus stumbled and fell directly onto the linen woman's carefully laid out arrangement of necklaces, bracelets and rings. His head smacked straight into an expensive looking, antique, small cabinet, containing the more expensive pieces. Amazingly, the cabinet didn't shatter.

The woman looked witheringly at him as he rubbed his forehead and mumbled his apologies.

An old man had just finished laying out his stall of gleaming jewellery and he smiled at them hopefully as they approached. Shannon introduced herself and Gus and both flashed their identity cards.

'Ok to chat for a minute or two?' asked Shannon.

The old man was impeccably attired in an old but well pressed suit and his face was finely featured with alert, appraising, sharp blue eyes. He nodded. He'd been arranging a beautiful gem stoned necklace, on an elegant red show-pad.

'Do you attend these fairs regularly, Mr…?'

'Fulford,' supplied the man. 'And yes, I've never missed a month in all the five years the fairs have been running. I used to have a shop in York but I've retired; I still like to make jewellery and sell it. Also, I quite like the company. I like to be around people who create and appreciate well crafted jewellery, if you will.'

'At last, someone who might have known her', thought Shannon, 'and chatty too.' Shannon retrieved a photo of Demmy from her pocket, 'Do you know this young woman, Mr Fulford. I believe she frequented the craft fair.'

'I do recognise her, Demeris, isn't it? A very talented young woman. Such advanced skill for her age. Her jewellery is a joy. Of course, I recognise her. She isn't in any trouble, is she?'

'I'm afraid she's passed away. We're investigating her death.' Shannon gave the man a few moments to collect himself as he digested the news.

His shoulders had slumped, 'That's terrible news: so talented, so young.'

'Did Demeris Harper attend these fairs regularly too, do you recall?'

'She did. Well, you pay annually for the stall, so it makes sense to use the monthly, or two monthly slot. They don't come cheap - but it's worth it with all the foot trade from the tourists and what not…such dreadful news.'

'It is. Did she ever have anyone with her?'

'Not serving on the stall, no, but her young man would help her set up sometimes. And then come back to help her pack away. He often stayed for a little while.' Shannon and Gus exchanged a look. Shannon fought to keep her excitement down.

'What did he look like, Mr Fulford? Do you know his name?'

'Frankie, or something like that, I think I heard her call him. Good looking chap, tall, dark, handsome. Always wore expensive clothes.'

'And roughly how old was he?' asked Gus.

'Around mid-thirties, I think, although I'm not great with ages.'

'Did you ever talk to him?' asked Shannon.

'Not really, they just seemed absorbed with one other. He didn't really invite chitchat. I once did try to talk to him, when we were packing away and everyone else had gone. He was one of those that talks about everything but never really tells you much, if you know what I mean? Still, Demeris seemed besotted with him. They only had eyes for each other. I wondered if he knew the gem trade a bit though, as he seemed quite knowledgeable about where I sourced some of the gem stones I use.'

Shannon hid a smile. The old man reminded her of her gran: rather garrulous and utterly unafraid to tell the truth; the privilege of old age she guessed.

'You've been extremely helpful, thank you, Mr Fulford. We're very keen to identify the man you've mentioned. Can you remember anything else about what he looked like? Was he thin or stocky, for example?'

'On the slim side, I think – but not puny, if you know what I mean.'

'And his face, can your recall his face? Colour of eyes? Hair colour?'

'Brown eyes, I think, but don't hold me to it. Longish nose, dark blond hair swept back.'

'That's great, Mr Fulford. If we have any more questions that we think of could we have your number, just in case?'

'Of course.' Gus carefully noted the old man's telephone number and address.

'We'll need some help putting together a picture of this man. Is that OK with you?' Shannon continued.

Fulford nodded his assent.

'One last question before we go though. Did the man, and Demeris Harper, ever seem to argue can you recall?'

'No, I don't think so but then most people wouldn't air their dirty laundry in public I would hope. You don't think this Frankie person might have done something to harm the young lady, do you?'

'We're just pursuing inquiries at the moment,' said Shannon. 'You know, working out who Demeris Harper was associated with – how she spent her time.'

The old man looked at her, 'What happened to her, if you don't mind me asking?'

'I don't mind you asking but I'm afraid we can't say too much other than that her body was found washed up on the coast, near Whitby.'

'I remember her mentioning she came from up that way. The old man sighed, 'And here I am, rattling around in my old bones, yet a young life like that is snuffed out before her time, poor young thing. Doesn't seem right, doesn't seem right at all.'

'No, it doesn't. Like I say, Mr Fulford, someone will be in touch, if that's alright. We'd like to put a proper picture together of Demeris Harper's companion.' Shannon smiled sympathetically at the old man before thanking him and moving on to the next stall.

They talked to all the other vendors and the man manning the door to take entrance fees. Some of the other vendors remembered Demmy but didn't add any more information than that which Mr Fulford had supplied. Many of the vendors had rotation type arrangements with others so didn't frequent the fair particularly often. Shannon rang the information that they had gleaned straight through to Elsie as soon as she got back in the car.

As they pulled out of York, Shannon asked, 'So, what did you make of Mr Fulford's aura, then?'

'Blue, which denotes attention to detail and general honesty.'

'And the rather elegant lady in the linen suit?'

'Who?' asked Gus somewhat disingenuously.

'Come on, Gus, the lady at the second stall we spoke to? The one where you mithered and mumbled before smacking your head on that cabinet.'

'I was too scared of the lady to even notice her aura.' Gus had a thing about confident older women.

'You fancied her, Gus. You did, didn't you?'

Gus frowned and spent the next ten minutes talking about the properties of tanzanite again. Shannon just knew what her birthday present would be from Gus in two weeks' time. She sighed, 'Thirty two years old - already.' She thought to herself, 'How did that happen?'

And then she remembered Mr Fulford's words: about Demmy being taken before her time. She shouldn't complain about having another birthday, for frig's sake.

I Popped Out

CHAPTER 30

Elsie had just got into the office when her phone rang.

'It's Mick Harper, Detective Storm.'

'Mr Harper, how are you?' Of course, it wasn't necessarily the best thing to say. How would anyone be if newly bereaved of a much loved one? He wasn't exactly going to reply, 'Fine, thank you.' Social niceties aren't exactly fuelled by human emotion but rather on trying to ignore human emotion, Elsie often thought. Mr Harper didn't reply. Elsie did not expect him to but she knew that if you edit completely your conversation with a grieving person, you probably wouldn't be able to converse with them at all - and that was even worse.

'I'd be really grateful if you could help me with some-thing, Detective Storm.'

'What is it, Mr Harper? If I can help I would be more than happy to.'

'Demmy used to wear a jet pendant - a family heir-loom. I believe she was wearing it…that night. She never took it off. She would have been wearing it that night. I was just thinking about it. It would mean so much to me to get it back – to remember Demmy and her mother by.' Mick Harper's voice was empty with loss.

Elsie knew that no necklace had been found on Demmy. She also remembered checking Demmy's belongings but there was no jewellery except for a silver bangle and a couple of inexpensive rings. These would be returned to the family when the in-vestigations were concluded. How to tell the father?

'Mr Harper, no necklace was found on Demmy, I'm so sorry. I wish I could have helped with this. She was wearing a couple of rings and a silver bangle - which, of course, we will be returning to you, but no, no pendant. Again, I am so, so sorry.'

Elsie sighed when she replaced the handset. She felt as if she had dismantled a bridge to the memories the man held of his daughter and wife. After Mick Harper had ended the call Elsie rang across to forensics straightaway asking if the necklace might have been misplaced. She knew it was unlikely but she asked anyway. At the moment it was the least that she could do.

CHAPTER 31

Later that day, Elsie and Sim visited the Skegwins again with the sole purpose of finding out if they knew anything more about Demmy's lovelife. Shannon and Gus' trip to York had proved illuminating. It seemed that Demmy had proved to have been a bit of a dark horse about her private life. It was raining heavily so there were few potential customers about. Mr Skegwin was rearranging one of the jewellery cabinets when Elsie and Sim entered the shop. Elsie asked him if he recalled Demmy having worn the jet necklace.

'Yes, I do,' he answered; a look of puzzlement crossing his face at the odd question. 'A family heirloom, I believe. Demmy was very attached to it.'

'Do you know if she was wearing it on the day she disappeared,' Elsie asked. She didn't really consider the necklace to be that important but she might as well get it out of the way before she and Sim broached questions about any relationships with clients or business associates.

'I wouldn't know as I wasn't here. I think Anna had given it back to her so she probably was.'

'Given it back? What do you mean?' asked Sim.

'The clasp had broken,' Anna had been fixing it for her. Well it was so old, the clasp had worn out and Anna is a trained goldsmith.'

'Is Anna here?' asked Elsie hopefully.

'Come through,' said Skegwin locking the shop door and leading the way down a short passage to the workshop cum office at the back of the shop.

'Anna was sitting at a workbench and performing the intricate manoeuvre of trying to fix some kind of trinket to a gold chain bracelet.

'Anna, can you remember anything about that pendant Demmy always wore, you know the jet stone with the strange engravings on it?' asked Mr Skegwin.

Anna turned and looked blankly at him for a moment and then replied, 'Yes, yes, of course I do. The pendant was very old. I fixed it for her. The clasp had worn away.'

'Have you still got it, Mrs Skegwin? Mr Harper will be so relieved to have it returned?' asked Elsie.

'Sadly no, I'd fixed it and given it back. Oh, what a shame,' she sighed. If only I'd kept it a bit longer but Demmy was so keen to get it back and wear it again. She was delighted at what I'd done. Was she not wearing it when they…found her?'

'Unfortunately not,'

'The sea is cruel - taking even that from poor Mick,' Anna sighed deeply, rubbing her eyes.

'We were also wondering if you can tell us of any particular relationships Demmy might have had with you know, special customers or people who came into the shop regularly,' asked Sim who had been looking at a notice board full of reminders and business cards.

'Well, we do have our regular customers who Demmy was a hit with naturally. She had a way with people. But our regulars tend to be older, who come in more for jewellery repairs and such like,' replied Mr Skegwin, 'The younger ones tend to be the tourist trade wanting the more special mementoes to take back home.'

'Was she particularly friendly with any of your business associates who visited the shop on a more frequent basis?' asked Sim again.

'No one in particular comes to mind,' said Mr Skegwin, 'although Freddie Bowland and she seemed to get along well,'

'Freddie Bowland?' echoed Elsie with a note of interest.

'His family have done trade with the local jewellery shops for many years - supplying precious stones and the like. They're a very wealthy family, of course. His father is retired now and Freddie runs the business. Mostly from his office at home, well it's easy to do that with all this modern technology, I expect. Of course, he doesn't keep the stock at home. He's more of a middle man - contacts all over the world, I believe.'

'Roughly, how old is he, do you think?' asked Sim.

'About thirty-five, give or take a few either side,'

'Hair colour?' he asked.

'A darkish blonde wouldn't you say, Anna?'

Anna nodded.

'Can you please give us his contact details,' requested Elsie.

'In fact, could we take his card from your notice board, I noticed it up there when you mentioned his name,' asked Sim.

'Please do,' said Mr Skegwin, 'we have his details anyway in the diary.'

I can't imagine he could tell you very much,' said Anna, 'he's a happily married man,' said Anna pursing her lips at any possible insinuation of hanky panky on her premises. 'But yes, he and Demmy did get along well. He enjoyed seeing her designs and often mentioned she was a true artist. He used to say she could turn a piece of coal into a gem, her work was so good. He used to come in around coffee time and he and Demmy would have a chat.'

'How often did he come in?' asked Sim.

'Oh, about once a fortnight. I think he was here last Wednesday.' She flipped through a large diary on her desk.

'Could we take a look in the diary, if you don't mind? asked Elsie.

'Of course,' she took the diary off the large oak desk and handed it to Elsie, pointing at the entry on the page.

'We'll need to keep this for now,' said Elsie.

Mrs Skegwin looked a little put out but nodded her head.

'Of course,' said her husband. 'And no, it's no inconvenience at all. Happy to help although I don't think it will tell you very much,' he added. 'We just tend to record visits by suppliers and things we need to stock up on, reminders and such like.'

The doorbell tinkled behind them as Elsie and Sim stepped out into the street.

'Why did you want that card off the notice board?' asked Elsie.

'It has a copy of Freddie Bowland's signature on it,' he replied simply.

'So?

'It's the same handwriting as that on the note we found in Demmy's house'.

'And the man seen with Demmy in York fits his description. He wore expensive clothes and Freddie is clearly wealthy. Right age too and brown hair. Although the old man thought he was called, 'Frankie'. Gus had apprised Elsie of their discoveries in York through a quick phone call.

'Easy mistake to make if he talked to him infrequently,' commented Sim.

CHAPTER 32

FRIDAY 17TH September 2018 The Bowland
Residence

Elsie and Sim decided upon an immediate visit
to Freddie Bowland. There was no address on
the card but a quick ring established yes, he was
in and yes, he would be happy to talk to them.
In helpful tones he gave them his address and
how to find it. He lived a few miles inland from
the coast and within the hour they were driving
down a narrow private road which led to a beautiful house. The large detached Edwardian house
was secluded and exuded wealth. It was gated
and Elsie had to speak into an intercom to be
buzzed in.

The gardens were magnificent with pristine lawns
edged by lavender and late, heavy-headed roses

that imbued the hazy afternoon with their lovely fragrance. It was a gardener's paradise with paved flags, rockery, and an elegantly placed summer house.

There were a couple of children on the lawn: a boy of about nine and a girl of about seven. Freddie Bowland's kids presumably. They were playing on a wooden adventure playground piece and their laughter and happy cries punctured the silence which pervaded the valley in which the house was set. Spying the detectives the boy stopped and stared for a few moments as he poised himself at the top of the slide. The girl barely noticed them as she was busy on her swing.

They rang the doorbell and a well-dressed woman appeared.

'Hello, you must be Detective Inspector Storm, we were expecting you.'

The woman wore grey linen trousers and a tasteful and expensive looking, cream, silk blouse. She had fine features and expensively cut, short, caramel coloured hair.

'It is, and you must be Mrs Bowland? The woman nodded and gave a nervous smile. 'Just call me Lydia.'

'And this is Detective Howard,' added Elsie. Sim nodded at Lydia Bowland.

'Come through, Freddie is in his study.'

The hall was paved with black and white chequered flags which looked original and led to a wooden set of stairs with a huge window at its mid-section before sweeping up to the next level. Off the hall itself, were some large solid-looking oak doors. Mrs Bowland knocked lightly on one of them and opened it when a softly spoken and well modulated male voice called, 'Enter'.

Freddie Bowland was on the phone to what sounded like a business associate. He smiled at them and beckoned for them to sit down. He was in his mid to late thirties with an expansive, good natured face out of which shone wide brown eyes. His caramel blond hair, flecked with a few emerging silver hairs, was cut, even more perfectly than Sim's, if that was possible. He wore a green shirt of some high end brand with its discreet logo on the chest. He seemed a very self-assured and prosperous man. He ended the call.

'Would you like a cup of tea?' asked Lydia Bowland.

'Erm no thank you', said Elsie. Sim smiled back and replied in the negative too. She left closing the door behind her.

'Terrible business', said Freddie.

'It is, can you tell me what you know about Demeris Harper, Mr Bowland?'

Freddie Bowland sat bolt upright in his seat. 'Demeris Harper. What's Demeris got to do with it? I can't see how for one moment she would have been involved.'

'Come again?' echoed a bemused Elsie.

'I can't see that Demeris is involved in the hacking. Obviously I have state of the art protection in place. It's the trade I'm in. To be expected in this day and age. I deal with some very high quality merchandise - quite lucrative too.' Greed lit his eyes as he spoke. 'But I can tell you right now, that Demmy won't be involved. You're on a false trail on that one. Her family are well off, for a start. I've seen her in the office at Skegwins: hated the computer. It wouldn't surprise me if she didn't even know how to use her mobile properly,' he chortled as if sharing some private joke with himself.

Clearly, Freddie Bowland thought they were talking about something else. Elsie also couldn't help forming the impression that he might be a bit of a buffoon.

She regarded a portrait on the wall behind Freddie that showed an old photo of a man who looked remarkably like Freddie, features wise; but the face in the portrait exuded wisdom and astuteness, unlike Freddie's boyish, frank but rather empty expression. Freddie was thirty five but there were no lowlights of experience in his features. Elsie guessed that he had not really experienced any hardship or obstacles which might have sculpted a more interesting face. She wondered how much of the family fortune was due to the father's foundation stones of business acumen. She became aware that she was making unfair assumptions. Something she'd promised herself not to do in the earlier days of her police career. She'd seen too many mistakes made that way.

It could, however, all be an act on Freddie's part. He was certainly giving an excellent impression of not being party to the knowledge that Demmy had been recently murdered. Yet he must have some business acumen to be able to still carry on the business successfully. All these thoughts and impressions flickered across Elsie's mind as she regarded the man in front of her who was momentarily distracted by a piece of thread hanging from his expensive shirt. He tutted, reached for a pair of scissors in his drawer and impatiently snipped it off.

'Mr Bowland, you appear to be under some kind of misapprehension. Demeris Harper was murdered last Saturday night.'

Freddie, who had started to fiddle with his Mont Blanc pen on the desk in front of him, dropped it with a soft clatter onto the well-varnished desk. He sat rigid in his seat and stared at Elsie, as if he couldn't believe what she had just said.

'Demmy, murdered. I don't believe you. Is this some kind of sick joke?'

'Unfortunately not, Mr Bowland; her body was washed up onto the beach at Robin Hood's Bay, last Sunday morning. Had you not heard?'

Tears rimmed the bottom of Freddie Bowland's lower eyelids and he tried hard to blink them back. 'I've been away on business - only just got back. She drowned then?'

'I'm afraid we cannot divulge how exactly she died, at the moment, Mr Bowland. I'm sure you understand.'

'Sunday morning? He echoed as if still unable to believe it. He slumped in his seat.

'Did you know Demeris Harper well?' asked Sim.

Freddie looked at him as if trying to clear his thoughts. He suddenly sat up again rigid. 'Quite well, she works...worked (he swallowed) at Skegwins in Whitby, I do a bit of business with them.'

'So, you just knew Demeris as a work associate?' asked Elsie.

'I only saw her the week before last,' said Freddie.

'When and where?' asked Sim.

'At Skegwins of course. It was just a courtesy call, ensuring all was well with the last delivery. It always helps to keep it personal and see clients face to face. On the Wednesday it would have been, about tennish.'

This tallied with the diary which Mrs Skegwin kept which recorded any meetings or professional visitors to the business.

'So you did not see Demeris after Wednesday of that week.'

'No, I don't think so.'

'You don't think so?' asked Elsie.

'No!' he said more forcefully.

'Mr Bowland, I am afraid that I will have to ask you to accompany us to the station, to help us with our enquiries.'

'What? Why? I can't just drop everything and come with you now. I've got work to do. Are you placing me under arrest?' he gulped.

'Not at this stage; although if you do not come voluntarily I may have to arrest you.'

'Why?'

'We can discuss it at the station.

Elsie and Sim were standing by now and reluctantly Freddie slowly rose out of his leather upholstered chair. Elsie saw Sim looking at a photo opposite Freddie's father's portrait. It showed a winning team at a Whitby rowing regatta (an annual event of rowing races for which the town was renowned throughout the rowing world.)

'Is that your father in the winning team?' asked Sim.

Nonplussed by the question, Freddie swivelled to look at the photo showing his father holding a trophy aloft with his rowing team members beside him, all of them standing in front of a rowing boat.

'My father? I don't know what relevance...' he frowned,

'It is your father isn't it?'

'If you must know, yes, yes it is. He was a champion rower in his day. He and his team, 'The Shanties' won every race going at the time. It was taken about forty years ago.' By now, Freddie had lost interest in this, what seemed to him, bizarre questioning and was gathering his phone and keys into his jacket pocket which he'd slipped on. His actions were frantic and confused - clearly wondering what he should take with him to a police station of all places.

Elsie peered at the picture. It was only a few feet away from the desk and thought one of the other faces looked familiar too. She dismissed the thought and they escorted Freddie from the house. After all, the same generations had populated the area for hundreds of years. Resemblances became common in the area after living there for a while.

Elsie was quite prepared to arrest Freddie but she knew that they would only be able to keep him for seventy-two hours if they did so; much better to try to get Freddie to come voluntarily. Elsie sighed almost imperceptibly. Another perfect home shattered.

CHAPTER 33

Before the interview with Freddie Bowland, Elsie gave Mick Harper a quick ring with the unfortunate news about the pendant.

'Mr Harper, DCI Storm. How are you?' she asked gently.

'Have you found out who did it?'

'We're still pursuing active leads, Mr Harper. If we have any concrete news I'll ring straightaway. I'm ringing actually about the pendant.'

There was a slight pause. 'Demmy's pendant. Have you found it?' His tone caught on a note of optimism which struck Elsie's heart.

'I'm sorry, Mr Harper, I've checked with Mr and Mrs Skegwin and it seems that the necklace had been fixed and returned to Demmy. Mrs Skegwin fixed the clasp. It seems likely that it is lost now, though.'

Another pause, 'I see,' he said quietly, 'Thank you for letting me know.'

'And of course, I'll ring as…' Mick Harper replaced the handset.

Sim approached her with an identifit profile in his hand. York police put this together with Mr Fulford, the gentleman at the craft fair who Shannon and Gus spoke to. It looks very like Freddie Bowland.'

Elsie concurred. 'Let's see what he has to say for himself.'

…………………………..

'Mr Bowland, I'll ask you again, when was the last time that you saw Demeris Harper?'

Freddie looked like a lost boy in the interview room. His confident demeanour had utterly deserted him. By his side sat a Mr Trowbridge, a legal representative Freddie had insisted upon before he would answer any questions at the station. It was probably a wise move given his predicament.

Freddie flushed red and his eyes were downcast as he spoke quietly. 'I erm, erm…

'Mr Bowland, please speak up, as you are aware this interview is being recorded,' said Elsie who had decided to interrogate him. Sim, Shannon and Gus were watching from behind the observation glass and were hooked up to the tape recording.

Freddie coughed nervously. 'I last saw Demeris on the Friday night. She and I were having an affair. I'm sorry if I didn't apprise you of this the last time that we spoke but my wife doesn't know. I didn't want to upset her. Although she has guessed, I think.'

Mr Trowbridge interrupted at this point, 'My client apologises wholeheartedly for not sharing this information with you, Detective Inspector, but we have discussed the matter in great detail and he wishes you to know that he will comply completely with your investigation, in order for you to apprehend whoever is guilty of this heinous crime.'

'That's good to know, but it doesn't help our perception of you, Mr Bowland, to have it on record that you have lied to us.' Elsie left that thought hanging for the moment. Freddie bowed his head.

'I know it doesn't but I felt ashamed and didn't want to admit to having had a relationship with Demmy. My wife has warned me that one more time…'

Elsie tried to stop herself from raising her eyes heavenwards.

'So you say you saw Demeris on Friday night. Did you pick her up from home? Work?

'She lives in Robin Hood's Bay; about halfway up the bank and that's too steep and narrow to park the car on. It's all double yellowed. I parked at the top of the bank and walked down to her cottage, at about seven-thirty. We just had something to eat and then I left about ten-thirty.'

'You left reasonably early then?'

'Lydia, my wife, was getting a bit suspicious so I couldn't stay out late.'

'Have you had affairs before then, Mr Bowland?'

Mr Trowbridge intervened. 'Detective, that question and its answer have no bearing on your case, and you know it.'

'Just trying to build up a picture here, Mr Trowbridge,' said Elsie before continuing, 'Can anyone verify that you were at the cottage until ten, Mr Bowland?'

'I don't think so, there are a lot of holiday visitors to the village. Many of the cottages are holiday cottages now. Even though it's classed as a village, in many ways it's like a small town. I see new faces every time I go there. Lydia will vouch for me having come home at about eleven though, we had another row when I came in.' He blushed.

'So you didn't see Demeris on the Saturday, at all.

'No, on the Saturday, I rang her a few times but got no reply. I had to get out of the house: Lydia was still mad with me so I spent all day at the golf club and then went to the gym in the evening. You can check on both those things, there are lots of people who will prove I'm telling the truth.'

'We will check your alibi thoroughly,' Elsie stated firmly.

'Alibi?' echoed Freddie weakly as he looked helplessly around the interview room.

'So what time did you arrive home on the Saturday?' asked Elsie.

'10.30ish, I think, or thereabouts,' answered Freddie.

Mr Trowbridge's had arrived late so the interview had been forestalled. It had done Elsie a favour. The forensic team already had fingerprints from the cottage. Freddie had been printed when he came in. The prints were instantly checked against those found in the cottage. The forensic team had found Freddie's fingerprints all over the cottage suggesting that he had been a frequent visitor, but there had been no evidence of violent activity. If it could be corroborated that Freddie had spent his Saturday, as he had said, and arrived home at around 10.30, it was going to be difficult to find out how he could have murdered Demmy in the timeframe. Unless he had somehow kidnapped Demmy, put her somewhere and then sneaked out from his home in the middle of the night and used a boat to take the body out to sea which was always a possibility. But then his home had sophisticated security, as Sim had instantly picked up on, there would presumably be a record of him leaving the house, if that had been the case.

'You have cameras presumably at your property, Mr Bowland.'

'Yes, yes of course. In my trade...' His voice faded away as it dawned on him that self-importance might work against him here.

'So you don't mind if a search is made of your property and we take a look at the cameras?' Elsie knew she could apply for a warrant but it was easier if the suspect gave their permission without them having to resort to that.

Mr Trowbridge intervened again. 'My client does not have to give permission. I'm afraid you'll need a warrant, Detective.'

Freddie intervened. 'No, Charles, I just want this nightmare over. Things are going to be bad enough with Lydia as it is. Yes, you can search the house and see the cameras, you have my permission.' He turned to Mr Trowbridge, who was trying hard not to show his displeasure with Freddie's decision. 'I've got nothing to hide, let them find out for themselves.'

'I'd like to take a short break, Mr Bowland, Mr Trowbridge. Interview suspended at 6.30pm,' Elsie stated into the recorder. She left the room and immediately sent the team to search the Bowland property and to seize the CCTV tapes. Her feelings were mixed: pleased at having trouble free access to the property but uneasy about Freddie's candour. He was a prime suspect but cloaked in all the trappings of innocence. Still evidence would hold the incontrovertible truth. She would just have to wait and see.

'Interview with Mr Freddie Bowland by DI Storm re-commencing at 6.45pm, Mr Trowbridge, Mr Bowland's legal representative also present.'

'Mr Bowland, you've told us that your father was a champion rower.'

Freddie looked confused at the line of questioning. 'Yes he was. He was famous in the area for his rowing during the seventies. Why? What on earth has my father's pastime got to do with Demmy's murder?'

'So he presumably was able to manage a boat better than most in the choppy seas around this coastline?'

'He could take a boat out in most weather. He wasn't daft though, he could read the sea and knew when not to risk his chances.'

'And did he teach you to read the sea, as you put it?'

'He wanted me to be a champion rower like him. We would go out in most weathers and yes, even if I say it myself, I can read the sea better than most. He taught me everything I know.'

Mr Trowbridge by now had twigged the direction the interview was going in. 'DI Storm, Your turn of questioning is irrelevant: Mr Bowland's father and his hobby are of no relevance to this investigation.'

'Demeris Harper was taken out to sea, by boat, at a time when a storm was on its way. The seas would have been choppy and only a keen and experienced sailor would have attempted such a journey.

It is highly relevant that Frederick Bowland, from his family history, would have had the skills to attempt such a journey.'

'That is completely circumstantial, Inspector and you know it,' said Mr Trowbridge contemptuously. 'Have you any more questions for my client?' he asked sourly. 'Mr Bowland is a very busy man. He has very generously allowed you access to his property and possessions and I can't see how his being detained here further can help you further in any way with your enquiries.'

Freddie managed to splutter. 'It's because I know the dangers of the North Sea that I would be the last person to set out in a storm.'

The door to the interview room opened and Sim stepped in. He took a seat next to Elsie.

'For the purposes of this interview, I have been joined by DS Howard. The time is now 7.00pm,' said Elsie, leaning into the tape recorder as she spoke.

This was a tactic usually employed by Elsie and Sim. The good cop, bad cop routine was effective but neither of them often resorted to it. It was clear that Freddie Bowland appeared to be scared wit-less. It was best to take advantage of this by plying him with detailed questions to account for the time leading up to and including the time of the murder.

Sim began, 'Tell us again, Mr Bowland, how you spent the Friday evening of the 10th September…'

CHAPTER 34

SATURDAY 18th September 2018 Scarborough
Police Headquarters

The next morning, Elsie called a meeting in the investigation room. As the investigation was at such a crucial stage it had been agreed that the team would work on the Saturday.

'Right everyone, I want every single detail verified as to Freddie Bowland's account of how he spent his Friday evening with Demeris. I want the TV schedule checking to see if he watched the programmes he said he watched; the contents of the bins checking to see if they ate what he said they ate; forensics to check Demeris' house again in light of Bowland's admission. A full forensic check of Mr Bowland's house is taking place at present. We should have the full results shortly but so far there is no trace of Demeris at the Bowland house. Not that I really expected there to be but we need to cover all bases. I've drawn up a list of who checks what.

'I understand Mrs Bowland and her children have gone to stay with her parents in Scarborough. I want a full search of Freddie Bowland's car and interviews with staff at his golf club and the gym he attends. Leave no stone unturned. We also need any CCTV footage from the golf club and gym to verify the times Mr Bowland said that he arrived and left from both venues.'

'Have the security cameras been checked yet on Freddie's house yet, Maam,' asked Shannon.

'We're double checking it for any tampering but so far preliminary viewing shows that he left at 6.30pm and arrived home at 10.58pm of the Friday evening and then left again early on the Saturday morning and arrived back later that evening at 11.27pm. It's crucial that we track Bowland's movements from the time that Mr Bransdale said he last saw Demeris up to her time of death.'

'Suniya has confirmed that Demeris was murdered at around 3 or 4pm on the Saturday afternoon. We need to check Bowland's movements in particular around this time. He says he was playing golf so we to check possible witnesses and any cameras at the course premises.'

Luckily the Super had granted them two extra DC's to help with the vast amount of information gathering: DC Gianelli, a young woman who had just passed her DC qualification and DC Thomas a young man who had been a DC for about a year. Both were conscientious and efficient and keen to make their mark.

Elsie gave out the rostas detailing the precise tasks each pair of detectives needed to focus upon.

'Let's get to it, team.

The sense of energy as the team left the room was tangible. A lull settled over the investigation room as they left, clutching their schedules.

'Do you think Freddie Bowland is guilty, Ma'am?' asked Sim.

'I don't know, Sim, I really don't. But someone did it and he is the most likely suspect so far.' She said frankly. 'If nothing else we need to completely eliminate him.'

CHAPTER 35

Whitby - 1827

Nellie Whittaker was walking up the steep hill to the market with her ten year old daughter Lizzie. It was mid-October and a keen wind blew off the sea. The clutch of whaling ships, with their tall masts in the harbour, rolled and rocked in the breeze as the indifferent Abbey stood loftily above them on its cliff overlooking the town.

'Fasten your cloak well, Lizzie. I think that's the last we have seen of summer.'

It'd been a glorious summer season but within the last week or so the temperature had dropped and the fresh breeze had begun to assume a winter bite. Scrutiny of the sky to the west showed

dark clouds scudding their way toward the town –
probably heralding the fog which the older fishermen had predicted as being on its way.

'Ow,' yelled Lizzie, as a small stone whipped
through the air and caught her on the arm extending from her cloak. Lizzie stopped and gazed fear-
fully at a boy, about her age, who had a vicious grin
on his face - clearly the source of the missile. Nellie
stopped abruptly and turned around. She stepped
briskly in front of Lizzie and was about to upbraid
the small, undernourished boy who stood defiantly, on his dirty bare feet, in front of her. The rags
he was dressed in earned Nellie's sympathy but his
snarling malicious face did not.

'Don't do that again child, do you hear me or I
shall report you for vagrancy. You have injured my
daughter. I should report you even now.' By now
Lizzie was trying not to cry as Nellie bound up her
bleeding arm with a handkerchief.

The boy was stood beside a pile of rags. The rags stirred and the bony face of a woman emerged from them and sat up blinking blearily. Her face was covered in sores. At first Nellie clutched Lizzie before stepping back and dragging Lizzie with her.

'Leave my boy alone. You don't know it was him that done it.' The beggar woman then coughed making a horrible rattling sound.

Lizzie was expecting her mother to turn and go on her way but she didn't do this. The beggar woman and Lizzie seemed struck silent for a moment before her mother stepped forward toward the other woman. The boy raised his hand, another stone at the ready.

'Martha, is that you?' Nellie's voice cracked in disbelief as she said these words. Nellie looked in astonishment at her mother. How did she know this vagrant and by her first name too? Her mother was married to a sea captain and only tended to mix with the more well to do women who lived in the gentile houses at the top of the bank in Robin Hood's Bay. And she had high standards for her daughter. She was always exhorting Lizzie to comport herself in a measured and ladylike way and preferably, only to mix with others of similar behaviours..

'My, my, if it isn't our Nellie?' chortled the beggar woman with a rattley laugh. 'Ain't you the lady now, and who's this? One of yer offcuts.'

'Leave Lizzie out of it, Martha,' warned Nellie.

'You're the one who 'ccused my boy, Nell. I was just layin here mindin me business.'

Nellie looked at the boy, who seemed equally non-plussed that the two women knew each other. 'This is your son,' she eventually replied, aghast.

'My son and your nephew, Nell. Just like your miss is my niece.' Martha's face lit with glee as she noted the horrified expression on Lizzie's face.

'Martha, why didn't you come home? Grandma searched for you everywhere.'

'Too many don't do this, don't do that. Wasn't for me. Besides you were always the favourite.'

'You went out of your way to upset Gran, and you know it, Martha.' Nellie's face took on an expression of resolve and she stepped toward Martha and crouched down. 'Come home with me, Martha. You're sick. You and your boy, come home with us.' Truth to tell, she knew that Samuel, her husband, would have an apoplectic fit if she brought the two vagrants home with her, but she had no choice.

'Don't think so, Nell. Don't think I could spend one minute in your kind of house.'

'Then let me take the boy. He'd get good schooling, clothes, food…What's his name?' she added weakly.

'Jack, if you must know. Ere, Jack, do you want to go with the fine lady and go to school?'

'Leave me mam alone, you old hag. Ain't going to no school,' he uttered stubbornly - the feral ways of the street already engrained in his scowling features.

Martha chuckled. 'I think he says no.' Her eyes narrowed menacingly. 'Me and Jack, we're fine, as we are - don't need your charity. I'd leap into Hell before I took it.'

'You don't mean that, you're sick Martha. Listen, here's some money, for you and Jack here. Find yourself somewhere to stay, something to eat. I can bring more. I can come into town next week. I can be here at the same time next week,' she added determinedly. She drew a purse out of her cloak and withdrew most of the coins and held them out in her hand. Martha looked at them greedily and grabbed them with a scabbed skeletal hand. She then peered at the jet pendant hanging around Nellie's neck. She suddenly made a grab for that too, but was overtaken by a fit of coughing which made her put her hand over her mouth instead. When the coughing subsided her hand was covered in a gobbet of mucus and blood. Nellie looked at Martha's hand in horror.

'That's mine, Nellie, give it me.'

'The pendant?' Nellie looked at her sister in a perplexed manner. Was Martha still wanting to carry on this sibling feud over the jet necklace- the cause of so many past arguments between them?

'Come home with me, Martha and I'll give it to you?'

'Want it now, Nell. It's mine.'

Nellie could not believe that Martha was still obsessed with the necklace; she presumed that her illness was affecting her mind in some deranged way. Nellie was quite willing to give her desperate sister the pendant but she knew it would be likely traded for food, or more likely gin as Martha reeked of it. She wasn't willing to let it go for such reasons when it was such a fond reminder of their late mother. 'Come home with me, Martha and I'll give it to you then,' she repeated.

Martha reached out again and this time more forcefully. Taken by surprise, Nellie reared back and scrambled to her feet. She tried to talk to Martha again but was met with a hail of stones from Jack who had become agitated at the sight of violent movement.

Nellie and Lizzie fled back down the steep street: Nellie, in barely contained tears and Lizzie openly sobbing. At the foot of the steps Nellie turned to look back at Martha and Jack. She could still hardly believe that she had actually seen them but a fog had suddenly descended and wrapped the pitiful sight of the wretch and her son in eerie grey swirls. She thought that she could just make out their shapes as they ambled up the bank, the mother leaning heavily on the thin frame of the boy.

The strident clanking of the harbour fog bell shattered the silence shocking her from her reverie. She and Lizzie half walked/half ran to Samuel's landau which was parked at the harbour where one of the man servants was dutifully waiting for them.

The Sailor Likes His Bottle, Oh

Halyard Shanty

The Mate was drunk, and he went below,

To take a swig of his bottle, oh.

A bottle of rum, and a bottle of gin,

And a bottle of Irish whiskey, oh.

Chorus:

His bottle, oh, his bottle, oh,

The sailor likes his bottle, oh,

2. Tobaccio, tobaccio,

The sailor loves tobaccio,

A cut of the plug, and a cut of the Swiss,

And a cut of hard tobaccio,

Chorus:

3. The maidens, oh, the lassies, oh,

The sailor loves the Judys, oh,

A gal from Liverpool and a gal from the Tyne

And a lassie so fine and dandy, oh.

Chorus:

4. A bloody rough house, a bloody rough house,

The sailor loves a roughhouse, oh,

A kick in the ass and an all-hands-in,

A bloody good rough-and-tumble, oh,

Chorus:

So early in the morning

The Sailor likes his bottle-o

A bottle o'rum and a bottle o'gin

and a bottle o' Irish whiskey-o

So early in the morning

CHAPTER 36

All six of the team (including the newly acquired officers Gianelli and Thomas) settled into the investigation room at nine the next morning. Elsie allowed everyone to chat for a bit as they ate the doughnuts and drank the coffee she and Sim had brought in from the cafe across the street from the station. After ten minutes she began, 'Ok, can we make a start on findings so far; Sim, could you give us all an update, please?'

'There is no forensic evidence of Demeris being at Freddie Bowland's house. There is DNA from Demeris in his car but no more than would be expected in the light of Freddie's having had a relationship with her,' confirmed Sim. 'There is no sign of a violent struggle in Demeris's own cottage – there were traces of Freddie Bowland, but again that is to be expected. The contents of the waste bins confirm the meal that he said he and Demeris shared on the Friday night. Even the radio schedule matches what he said they were listening to when she was preparing the meal that they ate.'

'You'll be pleased to hear though Ma'am,' he continued, 'that more footage has been found of Demmy in Whitby. Gianelli and Thomas have been trawling shops in the town hoping to pick up footage of her. Demmy visited a chemist on Flowergate, maybe she remembered that she had to get something and that's why she turned back from her car. Street CCTV is woeful in Whitby and a significant number of cameras are out of action.'

'Yes,' added Elsie, Ian has been chasing up their full working for some time. The installation of new ones is imminent but of course that doesn't help us here.'

'So, we have street CCTV of Demmy on Church Street, one of the main tourist streets, of course. She leaves Skegwin's shop and walks over the Swing Bridge to meet Jimmy Bransdale at the harbour and then after talking to him for 20 minutes she walks toward her car in the car park near the supermarket behind the train station. For some reason, before reaching the car park, she doubles back to go to the chemist on Flowergate. And then there is no trace of her once she left the chemists.'

Sim had set up a powerpoint which showed the eerie footage of Demmy walking down Church Street, leaving work and sidestepping the many tourists which were sauntering down this ancient little street full of shops and which concluded at the cliff base of the Abbey steps. Demmy was walking briskly toward the other end of the street, toward the swing bridge which effectively connects the old town to the newer part of town on the other side of it. The image of Demmy switched to her actually crossing over the Swing Bridge.

'Of course, we're checking again to see if she crossed the bridge once more but it seems more possible that whatever happened to her would have happened on the far side of the town – on the other side of the harbour.'

'At last, something. Any footage of her leaving the chemists?'

'No CCTV in that street, Ma'am,' she seems to disappear again.'

'Ok, let's get hold of the footage of her in the chemists. Can you set it up pronto, Sim?'

'Will do, tech are just preparing it for us now.'

'Anything at all on Freddie Bowland's movements on the Saturday? Shannon, Gus?'

'We've checked everything Freddie Bowland has told us, Ma'am. And, mostly, it all seems to check out.'

For some strange reason, Elsie wasn't at all surprised. She was almost beginning to get used to all the major leads on Demmy's murder evaporating into the air, like the steam on the coffee she was sipping. The 'mostly' sounded hopeful though.

'Go on,' she said.

'The CCTV on Freddie's home has shown he left at 9.30am and arrived back home at 11.30pm. We timed the drive from the gym to his house and it takes just over thirty minutes; his car never left the drive after that, and stayed there all Sunday.'

'His golf club confirms that he stayed there all morning and lunched there - witnesses and CCTV

406

confirm this. He then left at half five. It's a short drive from the golf club to the gym - he actually beat the time it took us to drive it. His gym confirms that he arrived about 5.30pm and stayed until it closed. Again, witnesses and CCTV all confirm this,' added Gus quietly.

'It's a long time to stay in the gym – although I hear it has a pool, spa and café – the full works,' commented Elsie, 'but he is a bit of a narcissist and has admitted he'd fallen out with his wife and was reluctant to go home.'

'The gym however closes at 9.00pm so Freddie Bowland has about two hours missing from his account. He should have been home by 9.30, not 11.30, as was the time verified by his home security camera.'

CHAPTER 37

SATURDAY 19th September 2018 Scarborough Police Headquarters

'Interview with Lydia Bowland, commencing at 9.30am. Saturday 19th September. Present, DCI Elsie Storm, Mrs Lucille Bowland and her legal representative, Ms Ogwen.'

'Mrs Bowland, can you recall Saturday evening of the 11th of September, 2017.'

'Yes, I was in on my own. Got the children their tea, gave them a bath. We'd been in the garden most of the day as it had been warm. We (the children and I) watched a bit of TV, after tea and then I put them to bed. I watched a bit more TV and went to bed early – around ten. My husband came in at 11.30 ish.'

'Where had your husband been all day?'

'His golf club and then his gym. Or so he told me the next morning.'

'Had you rowed that morning, before he had left for the gym?'

'We had had words.'

'What about?'

'If you must know, I think my husband is having an affair. The signs are all there. Never leaving his phone about; the phone always on silent; late nights home with dubious accounts of where he's been. The usual.'

'The usual?' So he's had affairs before.'

'Yes, and I'm sick of it. He tries to project this image of being the perfect family man, but he's got a sickness, I think. Just can't help himself. I've given him too many chances, for the sake of the children, really. I'm not doing it anymore.'

Elsie had thought that it would be quite difficult to open Lydia Bowland up about her relationship with Freddie Bowland, she came across as quite reserved and self contained. It seemed as if Lydia was prepared to be candid – most likely, at the end of her tether with her philandering husband, with the publicity of the case probably stretching her to her absolute limits.

Do you know where Freddie was on the night of Friday 10th September?' queried Elsie.

'With his new girl, I expect. Of course, he wouldn't admit it. Told me he was having dinner with a client – a proprietor of a jewellery shop in York. He's too practised to admit exactly where they dined. And quite frankly, it's too demeaning now to ask. We rowed when he came in and rowed again in the morning. I gave him an ultimatum, anymore of it and I'd be petitioning for divorce. The house is too tense with all of this deceit. It's not good for the children. It's not right bringing them up to think that lies are normal.'

'You've clearly put some thought into this.'

'I have. Lots of thought. He only married me, I think, for my family connections. Respectability is every-thing in the jewellery trade. Clients have got to trust you to know that your goods and by implication that you are bona fide and trustworthy. I'm beginning to see that now.'

Lydia Bowland looked angry and determined but her large grey eyes were lined with tears as she spoke.

Elsie hated having to ask the next but crucial question, 'Mrs Bowland, Freddie left the gym at 9.00pm and yet he did not come home until 11.30pm on the Saturday. Did he say where else he went, after the gym?'

'Mmm, an unaccounted for slot of time, courtesy of Freddie Bowland,' spat Lydia, 'now that has 'female' written all over it.' She suddenly gave a dry sob and pulled out a tissue from her handbag. Elsie waited for her to continue but she just blew her nose before collecting herself and gazing at Elsie glumly.

'Did he say he'd been with a woman?'

'No, he would never admit to it; always looked exceptionally offended if I ever mentioned it, even - pathetic.' But then, curiously she added. 'Is this about Demeris Harper? I heard about it on the news just before I came here. I know that Freddy knew her. He's known her from way back, family connections. It wouldn't surprise me if they were having an affair – wouldn't be at all surprised. She was pretty; I've seen her photo on the news. And she was the right age. Freddie liked them gullible and young. To be honest, I think there's a big part of him too, that will never grow up.'

Lydia looked like she was still formulating her thoughts so Elsie remained silent.

'But I have to say, I find it difficult to imagine him capable of murder. I know he had a secret life, but he's too much of a child to keep it that hidden. Besides he's too much of a coward to commit murder, I think. And he would be revolted by murder. Too messy; it would spoil his suit,' she added with a bitter smile. Then she looked downcast, 'I'm sorry, that poor girl, I don't mean to joke. I shouldn't have said that, but he is so keen to project this immaculate perception of himself...But murder, Freddie? I just don't see it. But what do I know? I don't think I know anything anymore.' Again her eyes filled with tears.

It was clear that Lydia was at the mercy of her emotions: anger, bitterness, anxiety. Even the solicitor looked taken aback but she didn't try to check her client. Lydia was not saying anything to incriminate herself.

'Mrs Bowland, I believe Freddie Bowland's father was a champion rower, is that right?'

Lydia looked a bit baffled by the question and blinked at the turn of questioning. 'That's right,' she eventually replied.

'And was Freddie a great rower too, was it a hobby of his?'

'Used to be. That's where I met him, at one of Whitby's annual regattas. My dad's company is an official sponsor.'

'What company is that then?'

'Drury Accountants'.

Elsie had heard of them: a well-established and respectable practice across the region.

'That must be useful for your own business; having someone in the family who knows about accounts.'

'It's kept Freddie from making some mistakes,' Lydia said drily. 'Not mistakes done on purpose,' she added, 'just careless ones.'

It sounded as if Lydia Bowland was used to protecting her husband - even from himself. Elsie warmed to this woman who had so clearly been betrayed and yet still battled with some feelings of loyalty toward him and was trying to give an objective perspective of him.

'So Freddie is an accomplished rower?'

'Like I said, used to be. He had a rowing accident a few years back and nearly drowned. He's not been in a boat since. Won't even go on a cruise, I tried to get him to go on one with my parents and the children. He doesn't like swimming either. I'm not mocking him, by the way. It was a dreadful accident.'

'What happened?'

'He just went out rowing by himself and a sea fret came in. He'd gone out further than he'd thought. Got into difficulties. I'd called the lifeboat out – he'd always told me what time he was going out and when he was due back. He was a couple of hours over. His father had always drilled it into him to do that and it proved to save his life. Freddie wasn't as cautious as his dad as a rule. He generally took more chances than he should have. He should have seen the fret coming and turned back - not even gone out in the first place. At least he took on board his dad's old advice: by letting someone know he was going out, thank goodness. He always used to scoff at his dad for playing things too safe.'

Lydia's eyes filled with tears again, 'I remember thinking that perhaps he was with another woman and that I would feel a fool if that was the case and he wasn't in some kind of trouble. But the fret decided me. I've been around the North Sea too long to take chances: didn't want that on my conscience. Turned out he'd capsized and was too tired to get back in the boat. The lifeguards found him only just clinging to it.'

That threw a new light on things but it still didn't discount him. If he'd been desperate enough he might have overcome his fear and there were still the missing two hours to account for. Elsie thought to herself.

Lydia suddenly seemed to slump, it was as if she had aged five years during the interview. Elsie didn't think she was the kind of woman who liked to air her dirty washing in public: found it a bit too undignified, but she was obviously fraught and this had led to her being open, perhaps. Lines had become engrained around Lydia's eyes; her face had paled, only enlivened by the blotchy patches on her cheeks and her hair was messy from her fingers running frantically through it during the interview. She had stopped crying but she gazed, almost catatonic now, into the middle distance. Elsie had already dismissed her as an accomplice. Scrutiny of the security cameras at the Bowland premises showed her account of herself, on the Saturday, to be accurate: playing with the children in the garden and staying in on the evening. The footage showed that her car had remained in the drive throughout the whole of Saturday through until Sunday afternoon.

'Thank you for your time, Mrs Bowland. Interview concluded at 10.20am.'

CHAPTER 38

Whitby 1827 – Nellie 4 weeks later

Nellie was accompanied by two of the menservants as she traipsed up and down the cobbled street and steps where she had last seen Martha and Jack. She searched through all the alleys and ginnels of Whitby looking for them. At first, her steps were frantic but then they slowed as she discovered no signs of them and became more despondent. She even peeked into the myriad public houses which were thronged with sailors and fishermen but to no avail. Just to be sure, the menservants were despatched inside to ask numerous public house landlords, and their staff, if they knew anything about the whereabouts of Martha and her son. It was pointless. A few of them knew of Martha (and when they said her name it was with raised eyebrows) and usually appended with recollections of 'that rascal of a son of hers' but neither had been seen for a good few weeks.

Nellie had been ill with the influenza for the four weeks since she had run into Martha. At first, she had panicked that she had caught something worse – from Martha herself, as she recalled how sick Martha had been. It was simply the flu though, perhaps worsened by her overwrought condition at meeting her sister under such circumstances. Lizzie had been initially banned from Nellie's presence in case she too caught whatever ailment Nellie had succumbed to. Lizzie had been very quiet after meeting with her Aunt and cousin, as if a new frightening dimension had opened in her safe, cosy world.

Understanding how much the encounter had shaken her mother Lizzie had baked Nellie's favourite Moggy cake made with warming ginger and treacle and ensured a constant supply of scones and shortbread to coax her mother into eating. She had brought her the very last blooming roses from the garden and sprigs of gorse from the abundant wild bushes which dotted the moors around the bay, to sweeten the sick room. Lizzie was trying to draw her mother back into the world they had previously inhabited, which had now fractured due to dark hostile fingers trying to force their way in.

It was getting colder and the Whitby air was filled with smoke from the chimneys of the little cottages. The great smoky blanket it created, draped itself over the rooftops and around the tips of the tall masts of the whaling ships which were crammed into the harbour. Every now and then the harbour fog horn would throw out its blank-mouthed drone into the cold universe of the sea. The spectral outline of the Abbey could only just be seen through the mist and wafts of fuggy air.

The smell of fish filled the air as the fisherwomen on the quayside gutted the fresh catch which had just been brought in. But even their chatter and clatter of knives seemed somewhat muted in the dismal air. The sailors and fishermen busily tended their boats and ships in case the oncoming fog heralded a storm. Everyone wanted to disappear inside to the warmth and cheer of their glowing hearths.

Will, the older manservant, wise to the ways of the world, eventually felt compelled to speak to his mistress, 'Ma'am, you perhaps need to rest awhile; allow me and Matthew (his son of twenty three) to check with some of the men on the ships.' Nellie looked at him for a few moments. In her desperation she wanted to come with him but knew that Will's questioning of the sailors might prove indelicate; if any of them knew of Martha it would be unlikely to be conveyed through 'wholesome discourse.' She wearily nodded her assent and allowed herself to be escorted back to the carriage.

Nellie fretted whilst she waited in the carriage and pulled her cloak closer around her. The cold seeped into her tired flesh. After a while, Will and Matthew returned with the news that even though Martha had been known to some of the sailors, she had not been seen for a while. A boy fitting Jack's description had recently joined up as a cabin boy on a recently departed whaling ship. It was a Norwegian ship and the only one apparently which would take him. His reputation preceded him in the English speaking vessels ('Mad as hops, footpadder' as one fisherman put it). Apparently, he was a known thief and known for pilfering on the docks - and known for getting into scuffles whilst about his dubious business. Folk who knew of him had kept their belongings close when he ventured near.

A thought occurred to Nellie: 'Will, we must try the workhouse before we return.' She knew that the workhouse was one of the only places to tend the sick and desperate.

The workhouse stood to the south east of the town, away from the main nugget of streets. It stood grey and forbidding as the fog encroached upon it. Its architecture was imposing, stark and unwelcoming - as befitting an institution which sought to blame the poor rather than helping them. Its numerous uniform windows gazed imassionately down upon her as Nellie clanked the bell set into the frame of the heavy oak door at its entrance. The sound of bolts withdrawing was soon heard.

An old lady peered through the crack in the door wearing a worn expression topped by a grey homity cap. Her eyes were brown and sharp though. She keenly looked Nellie up and down. Her eyes softened as she realised Nellie wasn't likely to be seeking board at the workhouse.

'Can I help you?' she asked in a cracked voice. 'I'm Mrs Dixon, the senior matron.'

'I do hope so. I'm searching for a relative of mine. She may have come here. She wasn't well you see. Martha, Martha Whittaker- about my age, with long brown hair. She was coughing dreadfully...when I last saw her. Has she called here, would you know?'

'And you are?'

'Her sister; her sister, Nellie.' Nellie could not hide the desperation in her voice.

If Mrs Dixon was surprised at a well to do woman making enquiries to the workhouse about a relative, she did not show it. Presumably she was inured to the manifold tales of human life which trailed their sad way to the workhouse door.

'We did have a Martha Whittaker here a few weeks ago. And fitting the description you gave. She was sick. Very sick...I'm afraid we couldn't help her. I'm very sorry. She passed away last Thursday.'

Sailors Farewell Hymn

It's our time to go now,

Haul away your anchor,

It's our sailing time.

Get some sail upon her,

Haul away your halyards,

It's our sailing time.

Get her on her course now,

Haul away your fore sheet,

It's our sailing time.

Waves are rolling under,

Haul away down Channel,

On the evening tide.

When my days are over,

Haul away for heaven,

God be by my side.

It's our time to go now,

Haul away your anchor,

It's our sailing time.

CHAPTER 39

SATURDAY 19th September 2018 Scarborough
Police Headquarters

'Interview with Mr Frederick Bowland, commencing
at 11.20am. Sunday 19th September 2018. Present
DCI Storm, Frederick Bowland and Mr Bowland's
legal representative, Mr Trowbridge'

'Mr Bowland, you have stated that you arrived home
on the evening of the 11th September at 11.30pm
and that you had attended your gym club until the
premises closed.'

Freddie briefly closed his eyes as if to brace himself. 'That's right.'

'Yet your gym closed at 9.00pm leaving two and a
half hours unaccounted for. By our reckoning it took
30 mins to drive from the gym to your house. If you

had driven straight home you would have arrived at 9.30pm. Please can you tell us what you were doing during the missing time from 9.00pm to 11.30pm?'

'I drove around for a while. Took a ride out to Sandsend, and walked along the beach for a while. I didn't want to go home and face yet another row.'

Sandsend was a village with a long beach just north of Whitby. There was a CCTV along the busiest part of its prom.

'So you did not see Demeris Harper during this time?'

Mr Trowbridge interrupted, 'My client has already stated that the last time he had seen Ms Harper was on the previous evening.'

'Yes, we have that on record, but it is highly likely that Demeris Harper's body was taken out to sea and dumped in the ocean somewhere along this stretch of coastline. Sandsend is just as likely as any other part of this stretch.

Freddie winced at the word, 'dumped'.

'Freddie, did anyone see you at Sandsend? Any other late night beach visitors or people walking along the prom, can you recall?'

There were a few people on the prom but I took no notice of them. I was still upset at the row with Lydia; my thoughts were full of that.'

'Why didn't you mention before that you had gone to Sandsend, after the gym?'

'You asked me where I had been and I told you.'

'But you didn't tell us where you went after the gym.'

Again, Mr Trowbridge interrupted, 'May I remind you, DCI Storm, that my client has never been arrested before; he has never had to account for his actions before in a criminal investigation. It is not surprising that he has made an error in accounting for all of his actions.'

Elsie looked sceptically at both Mr Trowbridge and Freddie, 'Nevertheless it was a strange omission to make under the circumstances.'

Freddie Bowland looked like a small boy who had been found out for some misdemeanour. 'It's true though, I have never been arrested before. I was hoping you would have found out that I was innocent by now. This just doesn't seem real, none of it. God knows what Lydia will be thinking. I guess it will be the divorce courts now, for sure. OK, I admit it, I didn't account for those two hours. I was hoping I wouldn't have to. I knew that I wouldn't have an alibi for them; I just went to the beach and walked about on my own for a while. That's what I did. Hell,

I didn't even register that I was there for two hours. I don't know what I will do without Lydia. I've known her forever. Our children, our house, friends, even the business is a huge part of Lydia and my lives together. I can't face doing everything on my own. I don't know how I would even start.'

Freddie dissolved into tears as the self-pity overcame him. Mr Trowbridge fumbled for some tissues and awkwardly handed them to him.

'Look,' Mr Trowbridge began, once Freddie's sobs had somewhat subsided. 'You have no proof whatsoever that my client murdered Ms Harper,'

'We have his admission that he does not have an alibi for the time Demeris Harper's body could have been put in the sea.'

'The lack of alibi does not indicate that Mr Bowland is guilty though. And you have no evidence to suggest he is. It is clear that without such evidence you cannot hold my client against his wishes for much longer. He has already been in custody for twenty hours. Are you going to hold him for any longer? He's told you everything that he knows.'

Trowbridge was right, of course, in that they could not hold Freddie indefinitely. A suspect could only be kept for 48 hours at Elsie's insistence. She would have to apply to the Super for an extension of another 24 hours. But was there any point? Another 24 hours would be unlikely to yield much at this stage and the extensive searching for evidence was complete...and inconclusive. She'd send Shannon in next to interview him; to try to hopefully gain some fresh detail as to those missing two hours. But as it stood, she would let him go in the next few hours... for now. If, that is, the Sandsend prom CCTV camera footage proved that Freddie had been there at that time he said he had been.

'Mr Bowland, where exactly did you park at Sand-send and which part of the prom did you walk along before going onto the beach? I need to know pre-cisely which direction you took on your walk…Could you draw me a diagram as a starting point?' asked Elsie.

CHAPTER 40

MONDAY 20th September 2018 Scarborough Police Headquarters

Chief Superintendent Ian Lansdowne was sat in his office when Elsie knocked on the door. 'Come in!'

Elsie had decided to appraise her boss of the developing situation, or non-development of it, as it was proving. Besides the Super had a keen mind and might have some insight which Elsie and the team had missed.

'Oh, Sorry,' Elsie uttered as opened the door and stepped in. A tall and elegant woman in her early fifties, dressed impeccably in a rather austere black suit and a crisp white blouse was seated opposite him. She had long brown hair threaded with silver, which was neatly tied back. A pair of large glasses was perched on her rather long nose. Her generous mouth was covered in glossy red lipstick. She looked out of place in the small scruffy space with its peeling paint, littered with coffee cups and sheafs of messily stacked paper. Ian had never quite embraced the age of IT.

'Aah, Elsie, how opportune. I would like you to meet Superintendent Whitmore,'

'Hello,' replied Elsie shaking the extended hand of the visitor. She wondered if the new plans for more coordination between regional forces was finally being put into action.

The other woman coolly and unblinkingly gazed at Elsie who felt slightly intimidated by this tall elegant creature. Elsie momentarily looked down and saw that her shoes were scuffed and that there was a coffee splotch visible on her creased skirt. Small spaces had recently become a problem to Elsie and for some unaccountable reason she felt the beginnings of a panic attack within the small confines of this office which was usually a kind of sanctuary. She blinked rapidly and concentrated on her breathing. She took deep breaths until she felt it subside - trying not to feel too angry at herself; she knew that acute emotion would just exacerbate the attack.

'Everything alright with the Demeris Harper case?' asked Ian.

'Yes, yes perfectly alright,' Elsie managed to respond breezily - a rather constrained smile etched on her face.

'OK, Elsie, as you are aware I've put in for retirement; I've worked in the force for over forty years – as we've discussed it's time.'

The words tumbled quickly out of Ian's mouth as if he had kept them pent up for too long and he was determined to show that his mind was made up. She could see the concern in his eyes though.

'Yes, Sir,' Elsie couldn't prevent the shock from entering her voice. She had tried to push their previous conversations on the subject out of her mind. She glanced at the woman who was watching them both.

'It's time, Elsie,' Ian reiterated briskly.

Elsie looked closely at Ian; his eyes looked strained with shadows and lines. This wasn't an easy decision for him, but he looked tired too. At sixty five he must be wanting to pursue other things, especially with his wife being unwell. She wouldn't make any emotional scene over it. She felt like doing so. She already felt the keen knife edge of loss which the decision would bring. She would make it easy for him. He deserved that.

'We will all miss you dreadfully, Ian, you know that but I think no one deserves some time to themselves more than you.' She blinked back the tears. She wouldn't, couldn't say any more.'

'Superintendent Whitmore will be my new replacement, Elsie. I'm sure that you will do everything you can to make her as welcome as possible'

Elsie looked at the woman who had a professional but distant smile on her face - about as warm as the winter sun up on the moors, Elsie thought to herself. Then she chastised herself for being so uncharitable. She didn't even know the woman yet. She wondered if some people had had similar misgivings when she had been promoted to the Scarborough force as a new Detective Chief Constable. She suspected a couple of them had as she had been selected over their applications for the same post.

'Congratulations and welcome, Superintendent Whitmore, very pleased to welcome you,' she injected enthusiasm into her voice. After all Superintendent Whitmore, would have worked hard to reach this position. Even so, her heart sank at the imminent loss of Ian.

'I've heard many good things about you,' said the new Superintendent, 'I look forward to working with you, DCI Storm.'

Elsie wondered if she should suggest that the new Super just call her Elsie, but her new boss looked as if she preferred a more formal approach. There was also a hint of scepticism in the new Super's eyes. Elsie was probably just imagining it - but she thought shamefully of the panic attack she had just nearly succumbed too. She wondered if she had not hidden it as well as she thought. She felt sure that Ian hadn't noticed it, but sometimes close proximity to another person had its own special kind of blindness.

'I think it would be good for Superintendent Whitmore to meet the rest of your team, Elsie, before I take her around the rest of the station. She has been fully appraised of your team's talents and success rate. Elsie inwardly groaned as she looked at the new Super who briskly snapped her briefcase shut and then stood up as if to military attention.

Elsie led the way into the briefing room where she had sent for everyone working the present case to be gathered together for a briefing.

Ian signalled for Elsie to make the new introduction as the team all looked quizzically at Superintendent Whitmore. Shannon was missing. Elsie hoped that she had got the message to come to the briefing room.

'Ok everyone, just to update you, I interviewed Freddie Bowland yesterday. His account of where he was on the Saturday has been checked out and it looks as if he was where he said he was – apart from the missing two and a half hours on Saturday evening, between 9 and 11.30pm. He claims he drove around for a while, up on the moors, before going to Sandsend beach and walking along the sand and prom. At present, he has no alibi or CCTV to corroborate this, although we are still checking CCTV from various places. First though, I would like to introduce Superintendent Whitmore to you.'

Seemingly as one, the team shifted their eyes to the new Super who stood poised and calm in front of them. She exuded control and ventured an utterly neutral thousand yard gaze with a fixed smile upon her face.

Elsie paused. She was hoping that Ian would take over at this point but it was as if he did not want to impose upon the new space which Whitmore was stepping into.

'Erm, Superintendent Lansdowne has tendered his resignation for retirement,' continued Elsie. 'I'm sure that you all feel, as I do, very sorry for his leaving but wish him all the very best for the future.' Groans of sadness reverberated around the room but were soon replaced with affectionate messages of good wishes for him in his new life, too. His resignation had been gossiped about for a while – all of the staff were aware of Ian's wife's condition

Elsie found it hard to find the right words. How do you phrase in a few sentences the loss of a way of life which had evolved over ten years: the time she had spent at Scarborough Police Force, under the excellent tutelage of Ian.

'Of course, we'll be giving Ian a proper goodbye, but for now, I would like you to welcome Superintendent

Whitmore, who is here on a preliminary visit to get to know us all a bit and to find out how Scarborough Police Force operates - which would be a major achievement, as none of us really know.'

The team laughed at this, knowing that this was only partly true. The Scarborough Police Force could be idiosyncratic but everyone worked effectively, within unspoken parameters to get things done.

Unfortunately, Superintendent Whitmore did not look amused but just peered at Elsie curiously before flicking her eyes over the team.

Whitmore stepped forward a little and Elsie quietened to allow her to speak.

'I'd just like to say a few words. I appreciate the high regard in which you have held, Ian and he has spoken very highly of you also. I just wanted to say a quick hello. I can see that you're busy so I shan't keep you. I can tell you that I am very much looking forward to working with you all and appreciate Ian is a hard act to follow. Thank you, and I'll hand you back to Detective Inpector Storm.'

For a moment, Elsie flicked her eyes around the room and saw it as the new Superintendent might see it: the grey paint which was once a kind of magnolia; the battered desks and chairs; the carpet which was so worn that foot trails like intercrossing serpents weaved their way lazily across it. Her eyes flicked back to Superintendent Whitmore who had reverted to her professional smile.

Sim seemed calm as ever: looking into the distance as if his thoughts were elsewhere. Gus was blinking rapidly like a lighthouse and was looking anywhere but at the new Super as he kept stroking his side parting down in nervous sweeps; he was rocking his chair back and forth as if trying to nonchalantly hide his nerves but this just gave the effect of him appearing slightly unhinged. Sensing the tension in the air, DC Gianelli was sat rigidly straight and it was difficult to ascertain if she was even breathing or not; DC Thomas just looked straight at the Super, his large brown eyes unblinking as if any movement by him might shatter the glass-like atmosphere in the room. And where was Shannon?

The door opened with a terrific bang as Shannon kicked it open bearing a tray full of coffees for everyone from the café over the road. 'Fuck!' she cried as the door re-bounded back onto her nearly upending the tray. She managed to step through into the room with tray and coffees mostly intact but one of the coffees wobbled on the tray and spilt a bit. Shannon did a little dance as she tried to regain her balance and stabilise it.

Elsie tried to ignore the interruption: 'May I intro-duce DS Sim Howard. And officers Katrina Gianelli and Ben Thomas. This is DC Shannon Cafferty' she said, 'and lastly, DC Gus Lambert.' She pointed at each of them in turn.

Whitmore nodded at each of them but her eyes lingered on Shannon - with her aqua fringe; her orange oversized shirt; black leggings ripped at the knee; and the coffee dripping disconsolately, off the tray she was holding, onto her Doc Martin boots.

As if to provide an encore, a loud smack shattered the tension once again. Everyone turned to look in the direction of Gus, who had mistimed the swinging back of his chair and had toppled backward, cracking his head on the wall behind him. He lay in a dazed heap on the floor for a few seconds and then, as if nothing at all had happened, he swiftly scrambled back into his seat and gazed solemnly, at no one in particular.

'Ahem, well Elsie, we'll erm, leave you to it. I'd like to push on and show Superintendent Whitmore needs to leave by 2 back to Middlesbrough,' said Ian.

As he stepped through the door, ushering Superintendent Whitmore in front of him, he whispered to Elsie with a bemused smile, 'Well, that went better than expected...' He scratched his head and rushed forward to catch up with the regimented clip of Whitmore's heels which were already clacking stridently down the corridor.

Just as Ian Lansdowne had stepped out of the door a young PC stepped through it,

'DCI Storm, I've been told to inform you straightaway. Face recognition software has identified Demeris Harper crossing the Swing Bridge in Whitby and half an hour later crossing back again. Apparently the bridge was crammed with tourists on the Saturday afternoon. Paul Lazonby asks if you will give him a ring.'

Elsie drew out her mobile from her bag and rang Paul, the tech supervisor straight away.

'We found her crossing back over the bridge again, Elsie. The first time she crossed, which you know about, it was easier to pick her up as there weren't many people walking across the bridge at the time. When she crossed back over the bridge it was much busier. There's only one quick shot of part of her face. It was very easy to miss as she was behind a couple of kids carrying balloons, of all things. But the kit picked her up from a fraction of a glimpse. It's definitely her.'

That was certainly understandable as one of the last sunny Saturday afternoons in Whitby would have been busy and the one bridge connecting the two major tourist areas of the town were often crammed, at times, on such days. 'Did you find any footage of her crossing back again?' asked Elsie, her heart in her mouth. A positive answer would likely confirm on which side of town Demmy had disappeared.

'Nothing, Elsie – although we're running more checks'.

'Did she seem to be on her own, Paul?'

'As far as we can tell but we can't be sure, Elsie.'

Elsie rang off and addressed the team who were waiting nervously for her reply.

'The face recognition kit picked her up returning back across the bridge afer leaving Jimmy and the chemists but there is no sign of her crossing it again and there is no evidence that she was with anyone when she crossed back, although, like I say, they're running more checks.'

'We scrutinised that footage but we just couldn't be sure, it was too busy,' said Gus, relieved.

'So, at least we know she went missing in the older part of the town on the other side of the harbour.

It's something, I suppose…maybe?' said Shannon uncertainly.

'So, she didn't go straight back to her car after going to the chemist and there is no evidence that she met up with someone in the main part of town and disappeared there,' said Sim.

'And she didn't go back to work as there is no trace of her on the CCTV in Church Street where the Skegwin's jewellery shop is; or of her actually in the shop,' said a mystified Elsie.

'And there isn't really a lot of area she could have got lost in on the older side of Whitby: just a few streets and the cliff steps up to St. Mary's and the Abbey. Shannon, Gus, I want you to contact all those who knew Demmy well. Find out if Demmy had any friends she could visit in the older part of the town.'

CHAPTER 41

TUESDAY 21st September 2018 Robin Hood's Bay

The black and yellow crime-scene ribbon was stretched across the door of Demmy Harper's cottage on Sunnyside Lane. Elsie peeled it back before plucking the key from her pocket and inserting it into the lock. She had decided to have one last look for the pendant at Demmy's cottage. Elsie knew it was a long shot but she wouldn't rest easy until she had exhausted every possibility.

'Now then! Detective Storm, isn't it?'

Elsie looked around and spotted Bill Tynedale walking along the alley toward her.

'Hi Bill.'

Bill stopped as he approached her.

'Any nearer to catching that poor girl's killer yet?' but then added after a pause, 'I don't suppose you're allowed to say. Sorry, foolish question.'

'It's alright, Bill, we're still pursuing enquiries. I wish I could tell you more.'

Bill stood back looking speculatively at the little cottage which was one of about twelve set in a terraced alley leading off the main street.

'This cottage has been in the Whittaker family for about three hundred years, you know. Demmy's mother's maiden name was Whittaker, you see. Baytown folk tended to stay put - many never set foot beyond a couple of mile radius. Those that did only tended to go as far as Whitby or Scarborough, maybe York - for the markets mainly.'

'Things have certainly changed, haven't they Bill?'

'You can say that again. When I grew up, Baytown was full of people who'd grown up here and whose families had before them…and families before them. Only a small fraction of those families live here now,' he added wistfully.

'Of course,' he continued, 'Demmy and Jess had ancestors in the smuggling years. This is an old smuggler's cottage. Jeb Whittaker, who they're descended from, lived here and he was the King of the Smugglers at that time - in Baytown that is. Of course, as he got wealthier he bought up other cottages in the Bay for his relatives. He never moved out of this one himself though. A lot of the wealthy smugglers in the Bay stayed put in their old cottages, you know. They didn't want to alert the excise officers to their unaccounted for wealth.'

Elsie had tuned out and was hoping that Bill would go soon. She wanted to try to find the pendant. It clearly meant a lot to Mick Harper and was worth one last look. Then she was struck by an idea.

'Bill, I guess you must be familiar with many of the hidden nooks and crannies in these old cottages? '

'I think so, but it's surprising how many hiding places there are within these old stones. Renovations of these cottages are still discovering old smuggling hidey holes within the cottages. Each one of the cottages is different, of course. And then there's the old smuggler tunnels beneath the alleys and ginnels – many of the tunnels can be accessed from the basements of the cottages. Of course, they're mostly blocked up now.' And then he mused, 'There's a whole other world beneath our feet; things hidden from the eye that we can't see; which haven't been discovered yet and very possibly never will be.'

But Elsie wasn't concerned about the tunnels, it was secret hiding places in this particular cottage that she was thinking about at the moment - which might lead to a discovery of the pendant.

'I'm looking for something that Demmy considered precious and might have hidden in the cottage, Bill. It's unlikely she wanted to hide it but you never know what else we might discover anyway.'

'And you want me to see if I can help you to find it. I'd be delighted to.' Bill's face had lit up. He was longing to use his knowledge for such an important enterprise.

She made him don, like herself, plastic gloves and foot coverings and then they stepped into the cottage.

'I'm afraid, Bill, that I must ask you not to touch anything. It is a crime scene. I know you'll understand. If you want anything to be touched or handled, please ask me to do it, won't you.'

Bill clearly didn't mind at all; if anything he looked rather excited than affronted.

'Absolutely, I'll just stand in the middle of each room and tell you where to look.'

'That would be great, Bill, thanks.'

There was no hall and the doorway led straight into the front room which had a small kitchen at one end. There was a sofa and a couple of armchairs set cosily around a real coal fire which lay grey and empty. There were of course, myriad small paintings on the wall, by Jess, and of course the larger wall hanging depicting the family tree which had interested Elsie in her previous visit to the cottage.

'I'll do my best Detective Storm, but you must understand that each stone and brick of the cottage, each piece of wainscoting and beam would need to be considered. The smugglers were highly intelligent; they were the masters and mistresses of concealment - to match any modern magician; had to be to dodge the curiosity of the custom's men, you see; it was a matter of or life or death. It wasn't uncommon for those caught with contraband to be hanged or deported to Australia.'

'I understand, but you'll have a better idea than me as to what to look for.'

'I'd start with the family tree hanging, I reckon. The larger pictures or hangings in the cottages often had hidden places behind them. Equivalent of many modern safes now, I suppose. And people tend to hang pictures in similar places so there's a chance something might have hung there generations ago.'

Elsie gingerly raised the family tree picture away from its mooring on the wall but nothing lay behind it.

'And knock around the wood surrounding the hearth. See if your knocking produces any echoes.' She did so, but all sounded solid.

'The trouble is that many of the more modern inhabitants have plastered or concreted over many of the hiding places.' Bill commented.

But still, on his direction, Elsie knocked around what felt like every square inch of the little sitting room.

'It could be that Jeb, knowing he was probably under more scrutiny than the others chose not to use his home as a hiding place,' said Bill. 'But it's worth continuing, I think.' Elsie took a short break whilst her eyes skimmed the room. Under Bill's direction she was now trained to look for any anomaly in the walls or woodwork which might give them a clue as to some kind of hiding place behind. Bill took advantage of the silence to bounce lightly up and down on his toes and moved around the room as he did so. At one spot he jumped in the same place a few times.

Every part of the floor sounded solid so he stopped.

An old corner cupboard built into the wall proved more interesting though. Elsie opened the little glass door set in a wooden frame and peered inside. At Bill's direction she removed the ornaments and tapped gently on the back of it. Nothing happened and exasperated she asked Bill to have a go. He applied pressure with his fingers and managed to get a piece of the wood to slide back revealing a hidden cavity inside. Elsie held her breath but there was nothing inside. She felt around it carefully twice with her fingers but nothing. She sighed with frustration. She would have loved to have found the pendant and given it back to Mick. She knew that if the pendant had been in an obvious place they would have found it by now but she knew that her conscience would not be clear until they had checked everywhere thoroughly. Not to mention other secrets which the discovery of a hiding place might uncover.

The first bedroom was of a wholly modern design with new flooring and wallpapered walls. It was clearly Demmy's bedroom. The furniture was fairly modern so not worth too thorough an investigation. Elsie still double checked the drawers and wardrobes in case the pendant turned up in them. She carefully checked the ornaments and jewellery box too, but nothing. The bathroom was of a modern design too and the tiles and plasterwork covered any possible hiding places from the smuggling history of the little cottage.

The last and second bedroom proved more interesting. It was clearly of an original layout with old cupboards built into the walls. An old brass bed took pride of place and Elsie wondered if this had been Jessie's old room. Various family photographs and ornaments, of an old fashioned taste, indicated that this might have been the case.

'Look, Bill,' Elsie conceded, 'you have a better idea than me about what to look for. I think you should try the cupboards, yourself.' She knew that the cottage had already been thoroughly searched for signs of crime and she was willing to take the chance of Bill being able to explore properly – under her observation. He was taking great care not to disturb anything. She thought that though unorthodox, it was worth letting him look properly. Finding the hidden cavity in the cupboard downstairs proved that he knew exactly what to look for and how to access these strange little hiding places.

Bill had been moving around the room anyway, unable to contain himself, knocking gently at walls for sound of a hollow echo but to no avail. Not that it would have been any use – even though the plaster was old, it was comprehensive. Bill stepped forward with the eagerness of a puppy and Elsie stood back. There were two floor to ceiling cupboards painted an old cream colour and the first one yielded no success. When Bill knocked on the back of the second however his knock did not meet with a solid thud like it had when he had done the same to the first cupboard, instead it made a barely discernible hollower sound. He turned and smiled at her. Together they removed the bundles of clothes and old shoes (clearly Jessie's) and two piles of blankets and then Bill proceeded to move two or three of the old shelves which slid out of their runners quite easily. They were left with a huge cavernous space.

'Can we raise the carpet, do you think?' He asked, a note of excitement in his voice.

Together they peeled back a section of the carpet at the bottom of the cupboard which, due to age, came away quite easily. Underneath the carpet was a hatch set into the wooden floor with a slender iron ring attached and perfectly set into the hatch itself – so as not to cause any visible rise on any floorcovering hiding it presumably.

'Of course, in Jeb's time, this would have been covered over with loose flags and rugs. A number of the cottages had these,' said Bill.

'What is it?' asked Elsie, 'a secret room to store the contraband?'

Bill smiled at her and raised his eyebows before grabbing the ring and raising the hatch. It creaked loudly.

They both craned their necks to peer down into the dark open space and a waft of stale damp air greeted their nostrils. Wooden steps led downward. Elsie marvelled at the ingenuity of the Bay-town smugglers and their building work. It seemed to be a secret, narrow, inner room, but so clever-ly constructed that from the outside you wouldn't even know it was there.

'We need a torch,' said Bill.

She knew that she just had to try the old wooden stairs which led down into it. The pull of history was just too strong. She also knew that there was no way that Bill could not be included too: his face shone with the eagerness of a child on a treasure hunt. And, after all, she never would have found the secret room without him.

They gingerly made their way down by the torchlight from their mobile phones. She went first and Bill followed. She slowly waved the beam of the torch around the space. Curtains of cobwebs draped the corners but otherwise the room was empty. Apart, that is, from a couple of empty shelves tacked along one wall.

'So it is a contraband hiding place then?'

'I would expect, it's a bit more than that,' said Bill excitedly. 'Jeb would have been too canny to hide stuff down here, or if he did, it wouldn't have been for long. Shine the torch at the shelving would you, Inspector.'

Closer scrutiny of the shelving showed a couple of hooks set into the lower one, possibly to hang foodstuffs off the floor. He twiddled with the hooks and the whole of the wooden panel, on which the shelves were fixed, slid away revealing an iron plate about a metre square which was too rusty to be prised away.

'Behind this is probably some kind of passageway connecting to other cottages or even leading down to the beck which runs through Baytown. It's probably all collapsed now. A lot of these cottages had interconnecting tunnels beneath or between them. The trick is to look further behind the hiding spaces themselves - as it fooled many a customs officer.

Elsie was fascinated but she had to remind herself she was looking for some kind of information relating to Demmy's case. 'This is amazing, Bill. So this room acts like some kind of double bluff: it would have made the customs officers think that they had found something and then realised they hadn't and not bothered to have looked any further: ingenious.'

'Exactly, the smugglers probably used this room for storage: blankets, ropes, general household odds and ends and it would have put the customs men off from bothering to explore further. And from the outside walls you wouldn't even know it was there.'

It was all fascinating but they hadn't found Demmy's necklace. 'Let's go back upstairs and see if we can find anything else, Bill,' said Elsie.

Predictably, they found little else of interest as sub-
sequent refurbishments over the centuries had hidden most of the traces of the family of smugglers
who had once lived in the cottage long ago.

As they were making their way to the front door Bill
suddenly stopped and looked up at a beam which
hung over the front door. 'That's strange,' he muttered.

'What is?' asked Elsie.

'That beam. 'It's out of sync with the others in the
room. The others are all evenly spaced but that one
isn't. You can only really tell from this angle.'

Elsie looked at the other beams running across the
ceiling of the room. Bill was right, they were evenly
spaced out between them but the one over the door
did not share the same kind of symmetrical pattern.

'It's probably nothing,' he said, ' the building of these
cottages was idiosyncratic and though solid, usual

building procedures didn't apply as the village in this lower part of the Bay is so short-spaced. Sometimes it was the families themselves which did the building work. Like I say, it's probably nothing but I wouldn't mind just checking something,' he added.

'Go ahead,' said Elsie, 'we might as well'.

Bill grabbed a wooden chair and placed it directly under the beam. He stood on it carefully and then gently tapped his fingers along it. One of the taps on the side of the beam nearest to the door produced a noise hollower than the others. He tapped it again and then placed pressure with his fingers on the same point. Elsie's heart started to beat loudly. She stepped forward to look up. All it seemed to take was the right kind of pressure in the right place and a small slat sprang open revealing a space within the beam which was like a tiny wooden cupboard. Facing the door it could not be seen from the main part of the room.

Bill turned his head down quickly and caught her eye. His own were gleaming, like an owl spotting a creature in the undergrowth. Elsie truly believed that in a former life, this mild mannered and polite man would have been happy to be a smuggler himself. The subterfuge seemed to wholly animate him. He gingerly scrabbled around in the space. Elsie, by now, had forgotten her exhortations to him not to touch anything. It would have been like trying to take a newly caught rabbit from a terrier. She had insisted that he wore the latex gloves anyway.

He gave a small cry of excitement as his fingers alighted on something and pulled it out of the small hiding space and clambered down from the chair clutching it.

'What is it, Bill?' she cried.

'I'm not sure, a piece of paper, I think.'

Elsie could see he was dying to open up the carefully folded paper but had remembered her previous instructions. He handed it to Elsie but couldn't help peeking over her shoulder as she read it.

It looked to be very old. On the front of the yellowing parchment and written in ink, was the one word, 'Alice'. Elsie carefully unfolded it.

My dear daughter, Alice,

If you have found this letter then you know that I will be in a better place, by now. Our hiding place, which no-one else ever knew about but you and I, has served some purpose. How you begged me to build you your own secret hiding place that only you and I would know about when you were a girl. On my passing I have instructed your mother to tell you to go once again to your secret hiding place. She knew what this meant even though she is unsure of where this place is. I have made equal provision for your brothers and sisters.

I have buried a chest to secure you in your future. I know that Wilf will spend it all. You know he will, and it is only because I am not in your immediate presence that I can tell you this without fear of your anger. Know that I love you and have kept your security secret for your own good. If Wilf has somehow managed to return to you, please try to keep knowledge of this security from him. You always were of too trusting a nature but I beg you to think of your future and of your children's futures. The path to the workhouse is an easy one - do not take it.

The pendant that I gave you has markings upon the stone – which are not merely for effect but mark out where the moneys lie which I have put aside for you.

The ovals mark the Butts; the smaller one you need is highlighted on the pendant. The waves are marked

– take your direction from the sea. Take the direction of the path directed by the arrow on the pendant and take the number of paces as indicated on the stone. I have buried the treasure about three foot beneath the moor. Your brothers will help you to dig for it.

Know that wherever I be, I will always be watching over you and loving you as much as when I breathed the air of the bay. And use this fortune wisely. Your brothers will take care to exchange the goods within the chest for the money you will need.

Your Loving Father, this day of 29th September, 1797.

Both Elsie and Bill looked at each other dumbfounded. This letter had lain here for over two centuries.

'Unless she saw the letter and then put it back she may not have got the letter, Bill.' Elsie said. 'If that's the case, I hope his daughter, Alice, managed without the money he put aside for her.'

Bill nodded misty eyed. It felt as if they had both for a moment, stepped back into history. The import of this precious family missive was not lost on them.

'Possibly she had the pendant and might have worn it for years, never really knowing what its markings meant. Never really knowing what her father had done for her,' murmured Elsie.

'Alice will probably be on that map of the family tree, Elsie.'

'Of course, Bill.'

They stepped excitedly toward the picture depicting the Whittaker family tree. Sure enough, there at its head was the name of Jeb Whittaker and Emma, his wife. Amongst their many brood was the name of their daughter, Alice.

'Do you know anything else about this Jeb Whittaker, Bill?'

'Only that he was the head of the smuggling in the bay for many years. I believe his son took over operations, after his father. Jeb died a violent death on a smuggling run. It's a remarkable and dramatic story. The excise men had apparently been tipped off and were lying in wait. He was shot, down there on the beach.'

'But why didn't Alice's mother, Emma, tell her daughter about her father's message:- to look in the hiding place after his death?'

Bill peered at the map of the family tree. 'It doesn't make sense does it? Something must have happened to either Alice or Emma to prevent the message being passed on.'

'I wonder if this pendant, in the letter, is the same pendant which Mick Harper is so keen to have back as a keepsake of his daughter.'

'So that's what you were looking for?' asked Bill.

'Yes, Mick said it was a jet pendant and moon shaped with odd markings on it. Apparently Demmy wore it all the time but it wasn't found on her. Probably lost to the sea.'

'The treasure itself might still possibly be there then,' said Bill, 'at the Butts'. 'If Alice and her brothers never retrieved it, it could still be there. People take metal detectors up to the Butts but if it is buried very deep it is unlikely to have been found. And it has become quite boggy up there in recent years. And it would take a very good, modern detector to find it, I would expect. Not to mention the fact that the ground becomes covered in more soil as the years go by.' Bill's face was lit with excitement at the thought of the possibility of finding the treasure.

'So who should we tell, Bill?'

'We should tell the British Museum and get them to have a look. Unfortunately, ordinary folk like us can't just appropriate treasure with historical value. What a story. It's probably worth a fortune. Jeb is likely to have acquired all sorts of valuable objects from all over the world at that time. That's if it hasn't been found at some point, anyway, over the years. If it has been, they kept it quiet. But then they would, wouldn't they?'

'We need to show the letter to Mick, first though. He should really be the first to see it. It is one of his ancestors after all. Just a shame I couldn't find the pendant. I might as well take the letter to him now. And you can contact the British Museum if you like, Bill.'

'My absolute pleasure,' replied Bill; his eyes gleaming. 'Do you know that there isn't hardly a month that goes past without me finding or discovering some piece of information related to the Bay's smuggling history. This is one of the most mysterious finds though. Honestly Elsie, the smuggling world is still here, isn't it: in the walls, the corners, the cupboards and beneath our very feet.'

Elsie smiled at his passion; discovering the secrets of the cottage had certainly been exciting but she still regretted not finding the pendant itself, or any further clues to Demmy's murder.

CHAPTER 42

TUESDAY 21st September 2018 The Harper
Residence

'I'm sure this does refer to Demmy's necklace,' said
Mick Harper. He was quiet for a few moments as
he looked at it the letter and then eventually said,
'Truth to tell, I find it difficult to get excited about any
treasure. It's meaningless to me. Thanks for looking
for the pendant anyway, Detective Storm. I think it's
likely Demmy was wearing it…when…and then the
sea must have…taken it.'

'It had been fixed by Mrs Skegwin fairly recently, but
she'd given it back to Demmy.'

'I'll ring the Skegwins, soon. I know Demmy thought
well of them. Demmy did mention that Anna Skegwin had been fixing her pendant. She'd got some

notion in her head that Anna was taking her time to fix it. Anna's just a perfectionist though. I tried to tell her, but you know what young people are like. No concept of time. Everything's got to happen today.'

'Have you known the Skegwins for a long time, Mick?'

'Since we were kids. We were all in the same rowing club, but Colin Skegwin was much better than me. Colin won loads with his rowing team.'

Earlier in the inquiry this would have been a good lead to investigate. It was likely someone conversant with the vagaries of the North Sea had taken Demmy's body out on the night of the storm but both Anna and Colin Skegwin had rock solid alibis. Colin Skegwin had been confirmed as having been in Scarborough all day and arriving home at the time he said: CCTV at various places - and witnesses confirmed this. Anna, of course, had been at the shop all afternoon; gone straight home and her car had never left the garage after that. CCTV in the shop and at their property at home confirmed all of this. Jimmy's alibi had now checked out. That meant that things were beginning to look very grim indeed for Freddie Bowland.

'Do you remember a man called, Harry Bowland, Mick, who was also in Eddie's rowing team, at the time?' Elsie asked.

'Course, Harry and I were friends for years. He became a multi-millionaire. He'd a string of jewellery shops in Whitby and then sold them all to concentrate on supplying jewellery to the shops instead. We kind of lost touch over the years, his wife and mine never really got on, you see.'

'Why was that?' asked Elsie.

'Amanda, Harry's wife, got turned a bit by all their money. Became a bit of a snob; Janice, couldn't stand her in the end. Janice never got like that about money, I'm glad to say - always grounded. She was a fine wife; a fine woman.'

Mick's eyes misted over but Elsie got the impression that he seemed to be keen on continuing to talk. Elsie hadn't the heart to leave just yet. It seemed a step in the right direction, at least, that he was no longer in his grief-stricken stupor.

'Did you ever meet his son, Freddie, Mick?'

'Couple of times but Amanda and Janice weren't getting on so well when the kids were small. I'm talking way back when…'

'I suppose Freddie became a keen rower too?'

'He was, but then had a dreadful accident in one of the boats. They couldn't get him to go out again.'

A cynical murderer could use such a story to thwart his involvement with such a murder, thought Elsie to herself.

'Did they have any other children?'

'Just Freddie and quite spoilt he became by all accounts. His mother doted on him - he had to have the best of everything. Few children would survive that and come out a well-grounded person. Why are you interested in the Bowland folks? Are they in trouble of some kind?'

'All sorts of things and people crop up in this job, Mick, you know. I'm just trying to get a feel for the background of things.' Elsie added vaguely.

Suddenly Mick glanced at the photo of Demmy placed on the mantelpiece. And his energy left him. He visibly slumped.

'I'll go, Mick. You look tired.' Heck, just what were the right words in these situations? Mick didn't seem to notice though and was once again drawn back into that suddenly imposed world of grief struck darkness.

'Just find whoever did it.' He said gruffly.

CHAPTER 43

WEDNESDAY 22nd September 2018 - Whitby

Elsie decided to retrace Demmy's last known steps before taking a walk along Whitby harbour front herself. She'd go back to the station after her lunch. Something niggled her and she didn't know what. Hopefully the retrace might shed a little more insight into what happened. Elsie didn't really hold our much luck but she felt compelled to try.

The town still thronged with tourists. The team were checking all the facts they had obtained so far about the case, to see if there were any anomalies that any of them had missed. She retraced the known steps that Demmy had taken on her last afternoon: leaving Skegwin's shop after her morning shift; meeting Jimmy on the harbour front; walking toward the car park near the major town supermarket behind the railway station, as a town camera had seen her do but turning back again toward town; the visit to the chemists to get some small personal items (as the shop's cameras and till receipts verified) and then, for some reason, recrossing the swing bridge but no record of her on the road the Skegwin shop was situated, or entering the shop, cameras verified that, so then…nothing. She had not returned to her car. She had not gone for a walk through the major tourist areas of the town (including the Abbey and the 199 steps leading up to it) as cameras would have picked her up in those places. She had vanished. The town cameras only covered part of the town though which added extra complexity.

So frustrating. It was like trying to piece together a jigsaw with half of it missing. She had to consider the possibility that a stranger, or more likely a friend or acquaintance had driven nearby where Demmy had last been seen and, for some reason, she had got into the car with them and been carried away to her dismal fate. But why would Demmy get into a car when her own was in the car park? Perhaps she had decided to visit someone who lived in the older part of town, near the Abbey, and her host had had malevolent intentions. A logical link to explore.

And now Elsie had wandered back to the harbour front and had got caught up with a crowd watching one of the street entertainers: a man dressed as a smuggler, or some kind of pirate, performing magic tricks to the tourist audience. Wearily, Elsie decided to stand and watch for a while before heading back to the station. She didn't usually like being amongst public crowds but didn't register it so much as she was so caught up in her thoughts.

The sound of fishing crates being hauled on and off the boats; the fishermen's shouts to one another; the lazy lapping of the waves against the quay; the creaks of the boats as they lilted and listed in the harbour waters; the gulls cawing as they sailed above on the September air all melded together and filled Elsie's ears with the timeless refrains of harbour life.

The sunshine poured down and it felt good to indulge the last of the summer rays. It was made more poignant knowing they would soon be replaced by the cold knife of winter winds. She glanced, at the majesty of the Abbey across the harbour at the top of the cliff above the town and then glanced back again to the magic performer dressed as a smuggler on the quayside. The performer clearly had his audience in thrall to which their light-hearted laughter attested. She became acutely aware of time and of how many of these sights, sounds and smells would not have been wholly dissimilar to a town dweller from past centuries.

Elsie approached the crowd and could see that the performer's hat, on the floor in front of him, was overflowing with coins.

She decided to watch the remainder of his first trick. A glass was turned upside down on a small table covered with cloth. On the overturned glass's base he placed a coin and then put a cloth over them both. Elsie had decided to watch this trick because she knew it. Her grandfather had taught it to her long, long ago when her spindly nine year old self was still suspended in that world obsessed by all things magical; when the sharp edges of reality were softened by the glow of fantasy.

She knew that the rim of the glass had material stuck across its empty top which resembled the cloth it was upturned on and that the audience would not see the difference. And that between the tablecloth and the stuck on piece of material was another coin – so when the magician whipped away the glass, the coin which had had the material positioned over it would now be visible, making it look as if the second coin was the first one which had fallen through the upturned base of the glass.

The crowd made its expected 'Oohs' and 'Aahs' before the magician moved onto his next trick with a rope procured from one of his 'magic' sleeves. Her mind drifted back to the case.

There were still no real leads; she felt that she was missing something. It was unlikely, yet still possible, that Demmy had been spirited away by a stranger or someone she knew. Yet something niggled - something to do with all the players in this grisly game. The answer, she felt sure, was lying hidden but there all along, just like the second coin in the trick she had just witnessed. That was her feeling but she just could not articulate why she felt like that. For some reason Bill's words about smuggling came to her, 'There's a whole other world beneath our feet, things hidden from the eye that we can't see.' In other words even things that can't be seen by the eye can still be there.

This didn't help her growing frustration though and she noticed that she had begun to breathe more heavily. She also began to feel hemmed in by the crowd. Why had she stopped here of all places? It wasn't the first time she had felt uncomfortable in a large public crowd. She tried to copy the rest of the audience as they clapped and made cries of appreciation as the magician worked his wonders with the rope but she was really trying to bear down on an impending panic attack. 'Oh, please, not here,' she silently implored herself. She focused on an area beyond the smuggler. By creating distance with the eye and away from direct surrounding it sometimes helped to keep the panic attack at a distance she had sometimes found.

Behind the performer there was a window to an old pub and its dark reflection mirrored the back of the magician and the crowd which Elsie was amongst. Elsie's breathing rate increased. She stared transfixed at her own helpless reflection which gazed solemnly back at her. That definitely did not help. She focused on the reflections of the faces behind her, in the window, and caught the reflection of a young woman facing slightly away from her, talking quietly into her mobile phone. The girl removed the phone from her ear and looked forward again at the performer. Her hair was dark and pinned up in a loose bun and her face was pale. Elsie gasped and had to make herself breathe: Demmy! She flung herself around to see the girl, but in Demmy's place was a young woman with long fair hair who looked curiously at Elsie because she had turned around so suddenly to face her.

She tried to tell herself that the apparition was merely a figment of an over-stressed imagination but her body did not respond and she began to hyper-ventilate. She glanced to her left but a large man in a white T shirt and blue flowered shorts blocked her view. She turned to her right and caught sight of a street hoarding which displayed a large map of Whitby for tourists. The crowd erupted into laughter at the magician's latest antics and Elsie took the opportunity to force her way through the crowd - keeping her eyes as much as she could on the hoarding. She reached it and with both hands leant against it, head down, breathing heavily. 'Breathe, just breathe. Your imagination… not real…it wasn't real…'

'You alright, love?'

Elsie took a deep breath and turned to see an old man and his wife, the large bag crammed full of day-trippers' necessities with a large blue flask jutting out of it. The old man tentatively put his hand on Elsie's shoulder and peered at her with rheumy eyes.

'Do you need to sit down for a while, pet?' asked his wife, who was had her arm linked through his.

'No, no I'm alright, thank you. Just don't like crowds much. I'll be better in a minute, honestly.' She tried to smile reassuringly at them. Her breathing had become more regular.

'You sure?' asked the old man. But it was clear that he could see Elsie was now improving. Elsie nodded and forced herself to smile reassuringly at him and not wanting to embarrass her further, he shuffled away after studying her for a few moments. His wife, her arm still linked in his, turned back to check with a puzzled look on her face and Elsie gave a small smile to send them on their way.

Elsie took her hands away from the board and looked back. The crowd around the magician had dissipated; the magic and charm of the moments he had created were now being packed prosaically away in a huge battered bag. Elsie's eyes flicked tentatively around the quay - as expected: no sign of Demmy.

She looked back up at the board and the map of Whitby and barely registered the various land-marks, thoroughfares and ginnels it depicted. On shaky legs she focused on getting back to her car.

By the time she reached the car park the panic attack had more or less gone but her mind was full of the reflection of the Demmy she had thought she had seen in the window, with Demmy speaking on her phone. Actually, she hadn't been speaking now she thought about it - more listening intently. As if it mattered she chastised herself, but the image would not recede. She felt embarrassed that the old couple had caught her in the middle of a panic attack. She was just glad that the map board had been there to help support her standing up otherwise she felt like she might have slid to the ground, overwhelmed by the attack.

Soon, she began to feel herself become more steady and she made her way back to her car. The shaking had subsided. She got into her car and drove away out of Whitby and was soon back on the road to Scarborough. With the driver window wound down she breathed in lungfuls of cool moor air.

As she entered the investigation room she saw Gus poring over his computer screen and staring at it intently.

'Gus, any progress?'

Gus was looking at one of the last images of Demmy as she was being served in the chemist in Whitby.

'I don't know, Ma'am. It's just the way Demmy is fumbling around in her handbag. Something seems odd.'

Shannon stepped into the room, carrying two mugs of tea, one of which she placed on Gus's desk.

'He's run through that bit about a hundred and fifty times today.' Shannon said bemusedly. They all stared at the screen. Demmy's face seemed frustrated as she rummaged through her bag. But then eventually, she retrieved her purse and after taking out a twenty pound note from it, put the purse back into her handbag after receiving her change. Gus stared fixedly at the screen and then rewound it to play it again.

Elsie thought it might be a good idea to call everyone together to try to draw together where they all were with the investigation and see if there was any new information. She stood upright from peering at Gus's screen. She glanced at Gus again. She knew that when a case got to this kind of non-stage, detectives could become obsessive about the details they did have, frightened that they had missed something. She needed to pull him out of it and focus on the bigger picture.

She bent down again to have a quiet word in his ear but then stopped as she focused on the image of Demmy fumbling in her bag; a look of consternation on her face before she then smoothly went to another part of her bag and confidently pulled out her purse. Elsie had a flashback to the girl who had appeared to be Demmy on the harbour front talking on her phone during the magician's performance. She took a deep intake of breath. 'What?' asked Shannon.

'I don't think she's looking for her purse at first,' she said. 'That's why it doesn't look right.'

'That's it!' Gus cried his fist gently hitting the desk in jubilation. 'She's found out that there is something else missing, hasn't she?'

He rewound and intently looked at the screen again, 'She's not looking for her purse. Her purse is in the right pocket of her bag and she's looking in her left side of her bag. When she wants her purse, she goes straight to it. Look again.'

Elsie, Gus and Shannon peered closely at the screen as Gus played the CCTV video images again. Gus was right. Demmy approached the counter by the till and whilst another customer was being served began to rummage around in her bag. When the other customer left, Demmy approached the till and continued briefly to rummage around anxiously in her bag before, seemingly becoming conscious of the assistant waitng for her to pay, pulling out the purse from a different part of her handbag.

'I'm guessing that she's looking for her mobile phone,' whispered Elsie. 'Her dad said she kept losing it.'

'So perhaps she went looking for her phone and that's why she didn't return straightaway to her car,' mused Shannon. 'But where could she have gone to look for it? Jimmy lives on the main town side of the bridge and the last known sighting is of her walking over the bridge to the other side.'

'She didn't go back to the shop or the cameras on Church Street or at the shop would have shown her there,' said Gus.

'Freddie Bowland was in the gym and didn't leave until much later. The only time he could have been with Demmy was much later on that evening – possibly between 9.30pm and 11.30pm. Where could Demmy have got to in those missing hours even if she had met up with him later?' pondered Elsie.

'And none of the people, in her regular haunts, saw Demmy that afternoon, and all have alibis,' added Shannon.

'We need to keep checking if Demmy knew anyone who lived in the old town, to see if she was visiting them,' said Elsie.

The next hour or so was spent going through, once again, Demmy's contacts, ringing around and visiting those of her friends, relatives and acquaintances who might have known. If Demmy had left the chemist to look for her phone, where exactly had she gone?

CHAPTER 44

WEDNESDAY 22ND September 2018 Robin Hood's Bay

It was a fine early autumn evening and Elsie had cooked herself a sea bass with some lightly steamed vegetables. She decided to eat it at the little table on her decking. The sea lay blue as far as the eye could see before it melted into the merging gold and pink sunset casting its arms across the bay. She retrieved a bottle of Chablis from the fridge, poured out a glass and tucked into her well-deserved meal. She savoured the exquisite flavours of the food and wine which complemented one another perfectly. Eventually, she pushed her plate away and perused two seals which were bobbing quite close to shore on their way, presumably, to join the rest of their colony at Ravenscar at the opposite end of the bay. The seals had developed quite a substantial colony on Ravenscar's rocky outcrop since the Sealife Centre at Scarborough had released a few into the wild a number of years previously. As fleeting as the waves the two seals soon dropped out of view.

Her doorbell rang. She plonked the used dishes and cutlery in the kitchen sink on her way to answering it.

'Bill! What a surprise! Come in.'

Bill beamed at her and came in carrying a slim paper wallet.

'I just thought I'd bring some news about the letter we found,'

'Would you like a cup of tea, coffee? I'm having wine.'

'Well, I wouldn't say no. To wine that is.'

Elsie smiled at him. 'It's too nice an evening to be sat inside - let's sit outside and you can tell me your news.'

With Bill duly settled on an iron chair across the table from Elsie, she poured out another glass for him. He pulled out a sheaf of papers from the paper wallet that he'd been carrying.

Bill took a sip of wine and the view looking out over the Bay. 'All the old fishermen cottages in the village are pretty special but the ones overlooking the sea really are something else, aren't they Detective Storm?'

'They are. I love this cottage, Bill, and please call me Elsie.'

He took another sip and after a few moments turned to face her. 'I've received an email from the British Museum. Do you remember how I told you that any information about treasure should be reported to them? Well, they were very interested – replied straightaway to my email. They're going to send teams, with enhanced equipment, to comb the area around the Butts. Although, as it's a place of special designated historical interest it has been done before, but they now have some new equipment which is more advanced than previous detectors. It's a shame that we don't have the pendant though, so that we can match the precise markings and steps on it with the instructions on the letter. It would make it complete, wouldn't it?'

'Indeed, but don't get your hopes up Bill. Jeb's hoard was buried over two hundred years ago. It might not be there anymore. Someone could have found it during that time.'

'You're right. Still, it would be wonderful if it was still there and we had helped to find it. There'd be all kinds of things from a smuggler's chest from that time: treasures from all around the world. But you're right, best not to get ahead of ourselves. Anyway, my other reason for coming is this.' Bill took out a piece of paper from the wallet and pushed it across to Elsie. It was covered in lines, dates and names.

'I decided to try to complete Jessie's family tree. I know she would have liked that. She had completed one branch of the tree from Jeb's daughter Nellie, leading down to Jess and Demmy, but the other branch leading down from Nellie's twin sister, Martha, was only half complete. I decided to finish it for her. It didn't seem right not to at least complete the part that she had started before she became ill.

Elsie loved family trees and she understood Bill's motivation. It was an exciting thing to do and perhaps Sam and Mick Harper would appreciate it. She peered at the paper in front of her and traced down Martha's line to a son called Jack: a sailor who had managed to work himself up from deck hand to the captain of a ship. Bill had helpfully outlined basic information about the new entrants on detachable stickers. Her heart saddened when she read that he had drowned in a shipwreck off the coast of Norway.

'This is interesting about Jack Whittaker, isn't it? Worked his way up from deckhand to captain but then died at sea.'

'Even more interesting considering his mother had died in Whitby workhouse. He certainly managed to drag himself up by the bootlaces, that young man. He was only 37 when he drowned.'

'And then.' Bill continued, 'the tree shows that Jack Whittaker had a son who was born in Whitby: Alfred. He worked as a shop keeper at a chandlers. He too died young: 35, leaving one child again, a daughter: Jemima, who seems to have taken over the chandlery shop. She too seems to have ended up in the workhouse and dying in there too.'

'Who knows? Perhaps she married a ne'er do well and he drank or gambled away the business. Jemima, you can see,' said Bill, his finger tracing down the line, 'had three children but two of them died in infanthood. The remaining son was born in the workhouse and attended an industrial school, then left and trained to become a carpenter. He came to work in Robin Hood's Bay for a distant cousin. I know that because the cousin is listed on Nellie's family tree, Joshua Harrison. See?'

Bill pointed out Joshua's entry on Nellie's branch.

'Martha's line doesn't seem to have had much luck, does it?' commented Elsie 'especially as Nellie's line lists one prosperous entry after another: Elizabeth, Nellie's daughter married a doctor; her children married farmers and captains or became business owners or members of the professional class - and mostly all lived to a ripe old age. Martha's in contrast, tended to die young and often in penurious circumstances, from one misfortune or another. The word 'vagrant' was listed more than once on Martha's side of the tree. Elsie traced Martha's line down with her finger through two hundred years of misfortune after misfortune.

'It's quite a tragic family history when all is said and done,' agreed Bill. 'But I only traced those who stayed in the area. It would have become too sprawling otherwise. It might very well be that those in the line, who moved away, might have experienced better fortune. It does make for odd reading though. I too was struck by the contrast in fortune between Nellie and Martha's family lines.

A shiver ran down her spine when Elsie came to the last entry for Martha's line: Anna Skegwin (nee Heggins). She gasped.

'You mean to say that Anna Skegwin is a family member to the Harpers? How bizarre, Bill.'

'I suppose it does seem a bit bizarre, Elsie, but I should imagine there are lots of people around here who are distant relations of one kind or another and don't know about it. It stands to reason as many folk roundabouts have families who have lived here for generations.'

'I expect you're right. Hey Bill, you might even be a cousin of mine twenty fourth removed or some-thing.' She joked.

'It's possible. This wine is very nice, cousin.' He added.

Elsie chuckled. 'It's still strange though, seeing it on paper in black and white though – how Demmy is descended from Nellie, and how Anna Skegwin is descended from Nellie's twin sister Martha from over two hundred years ago. So very strange. And Nellie married a sea captain, yet Martha ended up in the workhouse. I'd love to know how that came about.'

'Misfortune was much easier to fall into in those days - no welfare support that we rely on these days. And of course bad life choices or bad luck really did mean you were more likely to fall into a terrible life then.'

'I guess, we're never likely to know how Martha ended up in the workhouse, though. And then her only son who managed to do so well for himself, ended up drowning after raising himself as captain of a ship. It just seems so desperately sad, doesn't it?'

'It does,' agreed Bill. 'But whaling was a very dangerous occupation and it was likel a whaling ship that he captained, given its capsize in Norwegian waters. Many a whaling sailor lost their lives on the whalers. Greenland was a popular destination – for the whaling ships that is, and Whitby was a major whaling port in Britain. Very lucrative business it was too: whales supplied oils for lighting. This was before gas of course, which brought an end, more or less, to the whaling industry.

They both contemplated the tragic ladder of life which had descended from Martha. The waves lapped despondently on the sea wall below the cottage, as if they too echoed the sad thoughts of Elsie and Bill.

'Anyway, I must be getting along,' said Bill, 'I just wanted to give you an update. Fascinating stuff – and thanks for the wine.'

Elsie showed him to the door and then went and sat down on the decking area again. Curiosity struck her and she picked up her mobile phone.

'Mr Harper, DCI Storm here. I just wanted to ask you a quick question?'

'No news then?'

'We're following a few leads at present. I know it's not what you wanted to hear but believe me, we won't rest until we know what happened to your daughter. You can be assured of that. I know this is a strange question but were you aware that your daughter's necklace was possibly a map of sorts. Before you got the letter I found, that is?'

'No. We'd always wondered about the strange markings on it though. My wife thought they may have been some kind of runic good luck symbols but she never found anything that matched – she got some books on it once. But no, the markings never looked like a map. I suppose, thinking about it that it should have occurred to us, coming from the Bay and its smuggling history. They just didn't look like a map. Athough, to be truthful, at this moment I couldn't care less about any treasure.'

'That's completely understandable, Mr Harper. Completely. Perhaps it's something to think about another day. So, you can't tell me anything about the markings?'

'No. I told you. It just looked like a mishmash of incomprehensible dots and lines. None of us ever thought it might be some kind of map.'

'Mr Harper, thank you for your time. Once again, be assured that we are doing everything we can and will contact you as soon as we have some news.'

'I hear Freddie Bowland has been taken into custody.' Said MicK Harper.

'I'm afraid I can't comment about that at the moment, Mr Harper. But as soon as we have anything to tell you, I'll make sure that you are told.'

'Yes, you keep saying, you'll let me know. I didn't even know that Demmy knew him that well. She'd mentioned that he came into the shop sometimes. Spoilt little bastard, if I find out he had anything to do with it…'

'Mr Bowland is helping us with our enquiries, Mr Harper. He's not been charged. We're still at the investigation stage.'

Blimey, thought Elsie after she had finished the phone call. News certainly travels fast in this part of the world. She paused for a second and longed for the day that she could tell Mick Harper the news that Demmy's murderer had been caught.

Greenland Whale Fisheries

'Twas in eighteen hundred and fifty-three

In June, the thirteenth day

That our gallant ship her anchor weighed

And for Greenland sailed away, brave boys

And for Greenland sailed away.

2. The lookout on the cross-trees stood

With a spyglass in his hand

There's a whale, there's a whale

There's a whalefish, he cried,

And she blows at every span, brave boys

She blows at every span.

3. The captain stood on the quarterdeck

And a fine little man was he

Overhaul! Overhaul!

Let your davit-tackles fall

And launch your boats for sea, brave boys

And launch your boats for sea.

4. The boats where launched with the men aboard

And the whale was in full view

Resolved was each seaman bold

To steer where the whalefish blew, brave boys

To steer where the whalefish blew.

5. We struck that whale, and the line played out

But she gave a flourish with her tail

The boat capsized and four men were drowned

And we never caught that whale, brave boys

And we never caught that whale.

6. To lose that whale, our captain said

It grieves my heart full sore

But, oh, to lose four gallant men

It grieves me ten times more, brave boys

It grieves me ten times more.

7. The winter star doth now appear

So, boys, we'll anchor weigh

It's time to leave this cold country

And homeward bear away, brave boys

And homeward bear away.

8. Oh, Greenland is a dreadful place

A land that's never green

Where there's ice and snow

And the whale fishes blow

And daylight's seldom seen, brave boys

And daylight's seldom seen.

CHAPTER 45

THURSDAY 23rd September 2018 - Scarborough Police Headquarters.

When Elsie walked into the investigation room the next morning, there was a flurry of activity around Sim's desk. Shannon and Gus had drawn up their chairs and were staring at Sim's computer screen.

'What's happening?' asked Elsie drawing up a chair alongside them.

'We revisited all the CCTV footage again, Ma'am. And Sim thinks he might have found something,' said Shannon.

'Sim?'

'We got to thinking, Ma'am. If Demmy had lost her phone, she probably left it at work which was where she was most likely to have last had it. We took it in turns to replay different sections from that afternoon. Something odd happens to the camera at about three o clock in the afternoon and then at about four.' He said.

'Hang on, this footage is taken from the back door camera,' commented Elsie.

'That's right,' said Sim. Everything seems perfectly normal on the camera at the front of the shop: just Anna Skegwin letting customers in and serving them from time to time. No sign of a returning Demmy.'

'We checked the footage from the CCTV cameras at the front and the back of the shop didn't we?'

'We did but thought we'd check again and we found something which doesn't seem right with the camera which overlooks the back entrance to the shop. It's easy to miss it. We more concentrated on the front door where she usually entered and exited by.

It wouldn't make sense for her to enter by the back door. In the yard there is only space for the Skegwin's car.'

Sim forwarded the footage to just before three o clock, from the camera which covered the back entrance to the shop.

'Look at the timing of the footage,' he said, pointing to the time indicators in the bottom left hand corner.

Elsie peered closely and watched the tape. Sim was playing the footage slowly. Nothing at all happened on the tape. Just a steady image played showing a consistently empty back door with no visitors. But Elsie watched the slowed down numbers indicating the time: 14:58, 14:59, 15:00, 15:01, 15:03. Apart from a very slight flicker in the images from the camera, there was no indication at all that a couple of minutes had been lost. Just the same empty doorway again.

'There are two minutes missing,' said Sim, 'Either there's a fault with the camera, many of the older ones aren't perfect, or someone has deliberately been playing with the timings to stop something being seen which happened in those couple of minutes.'

'Like Demmy coming back to retrieve her mobile phone. It would only take a matter of seconds to press the digits in the key pad to allow the door to open and then step inside. And the Skegwins told us that Demmy knew the code to get in by the back door,' said Elsie, leaning back in her chair. 'Possibly, but I wonder why she didn't use the front entrance?'

'Maybe she was in a rush or didn't want to disturb Anna,' said Shannon. Then she suddenly stood up and went to the map of Whitby town centre which had been blown up and stuck on the wall. She peered closely at the map. 'There's a back lane to the shop – one of the many ginnels and ghauts which still exist in Whitby. Demmy didn't have to go by the main streets that we've covered. She obviously didn't retrace her steps back to the shop through Church Street, if she did come back to the shop. She might have accessed the back of the shop via the ginnels and yards from the back. But they ultimately back out onto the Abbey and its grounds, and the 199 steps leading up to it. Cameras covering the steps though, show no evidence that she came up or down them. Where did she come from? There seems to be no evidence of her approaching the back door from the land behind the shop or from Church Street in front of it.'

'There's an hour and fifteen minutes missing between Jimmy's last sighting of Demmy and her possible reappearance at the shop,' mused Sim.

'Perhaps she took a walk out that way to clear her head after her row with Jimmy. Maybe she didn't use the 199 steps up to the Abbey,' speculated Shannon.

'But it's all just cottages and fields between the shop and the Abbey,' said Gus.

Shannon paused for a moment or two before crying out, 'Caedmon's Trod!'

'What's that?' asked Gus.

'Caedmon's Trod!' It's a less well known pathway up to the Abbey – coming from the other direction. Maybe it can be accessed with a decent knowledge of the ginnels at the back of Church Street.'

'That's definitely worth exploring, Shannon. Let's have a look at which ginnels and yards she could have taken from Caedmon's Trod to the back of the shop.'

They all stood up to peer at the map. Elsie traced her finger over possible routes from Caedmon's

Trod to the back of the shop. 'It's possible if she veered off from the Trod across the lower line of the Abbey field and then enters one of the ginnels here,' she pointed out. 'If that was her route it would be a good shortcut to the back of Skegwin's shop.'

'And no CCTV cameras on that route,' added Sim.

'The map indicates a couple of ways through to the rear entrance of the shop and there is an opening at the rear of the yard at the back of the shop but it leads to some land which look like gardens belonging to some private cottages,' said Elsie.

'Many of these paths were used publicly at one time; the place was a bit of a warren. It's not too much of a stretch of the imagination to think that someone with an intimate knowledge of the area could find a way through. And probably without challenge as many of these cottages are probably holiday homes now,' added Sim.

'I'll get Gianelli and Thomas to see if they can trace the route and ask possible witnesses who might have seen her. One of the owners of the houses in the yards or ginnels might have spotted her. Good work, everyone. It's looking more and more possible that Demmy might have returned to the shop, isn't it? Maybe she took a walk up to the Abbey to clear her head after the row with Jimmy - and then she took a short cut through the yards and ginnels, to access the Skegwin shop via its back door to retrieve her phone. Right, Sim, let's see the coverage of the front of the shop at the time of the missing minutes.'

They all congregated around Sim's desk again.

Within moments Sim had retrieved the images from the camera at the front of the shop. The minutes were all accounted for but at 14:56 a customer, who Anna Skegwin had just been serving, exited the shop and Anna disappeared from view, presumably to retreat back to her office at the back of the shop. The countdown of minutes and seconds continued as normal from the camera in the front of the shop. As there was no coverage of the office itself (only the front shop and entrance and outside back door to the shop premises) what happened in the office and kitchen was hidden completely from view.

'The camera over the back entrance loses four minutes again, at 15:51 to 15:59, Ma'am, look,' said Sim. He had flicked the screen over to show once again the camera from the back of the shop and once again it steadily and continuously showed an empty undisturbed image of the back door and a couple of feet into the small yard used as a car park for the Skegwin's car. No one arriving and no one leaving. It was easy to miss the timer in the bottom corner jumping almost imperceptibly from 15:51 to 15:59.

'So the missing times could be when Demmy arrived and then departed,' said Shannon.

'So why didn't Anna Skegwin mention that Demmy had come back to retrieve her phone, or for whatever reason, if that's what happened?'

'It could be that she didn't know, but that's unlikely – she could argue that she was in the kitchen making coffee or having a late lunch. The missing times on the CCTV footage still need explaining, though,' said Gus.

'Is it possible for CCTV cameras to be messed around with in this way, Sim?' asked Elsie.

'You'd have to know what you were doing and it is easier on the older cameras, but yes.'

'But would Anna Skegwin have this kind of tech know how? She seems pretty old fashioned to me but then what does a techie look like – stereotypes are often wrong.'

'You can say that again,' commented Shannon, flinging her arm around a bemused Gus.

'When you think about it, her job as a jewellery designer involves attention to detail and I would expect that a modern jewellery designer uses technical expertise in their designs,' said Sim.

'And wasn't she the one in the office who kept all the accounts? The books which you brought from the shop were meticulous and very precise,' commented Gus.

'You'd think she would have solely used the computer for records, rather than books to record the daily workings of the shop, though,' he added.

'Maybe she kept the diary and accounts ledgers up to date as some kind of tradition – lots of people use both paper and computers in their work,' said Shannon.

There was a joint silence as everyone considered the implications of their theories.

'This is good thinking everyone,' said Elsie, 'at last we have something to go on.

'If it was Anna Skegwin who murdered her though,' said Sim, 'how did she move Demmy's body to the middle of the sea from the shop. Security cameras over the back door and yard, shows Anna leaving as usual at the end of the working day and then the security cameras, over the drive and front entrance of the Skegwin's home, show the car arriving half an hour later with the car entering and staying in the garage until the next morning. Demmy's body was found on Robin Hood's Bay beach the next morning. There wasn't any time for Anna Skegwin to move the body – or the means.'

'And if Anna Skegwin did kill Demmy, why did she do it? She and Skegwin spoke of her as if she were a model employee – almost a daughter figure. It doesn't make sense. What was the motive?' asked Gus.

'Some kind of dispute, perhaps? Maybe an accident of some kind that Anna Skegwin had to cover up,' said Shannon.

'The Skegwin's live on the coast on the edge of a rambling cliff. There used to be stairs going down the cliff face but they've crumbled away. But the steps are very near the house and the top of the steps can be seen on the security camera overlooking the back of the house.

Gianelli and Thomas checked it all out and retrieved the camera footage from the Skegwins and provided a full report. Sim, can you check the footage from the security camera at the back of the house again and see if it picks anything up. See if there's been any messing about on timing on that camera?'

'And I think we need to order a search warrant of the shop premises and the Skegwin home residence. See what that turns up. Although we still need to be cautious: how could she possibly have moved the body, if it was her?' concluded Elsie.

CHAPTER 46

THURSDAY 23rd September 2018 - Scarborough
Police Headquarters

Elsie knocked tentatively on Ian's door and opened
it when his loud voice shouted, 'Enter!'

'Elsie, sit down. How are things progressing?'

'I'm going to need a warrant to search the Skegwin
premises and their home, Ian.'

Elsie informed him of their recent findings. She liked
to run things over him anyway and she knew that if
there was no progress, it would be likely that they
would have to put Demmy's case to the side a bit.
New cases were always emerging: organised thiev-
ing in the tourist region and the organised crimes
involving drugs were the ever-present biggies. Ian
never pushed them to let go of a case but she was

well aware that some cases could never be solved –
crime was often a random enterprise and she had
been beginning to wonder if Demmy's murder was
some kind of random involvement of a stranger.

'The Skegwins, eh?' he mused.

'Mr Skegwin is not our primary focus, as such, Ian.
His movements have been accounted for: he was
with friends and had lunch with them in Scarborough. He was with them all day. He might have been
involved with getting rid of Demmy's body later on
but it is hard to see how that was achieved as both
of the Skegwin cars never left their home on the evening concerned. Mrs Skegwin's stayed in the garage
and Mr Skegwin's on the drive from Friday through
the whole weekend. He got a taxi back from Scarborough and arrived home at around 9pm. Security
cameras at the front and back of the Skegwin house
show that Anna Skegwin never left the house after

returning from work and neither did Colin Skegwin after arriving back home later on in a taxi. The tech department are double checked the cameras around the Skegwin residence to be sure but found nothing untoward. It's Anna Skegwin that we are investigating mostly at this stage, although, so far it's quite circumstantial, I have to say, but enough I think to incur a warrant to search, I believe.'

'The missing minutes on the camera warrants a search. I'll get one organised immediately. It's good work, Sim did well picking that up, especially. It's just...'

'I know. What could her motive have been, if it was her? I can only think it might have been some kind of accident and Anna Skegwin got scared and tried to cover things up. We never suspected her though. If it was her, then her reactions, when we questioned her, were chilling in terms of the lack of guilt.'

'It might turn out that there is an innocent explanation of the missing minutes. Has anyone checked to see if it has happened before and that it's not just a quirk of the camera?'

'The team are checking it now, with some help from the IT department, just in case.'

'Are there any missing minutes from the cameras at the Skegwin residence?'

'None at all – and nothing on the footage either, of a body being removed.'

'I expect the IT dept have checked to see if any more minutes are missing from other days on the shop camera. Even then they could be accounted for by Anna Skegwin wanting to cover her tracks by going through the tapes and deleting more missing minutes, on other days, to throw us off the scent and making the camera at the back of the shop appear dodgy. The crucial thing is that the missing minutes we have found match the timing of Demmy's disappearance. We need to send forensics into the shop and into the Skegwin home address.'

Everything seemed to happen at once, after that. Sim informed her that the tech department had found other missing minutes on other days. It might very well prove to be that the camera was faulty.

....

Elsie and the team met the forensics group at the Skegwin shop. A startled Colin Skegwin answered the buzzer and let them all into the shop. Elsie and her team and three other officers, as well as the forensic team made quite a sizeable and alarming number.

'Mr Skegwin, is Mrs Skegwin here?'

'She's at home,' he stammered. 'She always takes the afternoon off on a Wednesday. Unless it's the height of the tourist season or particularly busy,' he gabbled. 'What is all this?'

'I'm afraid you'll have to go to the station to answer more questions.' The two officers stepped forward to escort him to a police car waiting outside.

'Is this about Demmy? Is it? I've told you, I was with friends on the Saturday Demmy went missing and then went straight home. I don't understand.'

'We also have a warrant to search your shop and home residence, Mr Skegwin. Do you understand?'

'Of course I don't understand. Why would I kill Demmy? She was like a daughter to me?' Tears formed in Mr Skegwin's eyes.

'I want a s..solicitor,' he stammered, after a stunned silence; rallying a sense of anger and preservation.

'That will be arranged at the station, Mr Skegwin.'

The two constables took him by the arm and led him stumbling away.

Crikey, what if we've got this wrong, thought Elsie to herself but then mustered up a confident manner, 'Ok team, let's let the SOCOs do their job here while we pay Annie Skegwin a little visit,' she said.

They sped away to the Skegwin home on the coast to bring Mrs Skegwin in for questioning too. The forensic team would scour the residence after completing their search of the shop.

As they neared the Skegwin residence Sim's phone buzzed a text message, 'The techies have just confirmed that the security cameras around the Skegwin residence show no signs of untoward interference, Ma'am,' he said.

Elsie's face fell as she turned into the lane leading up to the Skegwin's drive. 'That's not good news and we just don't have a motive, do we?' said Elsie uncertainly. 'And I'm a bit worried that the shop security camera tapes showed other missing times on other days. Perhaps the camera does have a fault.'

'Our techies are working on that now to confirm possible interference,' explained Sim.

'I like to be more certain when I organise forensics to come in, that's all,' said Elsie. 'At the moment, I'm unsure if the Skegwins are involved. Mr Skegwin seemed genuinely mortified at having been taken in for questioning again. He really didn't expect to be, did he?'

'The Skegwins used to be champion rowers, your friend said. Someone took Demmy Harper and dumped her at sea when a storm was coming. Only people very practised and familiar with the vagaries of the North Sea could have accomplished that,' said Gus.

'True,' said Elsie, 'But how could they have transported Demmy, or her body, to a boat. Anna Skegwin's car never left the garage when she came home and her husband's stayed on the drive the whole weekend. And the times of the cameras and alibis confirm that the Skegwins never deviated from their routes. They came straight home. Anna Skegwin at five thirty and then Colin Skegwin at nine pm. They never had time to find a boat and take the body out to sea. The camera over the back door to their house shows no activity whatsoever on the evening in question, so far.'

'Gianelli confirmed that the steps down the cliffs at the back of the house are in complete disrepair, it would have been impossible, utterly dangerous to use them,' commented Gus.

I have to say,' said a worried Elsie, 'I'm wondering if I've done the right thing here.'

'It's the only thing we can do, Ma'am,' said Shannon.

'At least if nothing turns up we can completely discount the Skegwins from the enquiry,' mused Elsie. Her team was used to Elsie voicing her thoughts aloud about a case. She thought that it probably made her look weak but their opinions and views in response were of value. It was as simple as that.

'The Skegwins seem to have it all: successful business; relative wealth and comfort, if their house is anything to go by and their accounts seem healthy. Unusual for Anna Skegwin's family tree,' she mused

'What do you mean, Ma'am?' asked Gus.

'Nothing really,' replied Elsie absently as she turned the car onto the Skegwin driveway. A sea fret had moved in from the sea and it had almost obscured the entrance to the Skegwin drive; she'd almost driven past the gate.

CHAPTER 47

THURSDAY 23rd September 2018 - Whitby

Elsie knocked vigorously on the door. There was no reply and Elsie looked at the others quizzically. She knocked again but there was still no reply. She tried the handle and the door swung open. They stepped into the hallway and Elsie called out, 'Mrs Skegwin, North Yorkshire Police. Can you hear me?' There was no answering call. Gus and Sim checked the rooms which led off the hallway: the sitting room and the dining room: no sign of Anna Skegwin. Elsie boldly stepped toward the last door and opened it. There in front of her was the kitchen which had a huge glass front overlooking the sea with patio doors set into the glass. It was a fantastic feature and would have allowed the occupants a full view of the ocean on a clear day. At one of the chairs, placed by one of the glass patio doors, sat Anna Skegwin. She seemed dazed as if she wasn't really aware of where she was. She didn't even look at them as they came in.

'Anna we have a warrant to search your house. Your husband has been taken to the station for questioning and we'd like you to accompany us there too. I should tell you that a full search is being conducted of your shop,' began Elsie.

Anna Skegwin slowly turned her head to look at Elsie. Her eyes widened a little, as if she had only just become aware of her presence.

'Why are you here?'

'Mr Skegwin has been taken to Scarborough Station to assist us with our enquiries, Mrs Skegwin.' Elsie looked askance at the others because of Anna Skegwin's strange almost disembodied response.

'Mrs Skegwin, have you been drinking?' Elsie had spotted an empty glass next to a bottle of brandy on a nearside table.

Anna Skegwin just looked at her.

'Have you taken any medication?'

Anna just turned her head and continued to look back out of the window.

'Mrs Skegwin, we have more questions for you and would like you to accompany us to the station. Do you understand?'

Anna Skegwin turned her head back to look at Elsie again but her eyes were blank and showed no recognition of Elsie's words. Anna continued to gaze at her and Elsie thought that looking in her eyes was like looking at an Arctic wasteland: no sense of amination just a cold and settled blankness.

'We also have a warrant to search your house.' Elsie reiterated. Elsie nodded at Gus and Shannon to step forward to accompany Anna Skegwin to the car.

At that moment, belying her previous almost catatonic stupor, Anna leapt to her feet. Shannon and Gus readied themselves to catch hold of her and Elsie stepped in the way of the kitchen door to block Anna's departure. Anna didn't move forward to try to sidestep them but rather stepped back, wrenched open the patio door and leapt onto the terrace. It was as if she was consumed by some demonic energy. Startled, Shannon and Gus glanced at each other before making pursuit, with Elsie and Sim following closely on their heels.

Anna raced along the rear of the house across the back terrace which led to a little gate. She flung it open and raced along the cliff path. They raced after her but it was as if she had feet of

fury. At one point she hit a muddy patch and skid-
ded but righted herself and continued. The three
detectives kept pace with her but it was very difficult for them to actually catch her up, such was
her speed. And then, all of a sudden, she stopped
and peered down toward the waves below the
coastal path. Within moments the detectives had
caught up with her. All were breathing heavily
but Anna Skegwin seemed almost untouched by
her strange exertions. She did not turn to look at
them at all but just continued to gaze unpertur-
bedly down at the sea.

Elsie motioned the others to keep back.

'Anna, you need to come with us. Can you hear me?'

'I killed her, you know.'

'You killed her. Is that what you said, Anna? Do you
mean, Demmy?'

'It was an accident but she wouldn't let me keep the necklace and it was ours.' She said in a monotone voice.

'Ours?' queried Elsie. 'You mean yours and Mr Skelton's?'

'No, my family's:- the necklace belonged to my family. It always has.'

Elsie glanced at Anna's feet. She was standing awfully close to the edge of the cliff and she was worried about Anna's state of mind. She glanced at the others and shook her head not to make a move. From the hesitant and nervous looks on their faces she guessed that they were having similar thoughts to hers. She thought it best to just continue talking to Anna. A gull wheeled overhead and its lonely cry punctuated the sound of a wave crashing onto the rocks below.

'I don't understand, Anna. I thought that the necklace had been a family heirloom of Demmy's.'

'Demmy possessed it but it was an heirloom in the wrong family. My own grandmother told me of the pendant and her grandmother told her the story of it too. Demmy's family stole it. It was always meant to be in our family. That family took our heritage. It was left to us by an ancestor but Demmy's family stole it from the woman it should have been given to. It was always said that to bring the stone to a rightful heir would bring great fortune back to the family. Demeris giving it to me was a sign: a rightful sign.' Anna Skegwin related the story in a quiet monotone as if she were barely aware of her listeners.

Elsie could hardly believe her ears. The stone had been central to this case: unbelievably, bizarrely relevant. How on earth in this day and age could Anna believe that this pendant was some kind of talisman. But she clearly did. She had allowed this superstition to cast a dark and malignant shadow over her psyche.

A note of anger had crept into Anna's voice and with shaking hands she reached tentatively into her pocket. Elsie stepped forward slightly. The two men braced themselves ready to charge the woman, not knowing what her next move might be. She had already surprised them with the swiftness of her movements. Slowly she withdrew a long golden chain weighted down with a large black shiny stone: Demmy's pendant. Anna held the necklace in front of her face suspended on its solid chain like a dark little moon. Anna looked mesmerized at the sight of it.

'Is that Demmy's pendant, Anna?'

'My pendant, you mean.' A harsh expression crossed Anna's face and she gave a hateful glance toward Elsie.

'Yes, Anna.' Said Elsie soothingly. 'Was Demmy wearing it when she died?'

'No. She tried to steal it from me. The fool thought it belonged to her. She was obsessed with it. Never took it off. I knew what it was from the moment she walked into the shop looking for a job. It's beautiful isn't it?'

'It is, Anna; very beautiful.'

The gold of the necklace glinted as a shaft of after-noon sun bleached through the clouds and its black stone gleamed as it slowly twirled, suspended on its chain by Anna's fingers. Anna seemed almost hypnotised as she watched its ponderous swirl.

'She wore it so much the clasp broke. She could have lost it. I knew then I had to take it back…to keep it safe.'

'She gave it to you for repair?'

'Of course and I repaired it. And then one afternoon she sneaked in when I was busy in the shop.
I caught her stealing it from my desk. Said she'd
really come in to get her phone which she'd left.
The lying thief.'

Elsie decided not to challenge Anna's version of
events.

'So you argued about it. Did she manage to make
off with it?'

'I stopped her, of course. The idiot knocked her
head on the old marble mantelpiece when I tried to
take it back.'

'I see. Was she breathing after that happened,
Anna? Did she make any sound?'

'I managed to clean up the mess and then put her
in the car.'

'Was she still breathing, Anna?'

Anna just gazed at the necklace as if she and it were the only things in her world.

'Anna? What did you do with Demmy after you put her in your car?'

'I needed to get rid of her. Colin couldn't know. He liked Demmy. I brought her here. He was away.'

'Where was he?'

'Away,' said Anna in a monotone voice, still mesmerised by the necklace in front of her.

'It must have been very difficult getting rid of Demmy.'

'Why?' snapped Anna, seemingly breaking out of her trance.

Unnerved further by this switch in tone Elsie persevered. She was breathing heavily and she could feel the tension in the others beside her as they waited for the right moment to grab Anna.

'Trying to get rid of her: it must have been difficult. The camera at the back of the shop shows when you left and then you came straight here…' prompted Elsie.

'Of course, I did. Where else would I go?'

'Demmy's body was put into the sea, Anna. I know you're a proficient oarswoman but how did you manage to do that? The steps down to the shore are too broken and crumbled. You must have been very desperate to use them.'

Suddenly Anna gave a whoop of laughter, as mirthless as it was empty. 'The steps, oh, of course, I used the steps.' She seemed to find hilarity at the idea. Elsie and the two men were in Anna's eyeline but she was angled slightly to the right and was not aware of Shannon slowly but imperceptibly moving toward her on her left.

As she screeched with laughter she inadvertently took a step backward. Shannon quickly stepped forward. Elsie too stepped forward as if to stop her moving nearer the cliff edges. Startled by Elsie's movements, Anna reared back. Inevitably, she stumbled to catch her balance but to no avail. Elsie and the others moved as if as one to try to reach her. Shannon was the nearest at that point though and managed to grab Anna's hand, hauling her back toward them but then Anna's feet slipped on the wet grass. With a scream she lurched backward even more.

Shannon was suddenly pitched forward still holding onto Anna's hand. Gus frantically tried to reach toward Anna who was leaning backward over the cliff. He managed to grab hold of Anna's jumper but Anna's panicked movements made it slip out of his grasp. Shannon tried hard to keep hold of Anna's hand. Her fingers just couldn't hold on to her. Anna's eyes were writhing in panic. Slowly, inevitably, Anna's fingers slid away from Shannon's as gravity claimed her and she fell onto the rocks below with an ear piercing shriek.

At that moment a lone wave crashed over her twisted body as if the doings of human life were of no moment to the foaming elements of the great North Sea.

For those still on top of the cliff the drama was far from over as Shannon too pitched forward hindered by the wet and crumbly ground. She too slid, a foot or so down the cliff on her back. Elsie was the nearest to her and she sank to her knees and grabbed Shannon's hand which was outstretched behind her frantically scrabbling at the muddy ground trying to prevent her decline. And Elsie froze as part of the cliffedge crumbled with clods of mud falling silently but remorselessly into the sea below.

Elsie gasped and began to shake all over. 'Not now, please God not now,' she pleaded silently to herself as the blanket shadow of panic descended. She forced herself to keep hold of Shannon's hand. Sim, seeing the precariousness of the cliff edge and that it could crumble at any moment taking all of them to the crashing waves below also sank to the ground and edged toward both women. At the same time he waved Gus back as Gus had made a sudden movement as if to also grab Shannon. 'Gus, go and find some rope from the Skegwin's!' muttered Sim hoarsely. Gus blinked once. His face had paled. He quickly turned and sped back to the house and was soon swallowed into the mist.

Elsie felt as if she had turned to stone and her ratching rasping breaths felt as if they were her last. She forced herself to breathe and not pass out. The rest of her energy was spent concentrating on holding onto Shannon who was too petrified to move. She knew that if she fainted now that Shannon would be lost to the rocks below. With her other hand, Shannon had grabbed onto a clump of gorse growing out of the side of the cliff. Pinpricks of blood appeared on her hand from gripping the prickly shrub, but it wasn't enough. Clods of mud, grass and rock continued to dislodge all around Shannon and fall onto the rocks below.

'I don't think I can hold on, Elsie.' She moaned. At the edges of her eyes, Elsie felt the darkness close but willed herself to keep it at bay; keep breathing and keep holding on. It seemed like a lifetime. 'Hold on Shannon,' she managed to say, 'Just hold on!'

'I'm right here, Ma'am,' Sim uttered – he had been inching closer and closer to the two women aware that every one of his movements threatened the stability of the cliff top. He grabbed Elsie's ankle sparking another great clod of earth to tumble into the sea at the vibration of his movement.

Soon, although it seemed as if the seconds had turned into hours, the sounds of footsteps were heard and Gus appeared breathless and pale, half carrying, half dragging a large coil of rope behind him.

'Stay behind me, Gus! Keep hold of one end of the rope and pass me the other. No sudden movements!' Sim then edged very cautiously toward Elsie and Shannon and gingerly stretched out to grab Shannon's outstretched hand which was clinging desperately to Elsie's. With a practised deft movement, testament presumably to his army training, he knotted the rope around Shannon's wrist and then edged gingerly backwards. Soon he had managed to secure the rope around Elsie's middle before edging further back.

He and Gus began to carefully pull the rope. Suddenly Shannon screamed as the gorse bush she had been holding onto came away in her hand sending about two foot of crumbling mud onto the hungry waves and rocks below. All that was now holding her was Elsie's hand and the rope. Elsie felt herself beginning to black out but she forced herself to breathe. 'We've got you, Shannon' she rasped, 'Just stay as still as you can.

Slowly and inch by inch the two men pulled Elsie and Shannon back toward them. At long last, they were pulled clear of the top of the cliff edge.

Elsie lay on her back. She felt as if she were no longer part of her own body. Her mind whirled and careened as the back of her head sank into the wet grass. She could hardly breathe. The sea fret gently encroached as if to blanket the horror away. It momentarily cleared - much like mist on a window that has been rubbed away. Something made her turn her face and she saw a girl stood between where she was lying and the cliff edge, twirling a necklace by its chain and staring transfixedly at it...Demmy. A swirl of sea mist enveloped the girl and when it cleared she had gone.

At last, Elsie took a deep shuddering breath and sat up to put her head between her knees

'Ma'am, Ma'am?' said Sim.

'I'm sorry, Sim, I'm alright, really.' She glanced at him and then back to where Demmy had stood - where now only remained a billow of eddying mist. Her breathing was back to normal. She took a few moments and then shakily stood. Sim didn't let go of her arm.

Gus was sat with one arm around Shannon who was in too much shock to speak but was just sat there taking huge dragging breaths. With his other hand Gus rang for an ambulance.

CHAPTER 48

FRIDAY 24th September 2018 - Scarborough Police Headquarters

All of the team came into the station the next morning. Elsie felt as if she was on auto-pilot and was worried that if she stayed at home for the day her thoughts would be full of fretting about the previous evening's events. She preferred to have something to do. Even Shannon was at work after discharging herself from the hospital as there was nothing physically wrong with her. Elsie guessed, that like her, Shannon preferred to be with the people who had shared the horror of the previous day.

Elsie was quiet for a moment as the team congregated around her desk. She decided to tell them about Bill's discovery of Anna Skegwin being related to Demmy.

'You know that letter which Bill and I found at Demmy's cottage in Robin Hood's Bay?'

'Yes, the one that seems to mention Demmy Harper's pendant,' replied Gus.

'Well, while we were looking for the pendant at the cottage – just before we found the letter, Bill took a closer look at an incomplete family tree which her Aunt Jess had been working on. It traced Demmy and Jess's family tree back to a famous smuggler, Jeb Whittaker, in Robin Hood's Bay – right back to the late 1800's. The smuggler's daughter, Alice, had twin girls and Demmy's line is traced through to one of them: Nellie Whittaker. But Jess had only got partway to completing the tree for the other twin girl, Martha Whittaker. Bill decided to complete it as a means of paying his last respects to Jess. He and Jess were at school together and he likes that kind of stuff anyway – a local historian. Anyway, it turns out that Anna Skegwin is at the end of Martha's line. Just local history stuff.'

'Many people roundabout are very possibly inter-linked in this way if their families stayed in the area. Those connections would probably be found if you went back far enough,' added Sim.

'That's what Bill said,' said Elsie.

'It's a coincidence though,' said Gus.

'Not really, if you think about it,' said Elsie. 'It's the same for any community the world over, I would have thought.'

'Not just the family connection but the relevance of the pendant to Demmy's killing,' said Gus. It seems odd that the pendant had relevance then. And, now, over two hundred years later, it pops up again, in the middle of a murder investigation, with the descendents of the original people who were involved with its ownership.'

This crystal obsession of Gus's belied the fact that he was a meticulous and very rational minded detective – the ultimate detail man. Elsie smiled to herself and wondered how he could persist in such esoteric irrational beliefs. And yet, and yet…this jet pendant had turned out to be key to the whole case. Perhaps they would have had earlier success if Elsie had mentioned it to Gus earlier; he might have picked up on the stone's significance, she thought guiltily.

'Anna Skegwin obviously thought that Demmy's pendant had some kind of meaning for her – was some kind of charm of good fortune.' Gus added.

'It seems incredible that this kind of belief can persist in the modern age?' said Sim.

'In the cold light of day, it isn't credible at all, but murderers rarely commit their crime under the full beam of light, do they? They usually commit their work in the shadows – of one kind or another.' Gus pointed out.

Gus's words sparked something in Elsie. Studying the family tree had been very peculiar with all of the children descended from Nellie experiencing good fortune in their lives (but that could be down to sound life choices and most likely once a wealth base was set up it would be easier for descendents to succeed down the line she rationalised), whilst those descended from Martha seemed to experience a lot of misfortune in one way or the other: vagrancy, ill health, early deaths, business problems.

'It's a study in catastrophe following Martha's line,' commented Elsie, 'I really wish I'd mentioned Bill's findings on Jess's family tree sooner, Gus, I have to say. Maybe you could have pointed us in the right direction.'

Gus blushed, 'I'm not entirely sure the relevance would have been that apparent to me in hindsight, if I'm honest, Ma'am.'

'Maybe, maybe not, but I still think I didn't draw properly upon all the different insights of the team, Gus. No more mocking your crystals from now on, I promise.' said Elsie.

'I didn't know you did,' replied Gus, with a raised eyebrow. Whether the eyebrow was raised in humour or mild affront, Elsie couldn't tell.

'I wonder if Anna Skegwin did intentionally murder Demmy, or if it was an accident like she said?' pondered Shannon.

'I guess we'll never really know,' said Elsie. Anna Skegwin was in no fit state to tell the difference, I suspect. Forensics aren't conclusive about whether it was a blow caused by the skirmish between Anna Skegwin and Demmy, or by Anna forcefully causing Demmy's head to be hit on the corner of the mantelpiece'.

'But how did Anna put Demmy's body out to sea?' Sim queried. 'She can't have used the steps.'

He thought for a moment before adding, 'In fact, I wonder why there are steps there in the first place. Where do they go? It's a shame that the overhanging cliff prevented us from at least being able to take a good look down there.'

'There aren't any other steps, are there?' interposed Shannon, 'Maybe on the far side of the house?'

'Thomas checked that,' replied Sim. 'There's no way down. And the cliffs on this part of the coast are often crumbling into the sea.'

Elsie had a sudden recollection of Bill's words on the day that they had explored Jess's house: 'There's a whole other world beneath our feet, things hidden from the eye that we can't see…which haven't been discovered yet – possibly never will be.'

'Of course, why didn't I think of it before!' she exclaimed and stood up suddenly.

'I want every inch of the house searched – there has to be a tunnel down to the shore. It's old enough to be a smuggler's house. It's the only way she could have taken Demmy out to sea.

Elsie's phone rang. After a few minutes, of mostly listening, Elsie rang off. 'The SOCOs have found traces of Demeris Harper's body in Anna Skegwin's car boot; in the garage, hallway and in the basement.'

Within the hour the team was at the Skegwin residence again. The SOCO were already there. Jim, the chief officer in charge of the Scene of Crime investigation had spotted their arrival and was at the door waiting for them.

'We're finishing up now, Ma'am and we'll be gone in ten, so we'll leave you to it.'

Within fifteen minutes Elsie and the others were standing in the hallway of the, by now, empty Skegwin house.

'The cameras showed Anna never left the house after putting her car in the garage. There has to be a way down from inside the house. Bang on walls and floors to see if anything sounds hollow,' instructed Elsie as she opened all the doors in the hallway. Most led to rooms on the ground floor but one led to a descending flight of stairs down to a darkened room. Makes sense to start here,' she said flickering on a light which illuminated the stairs leading down to the basement.

They clattered down the cellar stairs. It was dark but Sim managed to find a light. It was full of old boxes and rowing paraphernalia. She touched one of the two wetsuits which were hanging up from hooks on the far wall. She moved some of the box-es around and stamped her foot on various parts of the cellar floor hoping to hear anything but the dull low thud of solid ground below the floor line. To no avail; her heart sank. Were Anna's words just the ramblings of a deranged person? Maybe she had managed to drag Demmy's body down the cliff face with the impetus of the desperate. And the Satur-day, on which Demmy had died, had been much drier weather. But if she had done so, would there not have been a boat already down there? How would that have got there? Perhaps Anna Skegwin, in her deranged state, had imagined that she had played a part in Demmy's death. Perhaps Demmy had never retrieved her necklace. The murderer could still be Freddie Bowland who had perhaps managed to acquire a boat in his 'lost' hours. Elsie thought gloomily to herself. One thing was certain, if there was a secret smuggler's tunnel, she was determined to find it. She wished she had Bill with her. He seemed to know which overlooked places were actually the best places to look. 'There's a whole other world beneath our feet, things hidden from the eye that we can't see.'

Within a few minutes all four of them were tapping on walls; jumping up and down on flag stones and checking under, in and around, storage areas. They would have looked quite mad to an onlooker. But the cellar was solid and gave no hint of any secrets from a past time. Eventually, they admitted defeat and all four of them stood and stared at one another – their eyes scrutinising the nooks and crannies of the cellar to see if there was anywhere else they could search. Elsie sent Shannon and Sim to investigate the other parts of the house which might contain the entrance to a basement but to no avail; they came back shaking their heads.

'Maybe, I was wrong,' said Elsie sighing with frustration.

'It was a good idea, anyway, Ma'am,' and who knows with these old Smuggler's houses. I've heard of plenty of strange findings in old houses in the area,' said Sim.

'Yep, history never quite leaves us,' added Gus.

Elsie smiled at them, silently thanking them for their well-meant words. She still felt a bloody fool though. Shannon stood there with a disappointed expression on her face rubbing her sore wrists. Yes, it was time to go. The best thing to do would be to come back with Bill, Elsie thought to herself.

They clumped back up the stairs. All four knowing that once again, they would be tormented back at the station for their unorthodox approach – looking for secret tunnels indeed. Their 'quest' was bound to leak out somehow – these things always did. Gus hoped Shannon would soon get back on form; she had been understandably quiet today. She was more than able to parry any of the usual mick-taking which was covertly or often overtly directed at the team. He knew that they wouldn't say much to Sim – he was too big and exuded a natural authority when he had to, and was probably used to counterpointing laddish banter with his army record. Elsie wouldn't get much teasing either as she was in a position of command. He knew that being diminutive, non-confrontational and odd, he would be the one facing the worst of the onslaught of comments in the next few weeks and beyond. Once the shock of the team's previous day's adventures had worn away, then the jokes would come – always the rearguard of drama. Actually, was it really worth worrying about, he thought to himself – given yesterday's almost tragedy?

When he reached the top of the stairs he realised that he had left his jacket in the cellar – moving all the gear around had been hot work. 'Be with you in a moment,' he called out to the others who had already climbed up the hallway. 'Just need to get my jacket.'

'Alright, Gus, will meet you back at the car,' called Elsie.

He ran down the steps, retrieved his jacket and then ran back up them again. He went to switch off the light and then stood stock still for a moment. Then he spun around and went down the stairs again – more slowly this time. With each tread he paused and then when he reached nearer the bottom he turned again and ascended slowly. The bottom half of the stairs made a hollow sound but not the top half. He went down again, even more slowly. He was convinced that the bottom stairs made a hollow sound. Understandable, he told himself, stairs often are hollow and it could be to do with their structure. Nevertheless, he investigated the bottom stairs more thoroughly. He started at the bottom and inspected each one. On the fourth step up he could see that the inner wood, supporting the step was a bit looser than the others. He poked at it and eventually pushed it quite firmly. To his shock it gave way and folded in on itself exposing what looked like to be some kind of lever. He pushed it one way but nothing happened so pushed it another. To his amazement around seven of the lowest steps folded to the right, away from the stone wall which the steps were set against. A dark space was revealed in part of the exposed wall. Rough-hewn steps seemed to stretch downwards, further to the left, as far as his torch would allow him to see. He pulled the stairs back into position and rushed back up them to find the others.

……………………..

'Who's going first?' asked Gus.

'You should do the honours, Gus, seeing as though you found them,' said Elsie, peering into the gloom. They stepped into the tunnel. The faint sound of waves crashing on rocks reached their ears after a short while. The tunnel was steep and stepped in places but generally stony. It widened as they went down it. The first part of it was clearly man made with thick wooden panelling surrounding them on all sides. Before long, though, the tunnel took on more of the feel of a natural cave with a rocklike face that looked as though it had been formed from century after century of pummelling waves.

The last part of the cave opened onto a small rapidly emerging sandy cove as the tide had not long turned and was ebbing away. It also had a small rowing boat tucked deep inside the driest part of its recess and secured in place with a rope.

CHAPTER 49

Stoupe Brow, The Butts – Robin Hood's Bay

The two archeologists, which had done the main digging, stopped as their implements tapped against a wooden object.

Bill gripped Elsie's arm in excitement. The small group of ten or so historians, officials and archeologists were silent as the realisation struck that the sophisticated equipment had possibly found Jeb's treasure hidden all those years ago.

The two archeologists were joined by two more who skilfully and carefully dug around what turned out to be a wooden chest - all its four sides were exposed as it lay in the nadir of the crater which they had dug around it. A special lifting device extracted the heavy chest and carefully placed it on the canvassed pallet especially prepared for it. The chest was surprisingly intact and seemingly robust. It measured about eighteen inches wide by ten inches deep and about the same in height again.

The peat had done a remarkable job in preserving its dark timber and tarnished brass. The head archaeologist took some time carefully cleaning around the lock. She probed the brass fitting of the lid with a special master key type implement. She tentatively turned it after the key engaged with the lock, fully prepared to cease if there was any force needed. No force was needed as the turn of the key was surprisingly smooth. She gently pushed back the lid to reveal one of the most beautiful collection of colours Elsie had ever seen: sapphires, tourmaline, jade, emeralds, topaz, rubies, garnets interspersed with the inimitable gleam of pure gold; like some sparkling vision from a storybook; The contents of the chest glowed as they glittered and danced in the light of the mellow morning sun.

Despite what had been a damp start, it was promising to be a fine day. The heather was brightening to amethyst, and the azure sheet of sea melded with the beautiful blue of the sky whilst the skylarks careened overhead. A sight to rival even the contents of a treasure chest, Elsie thought to herself.

APPENDIX

Selection of traditional shanties :

(Mostly anonymous as names have been lost)

The Mermaid

It was Friday morn when we set sail,

And we were not far from the land

When our Captain he spied a mermaid so fair

With a comb and a glass in her hand.

Chorus:

And the ocean waves do roll

And the stormy winds do blow

And we poor sa-li-ors go skippin' at the top

While the landlubbers lie down below!

2. Then up spoke the captain of our gallant ship

And a fine old man was he!

"This sweet mermaid has warned us of our doom;

We shall sink to the bottom of the sea!"

Chorus:

3. Then up spoke the mate of our gallant ship,

And a fine spoken man was he!

Said "I have a wife in Brooklyn by the sea,

And tonight a widow she will be!"

Chorus:

4. Then up spoke the cabin-boy of our gallant ship,

And a brave young lad was he!

Said "I have a sweetheart in Salem by the sea,

And tonight she'll be weepin' there for me!"

Chorus:

5. Then up spoke the cook of our gallant ship,

And a crazy old butcher was he!

Said "I care much more for my pots and my pans

Than I do for the bottom of the sea!"

Chorus:

6. Then three times round spun our gallant ship,

And three times round spun she;

Three times round spun our gallant ship,

And she sank to the bottom of the sea!

Chorus:

The Common Sailor

I'm the man before the mast that ploughs the raging sea

And on this simple subject will you please enlighten me

Common sailors we are called, come tell me the reason why

And on this simple subject I'll reply

CHORUS sung after each verse

Don't you call us common sailors anymore

Don't you call us common sailors anymore

Good things to you we bring. Don't you call us common men

We're as good as anybody that's on shore

The young girls of this country, their growing days we bless

We brings them silks and satins out of which they makes a dress

To gain the heart of some young man, as fancy dresses do

Don't never despise the sailor boys that sails the ocean blue

The young gents of this country, they're sitting at their ease

Not thinking on the stormy nights that we spent on the seas

We brings the leaves to make cigars to decorate their face

They wouldn't call us common if they were sometimes in our place

When speaking of a man ashore we never hear you say

He's a common this or common that, be his calling what it may

Be he a traveling tinker, or a scavenger, or a sweep

Then why call us common sailors, who battle with the deep?

Shanty - Traditional

I used to be a sailor, I sailed upon the sea,

And when I was at home my wife was very good to me,

But I commenced to worry and to wonder what she'd do,

When I was off a-sailing out upon the ocean blue.

What if I popped out and I caught her unawares,

Popped out sudden from the cupboard in the stairs,

Popped out, popped up, and took her by surprise,

Sometimes me boys it's better to be ignorant than wise.

I kissed me wife goodbye and told her I was bound to sail

Upon a Yankee whaling ship they called the Horse's Tail,

I told 'er I'd return again in six months or a year,

Then I hid meself beneath the stairs to see what should appear.

If I popped out and I caught her unawares,

Popped out sudden from the cupboard in the stairs,

Popped out, popped up, popped aloft to see

If my little wife was mis'rable and lonely without me.

Well, first there came the cabin boy, and then there came the cook,

She had 'em by appointment in a red appointment book,

The bo'sun piped himself aboard, and played a merry tune,

And last there came the captain with his bloody great harpoon.

Then I popped out and I caught 'em unawares,

Popped out sudden from the cupboard in the stairs,

Popped out, popped up, and popped 'em out the door,

And I vowed an oath I never would go sailing any more.

Now let this be a warning to all you jolly tars

Who leave your wives at home to go off sailing near and far.

Meself, I'm a greengrocer now, me flat's above me shop,

And any time I have the chance it's up the stairs I pop,

Yes I pop up and I catch her unawares,

I pop her in the parlor and I pop her on the stairs,

Pop in, pop out, and pop back to the till,

And you can take your bloody sailing ships, and pop 'em where you will.

Strike the Bell

Scottish Traditional: Ring the Bell, Watchman

Up on the poop deck and walking about,

There is the second mate so steady and so stout;

What he is a-thinkin' of he doesn't know himself

And we wish that he would hurry up and strike,

strike the bell.

Chorus:

Strike the bell second mate, let us go below;

Look well to windward you can see it's gonna blow;

Look at the glass, you can see it has fell,

Oh we wish that you would hurry up and strike,

strike the bell.

2. Down on the main deck and workin' at the pumps,

There is the larboard watch just longing for their bunks;

Look out to windward, you can see a great swell,

And we wish that you would hurry up and strike,

strike the bell.

Chorus:

3. Forward on the forecastle head and keepin' sharp lookout,

There is Johnny standin', a-longin' fer to shout,

Lights' a-burnin' bright sir and everything is well,

And he's wishin' that the second mate would strike, strike the bell.

Chorus:

4. Aft at the wheelhouse old Anderson stands,

Graspin' at the helm with his frostbitten hands,

Lookin' at the compass through the course is clear as hell

And he's wishin' that the second mate would strike, strike the bell.

Chorus:

5. Aft on the quarter deck our gallant captain stands,

Lookin' out to windward with a spyglass in his hand,

What he is a-thinkin' of we know very well,

He's thinkin' more of shortenin' sail than strikin' the bell.

Chorus:

All Things Are Quite Silent

All things are quite silent, each mortal at rest,

When me and my love got snug in one nest,

When a bold set of ruffians they entered our cave,

And they forced my dear jewel to plough the salt wave.

2. I begged hard for my sailor as though I begged for life.

They'd not listen to me although a fond wife,

Saying: "The king he wants sailors, to the sea he must go,"

And they've left me lamenting in sorrow and woe.

3. Through green fields and meadows we oft-times did walk,

And sweet conversation of love we have talked,

With the birds in the woodland so sweetly did sing,

And the lovely thrushes' voices made the valleys
to ring.

4. Although my love's gone I will not be cast down.

Who knows but my sailor may once more return?

And will make me amends for all trouble and strife,

And my true love and I might live happy for life.

Roll the Old Chariot Along

Oh, a drop of Nelson's blood wouldn't do us
any harm :
Oh, a drop of Nelson's blood wouldn't do us any harm
And we'll all hang on behind.
Chorus:
So we'll roll the old chariot along
An' we'll roll the golden chariot along.
So we'll roll the old chariot along
An' we'll all hang on behind!

2. : Oh, a plate of Irish stew wouldn't do us any harm :
Oh, a plate of Irish stew wouldn't do us any harm
And we'll all hang on behind.
Chorus:

3. : Oh, a nice fat cook wouldn't do us any harm :
Oh, a nice fat cook wouldn't do us any harm
And we'll all hang on behind.
Chorus:

4. : Oh, a roll in the clover wouldn't do us any harm :

Oh, a roll in the clover wouldn't do us any harm

And we'll all hang on behind.

Chorus:

5. : Oh, a long spell in gaol wouldn't do us any harm :

Oh, a long spell in gaol wouldn't do us any harm

And we'll all hang on behind.

Chorus:

6. : Oh, a nice watch below wouldn't do us any harm :

Oh, a nice watch below wouldn't do us any harm

And we'll all hang on behind.

Chorus:

7. : Oh, a night with the gals wouldn't do us any harm :

Oh, a night with the gals wouldn't do us any harm

And we'll all hang on behind.

Chorus:

Greenland Whale Fisheries

'Twas in eighteen hundred and fifty-three

In June, the thirteenth day

That our gallant ship her anchor weighed

And for Greenland sailed away, brave boys

And for Greenland sailed away.

2. The lookout on the cross-trees stood

With a spyglass in his hand

There's a whale, there's a whale

There's a whalefish, he cried,

And she blows at every span, brave boys

She blows at every span.

3. The captain stood on the quarterdeck

And a fine little man was he

Overhaul! Overhaul!

Let your davit-tackles fall

And launch your boats for sea, brave boys

And launch your boats for sea.

4. The boats where launched with the men aboard

And the whale was in full view

Resolved was each seaman bold

To steer where the whalefish blew, brave boys

To steer where the whalefish blew.

5. We struck that whale, and the line played out

But she gave a flourish with her tail

The boat capsized and four men were drowned

And we never caught that whale, brave boys

And we never caught that whale.

6. To lose that whale, our captain said

It grieves my heart full sore

But, oh, to lose four gallant men

It grieves me ten times more, brave boys

It grieves me ten times more.

7. The winter star doth now appear

So, boys, we'll anchor weigh

It's time to leave this cold country

And homeward bear away, brave boys

And homeward bear away.

8. Oh, Greenland is a dreadful place

A land that's never green

Where there's ice and snow

And the whale fishes blow

And daylight's seldom seen, brave boys

And daylight's seldom seen.

The Shoals Of Herring

With our nets and gear we're faring

Oer the wild and wasteful ocean

It's there on the deep that we harvest and reap our

bread

As we hunt the bonny shoals of herring.

2. It was on a fine and a pleasant day

Out of Yarmouth harbour I was faring

As a cabin boy on a sailing lugger

For to go and hunt the shoals of herring.

3. Now the work was hard and the hours were long

And the treatment sure it took some bearing

Her was little kindness and the kicks were many

As we hunted for the shoals of herring.

4. Oh we fished the Swarth and the Dogger Bank

I was cook and I'd a quarter-sharing

And I used to sleep standing on me feet

And I'd dream about the shoals of herring.

5. Oh! We left the home grounds in the month of June

And for canny Shiels we soon were bearing

With a hundred cran of the silver darling

That we'd taken from the shoals of herring.

6. Now you're up on deck you're a fisherman

You can swear and show a manly bearing

Take your turn on watch with the other fellows

While you're searching for shoals of herring.

7. In the stormy seas and the living gale

Just to earn your daily bread you're daring

From the Dover Straits to the Faeroe Islands

As you're following the shoals of herring.

8. Oh I earned my keep and I paid me way

And I earned the gear that I was wearing

Sailed a million miles, caught ten million fishes

We were sailing after shoals of herring.

Ye Mariners All

Ye mariners all, as ye pass by

Come in and drink if you are dry

Come spend, me lads, your money brisk

And pop your nose in a jug of this

2. O mariners all, if you've half a crown

You're welcome all for to sit down

Come spend, me lads, your money brisk

And pop your nose in a jug of this

3. O tipplers all, as you pass by

Come in and drink if you are dry

Come in and drink, think not amiss

And pop your nose in a jug of this

4. O now I'm old and can scarcely crawl

I've a long grey beard and a head that's bald

Crown my desire, fulfill my bliss

A pretty girl and a jug of this

5. And when I'm in my grave and dead

And all my sorrows are past and fled

Transform me then into a fish

And let me swim in a jug of this

To the North Sea

It's Christmas Eve and round me

Are dance and talk and jest, and I'm striving to

seem joyous,

Just as merry as the rest; but the faces and the

voices

They fade before my sight, and I see the Northern

streamers

Flush up the Arctic night.

Oh ! bright our hall is gleaming,

And warm the fire-gleams play on the holly other

eyes see,

But mine are far away, they see your lamp-lit cabin,

Not all they seem to view, and I fill them full with

gladness,

With a long, dear look at you.

You Landsmen May Have Plenty

You landsmen may have plenty

And dine at home at ease, but you'll never eat as we do,

Who are sharp-set by the breeze; you may have scores of dishes,

But on you they're wasted quite, while tough salt-horse we're munching,

With hunger that's delight.

You landsmen may have down beds,

And lie secure and warm, but can you sleep as we do,

Turning in from cold and storm?

From the keen night-watch in winter, tumble frozen down below,

And the bliss within a sea-bunk,

'tis then you'll learn to know.

A Drop of Brandy-O

The Landlady of France

from the 18th Century

A landlady of France loved an officer, 'tis said
And the officer he dearly loved his brandy-o.
Now said she "I dearly love this officer, tho' his
nose is red
And his legs are what the regiment calls bandy-o.

2. But when this bandy officer was ordered to the
coast,
Then she tore her lovely locks that looked so sandy-o
"Now goodbye, my love," said she, "when you
write please pay the post,
But before we part we'll take a drop of brandy-o."

3. "Take a bottle of it with you," to the officer she said,

"In your tent, you know, my love will be the dandy-o"

"You're right, my dear," said he, "for a tent is very damp

And 'tis better in my tent to take some brandy-o"

4. So she filled him up a bumper just before he left the town,

With another for herself so neat and handy-o.

And to keep their droopin' spirits up the poured the spirits down,

For love is like the colic, cured with brandy-o.

Blow The Man Down

Oh, blow the man down, bullies, blow the man down

Way aye blow the man down

Oh, blow the man down, bullies, blow him away

Give me some time to blow the man down!

As I was a walking down Paradise Street

Way aye blow the man down

A pretty young damsel I chanced for to meet.

Give me some time to blow the man down!

She was round in the counter and bluff in the bow,

Way aye blow the man down

So I took in all sail and cried, "Way enough now."

Give me some time to blow the man down!

So I tailed her my flipper and took her in tow

Way aye blow the man down

And yardarm to yardarm away we did go.

Give me some time to blow the man down!

But as we were going she said unto me

Way aye blow the man down

"There's a spanking full-rigger just ready for sea"

Give me some time to blow the man down…

One More Day

Have you heard the news, my Johnny

One more day!

We're homeward bound tomorrow

Only one more day!

2. Don't you hear the old man growlin'

One more day!

Don't you hear the mate a howlin'

Only one more day!

3. Don't you hear the old man callin'

One more day!

Don't you hear the pilot bawlin'

Only one more day!

4. Only one more day a-howlin'

One more day!

Can't you hear the gals a-callin'

Only one more day!

5. Only one more day a-rollin'

One more day!

Can't you hear the gulls a-callin'

Only one more day!

6. Only one more day a-furlin'

One more day!

Only one more day a-cursin'

Only one more day!

7. Heave and sight the anchor, Johnny

One more day!

For we're close 'board the port, Johnny

Only one more day!

8. Put on your long-tail blue, Johnny

One more day!

For your payday's nearly due.

Only one more day!

9. We're homeward bound today, Johnny

One more day!

We'll leave her without sorrow, Johnny

Only one more day!

10. Pack your bags today, my Johnny

One more day!

O, an' leave her where she lies, Johnny

Only one more day!

11. No more gales or heavy weather

One more day!

Only one more day together

Only one more day!

12. Only one more day, my Johnny,

One more day!

O, rock and roll me over.

Only one more day!

Printed in Great Britain
by Amazon

85614053R00350